"I Wouldn't Call This Swimming,"

Melissa said. "Why don't you let go of me?"

She wriggled in his arms, and Phil half released her. She scooped up a handful of water and threw it in his face, then darted away.

Phil watched her and likened her to a beautiful mermaid. It's been a long time, he thought, since she's laughed like this from sheer high spirits. Just as it's been a long time since she was last loved by a man. But these carefree moments were fragile. Nothing he said or did must cast a shadow across her happiness.

NANCY JOHN

is an unashamed romantic, deeply in love with her husband of over thirty years. She lives in Sussex, England, where long walks through the countryside provide the inspiration for the novels that have brought her a worldwide following.

Dear Reader:

Romance readers have been enthusiastic about Silhouette Special Editions for years. And that's not by accident: Special Editions were the first of their kind and continue to feature realistic stories with heightened romantic tension.

The longer stories, sophisticated style, greater sensual detail and variety that made Special Editions popular are the same elements that will make you want to read book after book.

We hope that you enjoy this Special Edition today, and will enjoy many more.

The Editors at Silhouette Books

NANCY JOHN
Champagne Nights

Silhouette Special Edition

Published by Silhouette Books New York

America's Publisher of Contemporary Romance

SILHOUETTE BOOKS, a Division of Simon & Schuster, Inc.
1230 Avenue of the Americas, New York, N.Y. 10020

Copyright © 1984 by Nancy John
Cover artwork copyright © 1984 Franco Accornero

Distributed by Pocket Books

ISBN: 0-671-53693-1

First Silhouette Books printing October, 1984

10 9 8 7 6 5 4 3 2 1

Map by Ray Lundgren

America's Publisher of Contemporary Romance

Printed in the U.S.A.

BC91

Books by Nancy John

Silhouette Romance

Silhouette Special Edition

Silhouette Desire

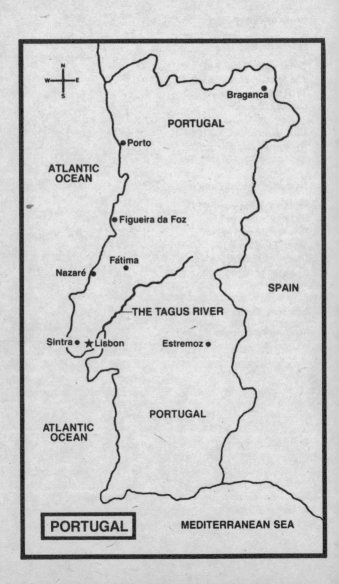

Chapter One

M elissa, you'll have to go to Lisbon tomorrow instead of me to handle this deal with Senhor Maxwell. Sorry it's such short notice, but it can't be helped."

Glancing up from the sales projections that she'd been checking, Melissa Colville stared in stunned bewilderment at her brother-in-law as he came striding into her office. A shaft of morning sunshine through one of the tall windows struck highlights of fire in the cloud of silk-soft, hazel brown hair that framed her face. With her delicately sculpted features, glowing complexion and warm golden eyes, she was more beautiful than she ever realized.

"For goodness' sake, Selwyn, what's this all about?" There was an untypically sharp edge to her voice. "I can't possibly go shooting off to Lisbon, as you well know."

"I'm afraid that I must insist," he said with a reproving frown. Selwyn Colville had a fair share of the family's good looks; but whereas Toby, his younger brother and Melissa's late husband, had been handsome in a carefree, charismatic way, Selwyn's face was graver. He had a weight of dignity

7

about him that was unusual in a man who wouldn't see forty for another couple of years.

"But what's stopping you from going yourself?" Melissa challenged.

Selwyn rattled the sheet of cream-laid notepaper he was carrying. "I hope to heaven that I'm worrying about nothing, but I don't like the tone of this letter that arrived from Munich this morning. Since Franz Mescher took over from his father last winter, he's been throwing his weight around more than a little. Now he seems to have the idea that he can find a better British distributor for the Mescher Vineyards than Colville's."

"That's crazy! We've been doing a marvelous job for Mescher's, upping their sales better than thirty-eight percent in the last six years. Doesn't he realize how difficult the market is right now?"

"Seems not. Franz needs to have the facts of commercial life spelled out to him in words of one syllable. Which is why I've decided to fly to Germany immediately to try and stop that young hothead from doing something stupid. Mescher's is too big a slice of our business for us to lose it without putting up a fight."

"Heavens, yes! Let's hope you can make him see sense." Melissa arched her slender eyebrows in query. "So why don't you call Senhor Maxwell in Lisbon and postpone your visit there, Selwyn?"

"Because I don't want to risk fouling things up with him. Getting the sole British agency for this new champagne-style wine they're producing at Caves da Silva Cunha could turn out to be a very big thing for us, Melissa. From the letters I've exchanged with Maxwell he seems a pleasant enough chap, but all my inquiries in the trade suggest that he's a tough negotiator. It's unfortunate that I can't go to see him myself, but if I don't send a senior member of the firm in my place he'd have good cause to be annoyed. What's more, he'd interpret it as a sign of weakness in our top management."

"Agreed. But I don't see why it has to be me," Melissa protested. "We have other senior people who could go. Graham, or Martin Pearce, for instance."

Selwyn sighed impatiently. "Get this into your head—Maxwell is a shrewd operator. Before he seriously considered appointing Colville's to handle his British sales he'd have done his homework about us, just as we've done our homework about him and the Silva Cunha setup. He'll know exactly how important you are in the firm, Melissa, and failing me, he'll expect to talk to nobody less than you. Why are you so reluctant to go, anyway? Lisbon will be lovely in April."

"Lovely," Melissa echoed ironically. "I can hardly wait to get there. But you appear to have totally overlooked the fact that I'm the mother of two young children."

"That's not a problem; you know it isn't. Pauline will be over the moon about having Jenny and Mark to herself for a few days. It could do you the world of good, Melissa dear, so why not treat the trip as a sort of vacation and enjoy yourself?"

He was right about Pauline, she conceded. Selwyn's sister, who ran the Colville family home in Kent with daunting efficiency, would be only too delighted to cope with the children. As for Jenny and Mark, both of them were fond of their Aunty Pauline and they'd be quite happy in her care—no doubt about that. But Melissa had for so long lived with the idea of not being a free agent that the thought of flying off into the blue at a moment's notice seemed outrageous. For years now her life had been loaded with responsibilities . . . to her two children and, until his death almost a year ago, to her disabled husband, Toby. Still, considering that it wouldn't even mean moving Jenny and Mark from their home or disrupting their daily routine, she could hardly put up a good argument against going to Lisbon in this present emergency.

While she dithered, Selwyn clinched matters by exerting his authority as head of the firm. "I have to insist that you go, Melissa, so don't let's waste time arguing the point. We're both going to be very busy in the next few hours. I've a lot of work on my desk to clear up before I leave, and you'll need to rearrange your schedule. Your flight tomorrow is at eleven-fifteen from Heathrow, and I'll have the hotel reservation and air tickets transferred to your name. I take it that your passport's in order?"

"Oh . . . sure."

Selwyn lingered in her office for a few more minutes, briefly running through the details of the preliminary negotiations he'd conducted with Philip Maxwell by letter. "Come to think of it," he concluded, "it makes a lot of sense for you to talk to Maxwell rather than me. Prospective clients always want to know how much of a push we can give their wines publicitywise, and with your PR background you can stun Maxwell with facts and figures." Selwyn leaned across the desk to give her a quick, brotherly kiss on the cheek. "I must be off now if I'm to get everything done in time to catch my plane. Thank the Lord I keep that overnight bag here at the office. I'll have to take the car to the airport, I'm afraid."

"That's okay. I never mind taking the train home."

"Fine. Well then . . . good luck in Lisbon, Melissa." His gray blue eyes took on a tender expression as he added, "I wish I was coming with you, my dear."

After her brother-in-law had departed, Melissa sat deep in thought for a few minutes. The sound of traffic from the street below was muted, as if any harsh noise would be in bad taste in this district of fashionable London clubs and well-respected firms that had catered to the needs of the aristocracy for centuries. Just out of sight down the street was the royal palace of St. James's, at one time a hunting lodge of King Henry VIII and his second queen, the ill-fated Anne Boleyn, and more recently the official center of court activities. The entire area was steeped in history, in tradition—and tradition was what the old-established firm of Colville's Wines thrived on. Not that tradition prevented

Colville's from keeping abreast of the modern world, a fact evidenced by the sheaf of computer print-outs which Melissa had been studying when Selwyn had walked into her office with his announcement.

She reached for the intercom and told her secretary about the sudden change of plans, adding, "You'd better come straight in to me, Linda, and we'll see what we can sort out for while I'm away. But first, will you please get me Pendlehurst."

Within seconds her sister-in-law was on the line. "Pauline, I've just had instructions from Selwyn that I'm to go to Lisbon tomorrow for a few days to fix up this deal with Caves da Silva Cunha. Selwyn can't go himself because he feels it's more important to go to Germany. In fact, he'll be leaving today." Melissa explained the situation briefly and finished up, "So is it okay with you if I leave Jenny and Mark in your charge?"

"Let me see . . . no, I can't think of any reason why that won't be possible. As you know, Melissa, I'm always ready to put myself out to help in any way I can." Though the crisply spoken words carried a hint of martyrdom that was familiar to Melissa, she could tell that in reality Pauline was almost purring with pleasure. She knew that it had been a source of great sadness to her sister-in-law that she'd remained childless through seventeen years of marriage. Now that Pauline was in her forties the possibility of her ever producing a child was receding into an improbable dream.

"You're sure it won't interfere with any plans you and Edward might have made?" Melissa queried.

"There's nothing that I'm not willing to cancel." The reply caused Melissa to smile to herself. It never occurred to Pauline that her husband might have an opinion to offer on any matter that concerned the family.

Though she invariably acted with the best of intentions, Pauline was the bossy, managing type. The role had been thrust upon her early in life, when her parents had been drowned in a sailing accident. At eighteen, the care and upbringing of her two younger brothers—Selwyn, then fifteen, and Toby, just turned ten—had fallen upon her shoulders. And extraordinarily capable shoulders they'd proved to be. While the boys grew up Pauline conscientiously acted as surrogate mother, organizing the domestic arrangements at Pendlehurst Manor with amazing skill for one so young. She was assisted by a married couple, Freda and Tom Huggett, who lived in a cottage on the grounds and did housework and gardening respectively. But there had never been any question about who was in charge. When Pauline married Edward Drake, a dental surgeon whose practice was at nearby Tunbridge Wells, she had apparently taken it for granted that her husband would move in with the rest of the family at Pendlehurst.

Similarly, when Toby and Melissa were married, nine years later, Pauline had expected that the newlyweds would make their home at Pendlehurst. Toby had been happy enough to go along with the plan. As they would have their own suite of rooms, he'd pointed out cheerfully, they could keep to themselves whenever they chose. Melissa, though, had been dead set against the idea. Toby was far too easy going to make any kind of stand against his sister, and she'd feared that their private life would be submerged under Pauline's benign autocracy. For her stubborn determination that they should have a home of their own she had been labeled by Pauline as a difficult, selfish girl. Though burning with resentment at such unfairness, Melissa had nevertheless set out to win her sister-in-law round in the interest of family harmony. It had been a hard struggle, but she'd finally made it. She and Pauline would never really like one another, she suspected, but they were at one in having a grudging respect for each other.

Fate had finally stepped in and put an end to Melissa's struggle for independence. One wet Saturday evening Toby had set out alone in the new sports car he'd acquired just the day before, and had crashed into a tree while taking a bend.

When, three months later, he was discharged from the hospital, the argument in favor of giving up their small second-floor apartment in town had been overwhelming. As a permanent invalid Toby had undoubtedly been happier at Pendlehurst where there was more space and comfort, where he could sit outdoors in his wheelchair on fine days, and where he was surrounded by a bevy of caring relatives. Furthermore, the arrangement had permitted Melissa— with Pauline's help in caring for the children—to take over Toby's job at Colville's Wines and provide them with an income so they wouldn't have to rely on handouts. The job, too, had been a merciful escape for a few hours each day from the pain of watching Toby's slow decline; from the frustration of being unable to reach the charming man she had married, and finding herself instead the main target for Toby's sudden outbreaks of bad temper. Since Toby's death the idea of moving elsewhere had never been a serious proposition. The children were happy where they were, and she felt that it wouldn't be fair to disrupt their lives without good cause.

Melissa managed to get her desk clear by midafternoon. Then, leaving the office, she took a cab to Oxford Street and spent a busy hour or so shopping before riding the underground to Charing Cross. Whenever Melissa happened to travel home by train instead of with Selwyn in his car, she liked to walk the last part of the journey. From Fittlebury Station it was a pleasant half mile stroll along a quiet Kentish lane. She would have taken a taxi that day, but as there wasn't one waiting in the station yard, she decided not to bother; her purchases, though bulky, weren't that heavy. It had been fine all day and promised to be a beautiful evening. Birds sang in the overhanging branches of beech trees which, stirring gently in the breeze, threw dappled patterns of light and shade on the grass-verged tarmac.

The gates of Pendlehurst Manor stood open, and as she started up the graveled driveway the lovely old house stood framed between two giant cedars of Lebanon, its gabled brickwork and tall ornamental chimneys glowing with the rich patina of centuries. Hearing high-pitched voices coming from her left, Melissa changed direction and walked across the lawns to where she guessed Jenny and Mark would be playing in their sandbox. When they spotted their mother, the two youngsters came streaking toward her, followed by anxious admonitions from their aunt to be careful not to trip.

"Mummy, Mummy, come and see the big castle I've built," six-year-old Jenny chirped excitedly.

"Mine is heaps better," said her brother in a voice of heavy scorn. At five, Mark had already picked up regrettable delusions of male superiority from his nursery school friends.

"I'm sure they're both splendid," Melissa said evenhandedly, and bent to give each of her offspring a hug and a kiss. "Let's go and have a look." With a child clinging on either side of her, she walked to where Pauline was seated in a folding garden chair, occupying her time paying the household bills.

"Hi, Pauline!"

"Hello, Melissa." Maybe the more formal greeting wasn't intended to be censorious; it just sounded that way. Her sister-in-law was an impressive figure. She was a big woman, with angular features, good skin and striking violet eyes. Pauline's naturally ash blond hair was thick and straight, and she wore it in a short, shining bob. Her clothes were always of excellent quality, and she had her own distinctive style.

"So you managed to get away early," she went on in her full-bodied voice. "I haven't told the children yet."

"Told us what, told us what?" they chorused, dancing around their mother.

"I have to go away for a few days," she announced in a good-news voice. "To a country called Portugal, where they make lots of wine."

"Will we like it there?" asked Jenny, tilting her head

thoughtfully, and Mark demanded, "Is it by the sea? Can I take my new sailboat that Uncle Selwyn gave me for my birthday?"

"Sorry, darlings, I'm afraid I can't take you with me. Anyway, it wouldn't be much fun for you. I shall be talking business all the time, and I'd have to leave you in the charge of a stranger. So you'll be much better off at home with Aunty Pauline. We can talk over the phone while I'm there. That will be fun, won't it?"

Melissa didn't in fact need to do a big selling job on Jenny and Mark. Their cheerful acceptance of the situation was a relief to her, if slightly deflating. Their mother might be missing for a while, but why should they fret when they would still have a doting aunt and two fond uncles?

It was the best thing all round for the children to live at Pendlehurst, Melissa assured herself once again, even though she secretly longed for greater independence from her husband's family. It might have been different if she'd had a family of her own. She couldn't even remember her mother, and her father had died a few months before her marriage to Toby. He had been a university professor, and although he periodically applied himself to his daughter's welfare, and even showed her limited signs of affection, he really only came alive in the rarefied atmosphere of pure mathematics. Melissa, who had been left to the reluctant care of his various housekeepers, knew only too well the bleakness of a childhood without love or a sense of security.

Not least among the many advantages of living at Pendlehurst was that Jenny could have a pony of her own. She had pleaded for one passionately, and on her sixth birthday Melissa had contrived to make her dream come true. Tom Huggett, the gardener, who'd oftentimes deplored the fact that the Pendlehurst stables now served only as garages, had been delighted at the prospect of having a pony in his charge. Kimbo was a sturdy little brown mare with a neat white blaze, gentle as a lamb and infinitely patient with her small rider. Melissa herself had learned to ride as a child, so she'd felt competent to teach Jenny. She tried to give her as much time on Kimbo as possible. This was easy enough on weekends, of course, and she usually managed to get home early from the office at least once during the week for an extra riding session. She had done this just the day before, but even so . . .

"How would you like to have a ride before your supper, Jenny?"

"Oh, Mummy, can I?"

As the three of them approached the paddock, having collected the saddlery from the tack room on the way, they could see Kimbo contentedly grazing on the lush grass that was starred with golden buttercups. Suddenly the mare lifted her head and sniffed the air, then came frisking toward them joyously. Mark was still a bit timid, but he liked to spend a few minutes in the saddle, and then Jenny had her ride. Melissa was delighted at the progress she was making. She now sat confident and relaxed on Kimbo, with a nice straight back, knees close to the saddle, and hands and heels well down.

Afterward, as they were returning to the house, Melissa spotted Tom working in the greenhouse.

"Hello, Tom. I was coming across to your cottage to see you later on." Explaining about her trip to Portugal, she continued, "I wonder if you could find time to give Jenny a ride or two while I'm away?"

"No problem, Mrs. Colville. I'll be right glad to."

"Thanks a lot."

By the time the children had been bathed and put to bed, and she'd read them a story, Melissa realized that dinner was almost due. Leaving her packing until later, she changed quickly into a plum-colored jersey dress and went downstairs. Appetizing smells came from the kitchen, where Pauline would be putting the finishing touches on one of the superb meals that were regular fare at Pendlehurst. Melissa had long ago given up offering to help, having learned that Pauline jealously guarded any domestic activity that earned praise. Offering to wash dishes at the times when Freda Huggett was off duty was something else altogether.

In the cream-and-gilt-paneled drawing room, Pauline's husband was standing at the french doors to the conservatory gazing pensively at the evening shadows. He swung round as he heard Melissa and smiled a greeting, but there was always an element of caution in Edward Drake's attitude toward her. He was a pleasant-looking man, approaching fifty. His clean-cut features, silver-flecked hair and kindly gray eyes all helped to calm the fears of nervous patients in his dentist's chair. One would guess him to be a solid, dependable, utterly trustworthy man. Yet Melissa knew that he hadn't always been faithful to his wife. There'd been an occasion a year or so before when she was being entertained by clients of Colville's, a couple who ran a smart restaurant in Tunbridge Wells. Edward had been there, too, dining tête-à-tête with a slim, attractive woman. Their relationship had been embarrassingly obvious.

"For heaven's sake, Melissa, don't say anything to Pauline," he'd implored her the next morning, seizing an opportunity to catch her alone before breakfast. Avoiding her eyes, he'd added, "It doesn't mean anything, you know . . . not really."

Since that day Melissa had never been able to view Edward quite so warmly. She instinctively felt anger and resentment against any man who cheated on his wife. But deep down in her heart she couldn't blame Edward too much. Perhaps his main fault had been in allowing Pauline to be the dominant partner in their marriage. He invariably gave way to her wishes with smiling good grace, and to outsiders the Drakes probably seemed an ideal couple. But it had always been apparent to Melissa that their relationship wasn't a truly happy one. Childlessness had doubtless aggravated their problems. So possibly, Melissa had reasoned, the occasional lapse was necessary to Edward as a preferable alternative to a complete breakdown of his marriage. Believing that Edward sincerely cared about his wife, even if he was no longer in love with her, Melissa had promised to keep his secret. Whether or not Edward had continued the affair she didn't know, but it wasn't surprising that he never seemed wholly at ease with her these days.

"Can I fix you a drink?" he asked.

"A white wine spritzer would be nice."

Ice chinked, and soda gurgled. Edward handed her a tall glass. "Here's success to your trip."

"You've heard, then?"

He chuckled. "Pauline's cock-a-hoop, even if she won't admit it. You ought to get away more often, Melissa. You'd be doing her a favor."

"I'll think about it."

"Do that. You work darned hard, and you deserve a real break occasionally." He sighed enviously. "April in Portugal should be lovely. I wish I were coming with you."

Melissa laughed. "Selwyn said the same thing."

Edward gave her a shrewd sideways glance from beneath his bushy eyebrows. "Selwyn's very fond of you, you know."

"Aren't we all?" she quipped. "Fond of one another, I mean."

Edward shrugged and let the matter drop, but his words remained with Melissa all through dinner. During her marriage to Toby, Selwyn had always been a model brother-in-law—courteous, friendly and a stalwart support when the need had arisen. Just recently, though, she had detected signs that his romantic interest in her had never really died.

It had been Selwyn whom she'd first met. After graduating with honors in English she'd taken a job with a PR firm in Mayfair, and Colville's had been one of their clients. Melissa had conceived a novel idea for a series of wine tastings up and down the country, and her boss had sent her along to St. James's Street to discuss it. She and Selwyn had liked one another from the start, and she'd soon become her firm's main liaison with Colville's. The only small cloud on an otherwise sunny horizon had been Selwyn's obvious interest in her as a woman. Though he was neither a passionate man by nature nor impetuous, she'd been aware that he would eventually get around to proposing marriage.

The moment never came. Selwyn's young brother, Toby, who after university had been away on an extended safari in Africa, arrived back in England, met Melissa and fell in love with her. And she had fallen in love with Toby. It had been a whirlwind romance, and they were married within three months. Selwyn had accepted his defeat with good grace, and ever since he'd shown nothing but brotherly feelings for her.

Until now. Too often lately Melissa had been uncomfortably aware that Selwyn's gray blue eyes were resting on her thoughtfully and with growing warmth. She couldn't dismiss the possibility that he was once again thinking in terms of marriage. She could understand that from Selwyn's point of view it would make good, solid sense. They got along extremely well together, and in all modesty, Melissa knew that she was quite an asset to the family business.

From *her* point of view, Selwyn would reason, he had a lot in his favor as her second husband. The fact that he was an affectionate uncle to her children would seem an added bonus. And, of course, Selwyn *did* have a lot going for him . . . except for one vital factor. She didn't love him, and Melissa felt sure that she never could. Love, though, was a luxury she might well have to abandon hope of ever finding again; besides which, she reminded herself, love wasn't necessarily a pathway to lifelong happiness. She'd fallen headlong in love with Toby and for a time their life together had been blissful, but would their marriage have lasted? What if Toby hadn't had that accident, which had left him an invalid up until his premature death? If she were honest, it was difficult to imagine them still being together now. She would not be a contented, fulfilled wife, that much was certain. Poor Toby had always meant well, but his failings as a husband had been manifold. He had been happy-go-lucky, reckless, irresponsible. Even before his accident she had had to face the bitter truth that love alone was not enough.

Lisbon, Melissa had read in the guidebook she'd bought at London Airport, was a city built on seven hills. From the air, as the plane banked for landing, this was difficult to detect. But she could see that it was a beautifully laid-out city on the banks of a wide estuary that glittered in the afternoon sunlight. The most prominent building as they descended was an O-shaped edifice of red brick, which her street map identified as the bullring. Melissa had been happy to read that in Portugal the bull was never killed, but let go to fight another day.

As she alighted from the plane the air felt distinctly warmer than the April air she'd left behind in London three hours before. A bus trundled the passengers the short distance to the terminal buildings, and she was soon through the formalities. Emerging with her baggage, Melissa looked around for a taxi.

"You, I take it," said a male voice from right beside her, "are Mrs. Colville?"

Melissa swung around and met a pair of inquiring brown eyes that were the deep rich shade of dark sherry wine . . . and so extraordinarily riveting that she felt a jolt go through her. It was as if she'd received an electric shock. Dazedly she realized that he was exceptionally tall, well over six feet. He was altogether a large man, with a big-boned frame and a powerful physique.

"That's right," she said, pulling herself together. "I'm Mrs. Colville."

He bowed from the waist in a parody of Latin gallantry. "Allow me to present myself. Philip Maxwell, of the Caves da Silva Cunha wineries." His English was impeccable, the accent veering toward American rather than British. In response to his extended hand Melissa held out her own and was startled, and ridiculously unnerved, at the sensation of having it lifted to his lips. But she might have guessed he'd do that, she reflected wryly as she fought for composure. This man would know all the tricks when it came to women. Senhor Maxwell, she warned herself, would need watching.

"I wasn't expecting to be met at the airport," Melissa told him, conscious that three hours sitting in the plane hadn't improved the appearance of her tan-and-beige checked suit. She would very much have preferred an opportunity to settle in and present herself at his office in the morning, prepared to do battle. Doing battle was how she thought of her negotiations with the head of Caves da Silva Cunha, and nothing about Philip Maxwell's appearance or manner dispelled the notion. Without doubt he was one tough hombre. Those dark brown eyes of his, crinkled with laugh lines at the corners, had an intensity that threatened to see right through any attempt to put one over on him. At least their business discussions should be interesting, she mused, noting that her heartbeat had gone into overdrive.

Philip Maxwell picked up her suitcase, scorning the little wheels at one corner on which Melissa had been glad to trundle it, and tucked her canvas tote bag under his other arm.

"My car's right over there," he said with a jerk of his dark head. "Which hotel are you staying at?"

"Actually, it's not a hotel, but a guesthouse. My brother-in-law had booked himself there, and he transferred the room to me." Melissa consulted the slip of paper she'd kept handy to show to a taxi driver. "It's in Rua das Janelas Verdes."

Philip Maxwell nodded. "A discriminating choice! You'll find it greatly to your taste. That is," he amended with a slow, smiling glance, "if I've gauged your taste correctly, and I rather think I have." He didn't expand on that remark, and Melissa longed to know what he truly thought of her. In business deals, as in everything else, first impressions counted for a lot.

"This is very kind of you," she said, taking two rapid steps to each of his long strides.

"It was the least I could do, when Mr. Colville called me to say that you were coming instead of him. Have you visited Portugal before?"

"No, never."

"You'll love it here." There was supreme confidence in his voice, also a touch of pride which told her that, despite the fact that his father had been American, he regarded himself as Portuguese. He gave her a slantwise assessing glance. "I shall escort you to the various places that you must on no account miss seeing."

"I mustn't trespass too much on your time."

"Don't worry, you won't. Here's my car." He halted by a metallic green Jaguar, slung Melissa's luggage onto the rear seat and held the passenger door open for her. Letting his eyes meet hers and linger for a brief, significant moment, he added, "You and I will have no trouble combining business with pleasure."

Melissa slid into the car and smoothed her pleated skirt across her knees. Quite definitely a man to be watched! In fairness, she thought with a spurt of resentment, he ought to be short and slightly rotund; balding, perhaps, and well into middle age. Such a man might get ideas about her too, but she could have dealt with that; such a man wouldn't evoke this disturbing response in her. As Philip Maxwell settled into the driver's seat she felt conscious of a potent sensual charge crackling across the narrow space between them. Yet he appeared to be perfectly at ease. Dare she hope that she could deceive him into thinking that she was at ease, too?

"So you think I'll like the guesthouse?" She carefully made her voice neutral.

"I'm confident that you will. The place started its life as a convent, way back in the sixteenth century. It still retains something of the cloistered atmosphere. One can imagine the ghosts of the nuns gliding silently through those long hushed corridors, just out of one's view."

"You make it sound quite spooky."

"No, not that . . . not in any scary way. It's just that, as with so much of Portuguese life, there's a tremendous sense of the past." He grinned. "And we have a good deal of past to remember with pride."

"Vasco da Gama," Melissa murmured, keeping her end up with a scrap of knowledge remembered from school. "The sea route to India—fourteen-ninety-something, wasn't it?"

"Very good. But Vasco da Gama was only one of Portugal's famous sons who made their mark on the world. Britain and Portugal share a lot of history. Winston Churchill called us your oldest ally."

The word "ally" gave Melissa an odd feeling of warmth. "And now Colville's and the Caves da Silva Cunha are getting together to continue the tradition."

"Let's hope it works out." Philip Maxwell drew the car smoothly to a halt at a traffic light and sat with his strong, sinewy fingers lightly resting on the wheel. Beneath his short-sleeved khaki shirt he wore fawn cotton drill slacks, and the thin material was stretched taut across his powerful thighs. Melissa deliberately averted her gaze, glancing instead at a modern apartment building across the road.

"I see no reason why our negotiations shouldn't succeed," he went on, "as long as you can convince me that Colville's are in a position to provide what I require . . . a selling agency in Britain with flair and imagination, plus a first-class reputation."

"All of which you already know we possess in ample measure," she pointed out drily. "Otherwise you wouldn't have reached the stage of inviting us here to discuss the matter. Just as, in our turn, we've ascertained that Caves da Silva Cunha is solid and well respected. Colville's Wines values its high standing in the wine trade, Mr. Maxwell, and we wouldn't endanger our reputation by handling anything less than the best.''

He flicked her a lazy grin as the Jaguar smoothly surged ahead of the traffic again. "Which remark I can take as a warning or a compliment, just as I please?''

"I was merely stating facts," Melissa said. "I'm not devious in business matters. I prefer to lay my cards on the table.''

"Easy to say," he observed, "when you hold a strong hand.''

"I wouldn't be here if I didn't think so."

He acknowledged her point with an inclination of his head. The movement caused a lock of his glossy dark hair to fall across his wide brow until, with a flick of his fingers, he restored it to place. Immediately the faint look of boyishness which she'd noted, and found rather touching, was gone. Philip Maxwell was a man of thirty-eight—Melissa knew his age exactly—with mature, decisive features that were etched by the weight of the responsibilities he carried. He had a straight nose, a mouth that was firm even in repose, and a strong jawline with a small cleft in the center of his chin—a tiny indentation that she had a crazy longing to touch with tender fingertips. She swallowed hard, wishing that she could shake off the curious mood of unreality that was making her feel nervous.

"What are your plans for this evening?" he inquired, and Melissa knew that it was a potential invitation.

"First off, I want to shower and change my clothes," she said.

"Then?"

She shrugged. "Lounge around until dinner. Afterward perhaps I'll take a short stroll to get acquainted with Lisbon.''

"Alone?"

"Are you suggesting that it wouldn't be safe?"

"Not at all. As big cities go, Lisbon is remarkably law-abiding. I just thought that being alone would be a bit dull for you. How about having dinner with me? A preliminary skirmish, you might say."

"A skirmish, Mr. Maxwell?"

"As a prelude to our business discussions. And please call me Philip—or better still, Phil."

"I'd hate to be the cause of your breaking any other arrangement you have for this evening." Oh damn, she thought at once, that sounded pert, when she'd only meant to play it cool. She felt a sense of excitement that was entirely out of proportion.

"You'll have to live with the doubt in your mind," he said, his lips twitching in amusement.

"Or decline your invitation."

"Would that be polite? Furthermore, would it be good business tactics?"

She gave in. "Probably not, Mr. Maxwell."

"Phil," he reminded her. "And you haven't yet told me your first name."

"Didn't your inquiries about Colville's produce such a simple piece of information about one of their executives?"

He grinned amiably. "I seem to remember Melissa."

"You seem to remember correctly."

They had reached a point where the traffic swirled around the base of a grandiose statue from which wide, tree-lined boulevards aimed out in all directions. One of these ran down toward the sparkling waters of the Tagus estuary, a mile or more away. In another minute they had dived into the narrow, twisting cobbled streets of the old city, a maze through which Phil seemed to know his way uncannily. They passed a lovely church of cathedral dimensions, with two ornate bell towers and a creamy white dome that seemed to float against the blueness of the sky. On the balconies of tall old houses flowers rioted and fronds of greenery trailed. Lines of spotless washing strung high above the street added a note of gaiety to the scene, giving a nice feeling of real people living real lives right in the heart of this metropolitan city.

Phil turned a final corner and announced, "The Rua das Janelas Verdes."

"The streets seem to have such charming names," Melissa said.

"This one is poetic even in English. The Street of the Green Shutters."

"Is that what it means? How delightful!"

He stopped the car outside a glass-doored entrance in a high wall, bumping the wheels up onto the sidewalk to leave room for the clanking streetcars to pass. As they climbed out a doorman emerged to take Melissa's luggage.

"Thanks for coming to meet me at the airport, Phil," she said with a smile. "It was a kind thought."

"I'll just see you safely inside," he returned. "Besides, we haven't fixed about this evening."

Leaving the small, street-level lobby, they began climbing a flight of wide steps set between high, rough stone walls on which ivy clambered to form a trellised archway overhead. A shorter flight followed a turn, and they mounted to a shady courtyard, a sort of cloister, Melissa thought, remembering what Phil had told her of the building's history. Wisteria clung to the ancient walls, and tables and chairs were set out under gnarled old trees with dark bark and feathery green foliage. An air of tranquility seemed to pervade the whole place.

Inside, the same hushed calm prevailed. A scent of beeswax hung on the air, and the fine pieces of antique furniture gleamed with the patina of centuries of devoted care.

"How clever of Selwyn to find such a quaint place to stay!" Melissa exclaimed. "I'm going to love it here."

Phil smiled at her enthusiasm. "It's a lot nicer than those anonymous international hotels. Somehow you fit the ambience here, Melissa."

She tried to laugh off her sudden embarrassment. "Being ancient, you mean?"

"Being serene, poised, aware of your own worth."

"I feel anything but after a flight from London. Slightly shopsoiled, in fact."

"Not so that anyone would notice. You look . . . ah, here's the desk."

They came to a halt halfway along the cool, stone-flagged corridor, where elegant brass lanterns hung from the vaulted ceiling. A smiling young woman checked her in, speaking excellent English.

"About this evening," said Phil. "I want to take you somewhere special as your introduction to Lisbon." He glanced at his watch. "I'll call back for you at seven. Okay?"

"Thanks. I'll look forward to it."

The room to which Melissa was escorted surpassed her expectations. It was more like a suite, in fact, with the bedroom leading off the sitting room through a brocade-draped archway. Melissa went to a window and threw it open, breathing in the musky warm scent of crimson wallflowers that grew in a small pocket of soil just below. She had a panoramic view of the Tagus estuary, busy with shipping, its blue waters glistening in the sunshine. Far off to her right a graceful suspension bridge reached to the farther bank, where wooded hills rose in a low ridge against the sky. She sighed happily, feeling a glow of excitement. She had a sudden marvelous sense of freedom, a sensation that something inside her was thawing out, that she was beginning to come to life again after a long, hard winter.

You look . . . Phil had begun to say downstairs, and then he'd broken off. She wished that he'd finished his sentence. The thought that he so obviously approved of her gave Melissa such keen pleasure that she felt almost guilty. Heavens above, why shouldn't I be glad about it? she argued. If Philip Maxwell likes me, it will help our business discussions go that much more smoothly. But as she unpacked and hesitated over what to wear for their dinner date, business was the last thing on her mind.

Chapter Two

$\mathcal{H}$e wore a white tuxedo, and Melissa thanked the forethought which had provided her with a dress that lived up to it. As she descended the wide staircase to meet Phil, her fingertips gliding down the polished wooden handrail, she felt confident that she looked good in one of the garments she'd bought in such haste in London the day before—a paisley-patterned dress in a soft mauvy crepe, with a draped bodice and prettily cuffed three-quarter sleeves.

Even so, the approving gleam in those dark, velvety eyes of his was welcome confirmation. He came across the lobby to join her, and the raising of her hand to meet his lips seemed a natural gesture.

"You look beautiful," he said simply.

"Thank you." As they stepped into the courtyard Melissa drew her lacy mohair shawl about her shoulders against the slight coolness of the evening air. He took her arm as they went down the steps, and she thrilled at the pressure of those lean, strong fingers.

"You're very dressed up yourself," she commented with a smile. "Is such formality normal in Lisbon?"

"Not really. But I thought that the occasion called for something special."

"I'm honored."

"No," he corrected. "I'm the one who's honored."

In the little lobby at street level the porter jumped to open the door for them. The Jaguar was parked just outside, and Phil handed her into the passenger seat before going round to slide in beside her. Then they surged off, the tires humming on the cobbled roadway. Phil drove along a busy thoroughfare that ran parallel to the Tagus, past large ornate buildings and stately squares. Glancing back over her shoulder, Melissa marveled at the western sky, which was shot through with colors from smoky gold to fiery red.

Quite soon they left the waterside, and Phil found a parking space. At the restaurant she felt like a princess with his princely figure escorting her as they ascended a staircase into supreme elegance. They sat over drinks in a spacious lounge, surrounded by paneled walls and marble columns, beneath a glitter of huge crystal chandeliers. The menus they were handed while they waited were enormous, offering a vast variety to choose from.

"You must help me," she appealed to Phil with a laugh. "What do you recommend?"

"The cuisine here is international, of course, but I think that you should eat Portuguese tonight. To start with, what about smoked swordfish?"

"Swordfish? Okay, I'll give it a try."

"Pork is the best meat in Portugal, I think. There are a dozen ways you can have it."

"Perhaps you'd choose for me."

Phil grinned at her. "Now you've disillusioned me. I had decided that you were a make-up-your-own-mind sort of woman."

"I am. But there are times when it pays to be the helpless female."

"Is that how you propose to conduct our negotiations? Give me an innocent, little-girl-lost act and rely on my gallantry not to put one over on you?"

Melissa raised her glass and looked at him across the rim. "Not a chance!"

"Pity. I was busy thinking up some harsh clauses I could write into the contract."

"Then I'd better warn you that I'm especially good at reading small print."

"Yes," Phil said, "I guess you are at that."

She laughed, and so did he. The flippant exchange had been useful, Melissa decided. They had each of them made it clear that when it came to business there were to be no easy concessions, so now they could both drop their guards and enjoy the evening.

"Now to choose the wine," Phil went on. "What's your taste in that direction, Melissa?"

"Pretty catholic. It has to be, in my job."

"Let's try a *vinho espumante,* then. Portuguese champagne."

"The one you're going to market?" she queried in surprise. "I thought that it wasn't available yet, even here in Portugal."

"It isn't. But in any case, when I'm eating out I never drink my own wines. I prefer to sample the competition."

"Isn't that risky?" she challenged with a grin. "People might think you rated rival wines higher than your own. A bit like the president of a motor firm who drives around in a Rolls-Royce."

"Perhaps I just like living dangerously," Phil tossed back. He gave their order to the maître d' who had been hovering at a discreet distance, then asked her, "Shall we have another cocktail before we go through?"

"Thanks, but no. I must keep a clear head."

"Why?"

Because, her mind answered, in your company it would be only too easy to forget what I'm here for, too easy to forget that I'm a woman with responsibilities. She tried a dismissive smile to conceal the direction of her thoughts, but she knew from the amused expression in Phil's dark eyes that she had failed.

"I gather that you have two children," he said after a minute.

"Right. Jenny and Mark are six and five years old respectively."

"They must be a great consolation to you. It's not long ago that your husband died, is it?"

"Ten months." Melissa hesitated, unsure whether to say any more, but somehow it was important that he didn't think her unduly frivolous for a woman who had been widowed comparatively recently. "Before his death Toby had been severely disabled for four years, due to a car crash."

"So I understand." Phil paused a moment, then added sympathetically, "It must have been a difficult time for you."

"It wasn't easy," Melissa admitted. "Not for any of us."

It certainly hadn't been easy! Toby had never become reconciled to his disability, and sometimes his anger and frustration had made him resort to childish tantrums when he'd rail at his misfortune and throw things around the room. At such times the children had been really scared of their father, so it had never been safe to leave them alone with him for more than a few minutes. Yet he loved them after a fashion and enjoyed their company. Her husband had been immature in many ways, she reflected sadly, with a boyish charm that had made it difficult to stay angry with him. Before the crash Toby had lived his life with a boy's enthusiasm, a boy's lack of responsibility toward others. The police had estimated his car's speed when it failed to clear that fateful bend at more than a hundred miles an hour. Such an unnecessary accident, ruining his own life and affecting the happiness of everyone around him.

And yet she was well aware that she'd been exceptionally

lucky compared with most women with a disabled husband. She hadn't known the fear of being seriously short of money, and she'd had supportive in-laws. Despite her personal reservations about going to live at Pendlehurst after Toby's accident, she couldn't pretend that it hadn't worked out to her own advantage as well as Toby's. Pauline, for all her irritating, domineering ways, had been wonderful. She had shown infinite patience with her crippled brother, yet been firm with Toby's unreasonable behavior in a way that Melissa herself had found impossible. And the chance to get out of the house for a while each day had helped Melissa to keep sane.

At first she'd thought of taking up her PR career again, but then Selwyn had suggested that instead she should take over Toby's job at Colville's Wines. This had proved to be something that Melissa could cope with almost effortlessly, and she'd felt embarrassed to realize that for so long her husband had been drawing a generous salary for what amounted to a sinecure. She had quickly forged ahead in the job, taking on more and more responsibility. When the elderly Neville Langdon, who'd nursed Colville's through the difficult years until Selwyn had been old enough to take his father's place as head of the firm, finally decided to retire, Melissa had become the number two person. Her success in the business world had been a terrific confidence booster at those times when she'd felt most depressed in her private life. Her job had been an escape—she admitted it freely—but an escape that had enabled her to be a more agreeable companion to Toby and a better, more stimulating mother to Jenny and Mark.

"Who's looking after your children while you're away?" Phil inquired.

"My sister-in-law, Pauline. Actually, we all live together at the family home in Kent . . . Pauline and her husband, Edward Drake, Selwyn, myself and the children. So my trip hasn't meant an upheaval for Jenny and Mark. Pauline looks after them on weekdays in any case, when they're not at school. It all works out nicely," she added with a bright smile.

"I suppose so." Phil twirled his whiskey glass reflectively, making the ice clink. "Don't you find it . . . restrictive at times? I mean, living in the bosom of your late husband's family?"

"It has lots of advantages." Melissa was aware, and knew that he was aware, that she hadn't really answered him.

"How often do you have the chance to get away like this?" He was rephrasing the same question.

"This is the first time I've come abroad on business for Colville's. As a matter of fact," she went on, the thought just occurring to her, "I really believe that this is the first time I've spent a night away from home since Toby's accident."

"It's something to be encouraged, Melissa. You must certainly come to Portugal again."

"Won't that rather depend?"

Phil half closed his eyes so that they seemed heavy-lidded, giving him an incredibly sexy look. "I think it's a foregone conclusion, don't you?"

Thank heaven, she thought, that she'd refused a second glass of this potent dry white port. She'd have to go easy on the champagne.

"Shall we go in to dinner?" he asked.

"Sure. Just looking at that fantastic menu has made me hungry."

The dining room was even more palatial than the cocktail lounge. A quaint touch was provided by the little padded footstools at each table for the ladies.

"I've talked enough about me," she said when they were settled. "Tell me about *you.*"

Phil checked the sidestepping retort that sprang to his lips. With a sense of surprise he realized that here for once was a woman he would enjoy talking with seriously, but the sudden urge to open up his heart to her would have to be resisted. Melissa Colville was a business contact, first and foremost. What else she might become during her stay in Lisbon remained to be seen. In any event, he wasn't about to let it endanger their primary relationship.

In the instant while he pondered what to say he studied her face. She stood out from all the smart, sophisticated women in the room, women whose beauty was marred by a brittle veneer. Melissa's beauty was softer, gentler, entirely feminine . . . though he didn't for an instant doubt her business acumen. He'd been watching in fascination the way her lustrous eyes seemed to change hue with each passing mood, glowing with golden light when she laughed, sparking jewel-bright when she hit back at him, softening to tawny amber in contemplative moments, shadowing with pain when her mind dwelled on the past, as just now.

"I'm half-American," he told her, "as you'll have guessed from my accent if you didn't know already. When my father was a young man, just before World War Two, he inherited a vineyard in the Napa Valley from an uncle. That probably sounds like quite a legacy, but the years of prohibition had hit American wine growers badly and at that time they were only producing basic, low-quality wines."

"Not anymore, though. Colville's handles a few California wines that are quite the equal of anything produced in Europe."

"Yes, the scene in California has changed dramatically in the last few decades. But in the late thirties there was a lack of know-how, and my father, who'd studied law and knew nothing at all about wine growing, decided that if he wanted to learn something useful he'd better visit some of the major wine-producing countries of Europe. He spent time in Germany and France and Spain, and when he reached Portugal he met and fell in love with my mother. Soon after their marriage the United States entered the war and Dad returned home, leaving Mother here with her parents— Portugal was neutral, of course. But after he'd finished his army service he sold the vineyard in California and came here to settle. Eventually he took control of the vineyards belonging to my mother's family."

Melissa smiled. "So that explains how the head of Caves da Silva Cunha comes to have such a very un-Portuguese name. Did you get your accent solely from your father, or have you lived in the United States?"

"I spent four years there at university. Harvard. So I'm a real hybrid in every way."

"You're certainly a lot taller than most of the men I've seen around," she commented. "But otherwise . . . you have that same marvelous hair that's such a dark brown it's almost black, and yet it's full of rich color really. And . . ." She broke off, dismayed to find herself speaking her thoughts aloud so freely.

"Continue with the flattery," Phil prompted, his eyes glinting with amusement.

"I'd better not. It might give you ideas."

"I've got ideas already."

She flushed, and said quickly to cover her confusion, "Your father isn't still living, is he?"

"No, alas. Nor my mother. I have two sisters, one older, one younger. Both of them are married to Americans and live in the United States."

Knowing that he wasn't married, she inquired, "Does that mean you have no family left in Portugal?"

"There's just my maternal grandmother. You'll meet Dona Carlota when I take you to see the vineyards near Sintra. She's a fascinating old lady, I'm sure you'll agree."

Their appetizer of smoked swordfish had arrived, served with quartered lemons. The spicy flavor and sharp astringency were a delicious combination, and Melissa nodded appreciatively. "This is excellent."

"I knew you'd like it."

"I always enjoy trying something new."

"It seems," he said, his dark gaze on her face, "that I've met a woman whose tastes coincide with my own."

"Don't be too sure." The grin she gave him had an appealingly elfin quality that tugged at his emotions. "I might hate the style of pork you've chosen for me."

"As long as you don't hate the company."

The wine waiter arrived with their bottle of *vinho espumante,* making a little ceremony of displaying the label, expertly twisting off the wire and whipping out the cork with a satisfactory pop. The sparkling wine foamed into the tall, fluted glasses, and the bottle was lodged in a silver cooler beside the table.

"You'll like this, too," Phil observed, raising his glance in salute.

Melissa took a sip, wrinkling her nose against the icy bubbles. "Mmm! Delicious. Is it as good as your champagne will be?"

"Only nearly. I'd give this nine out of ten, and mine, nine and a half."

"Not ten out of ten?" she teased. "Such modesty. When am I going to have a chance to taste your wine?"

"Whenever you like. When we've finished dinner, perhaps, at my apartment?"

Certainly not that, she decided. It would be far too dangerous. "I think tomorrow morning at your office would be more suitable," she said lightly. "I'd be better able to make an objective judgment. By the way, what are you planning to call this superlative wine of yours?"

Phil laid down his fork, becoming serious. "I haven't settled on a name yet. It's one of the things I want to discuss with you before I make a definite decision. I can't expect you to think in Portuguese, of course, but you might feel that one name looks and sounds better than another."

"As far as marketing the wine in Britain is concerned, the name should be in English," Melissa told him. "In my experience—and this applies whether you're selling wine, or soap powder, or whatever—it's vitally important to have a name that's easy for people to get their tongue around so they won't be shy of using it. Foreign words can be a trap.

So much advertising is visual, and if customers aren't quite sure how a name should be pronounced, they'll hesitate about asking for the product in the shops. Each time that happens it's a lost sale for you, and your competitors get the benefit."

"That seems to make a lot of sense."

"Believe me, it does. And another thing, the name should have a relevance to the product. It should conjure up the right sort of image in the buyer's mind. Getting the name right is half the battle in marketing."

Phil quirked his lips. "So if I hit on a really good name for my wine, I won't need such an expensive distributor as Colville's?"

"*Half* the battle, I said. The other half is the really tough one."

He laughed, making tiny crease lines ray out from the corners of his eyes. "Want to know what I think, Melissa? I think you're one smart lady."

She felt absurdly pleased, but was careful not to let it show. "Why the surprise? Didn't your inquiries about Colville's elicit that fact?"

"Only up to a point." He gave her a long, intent look that sizzled the blood in her veins. "I'm going to enjoy discovering more about you over the next few days."

Their pork, when it came, was meltingly tender— medallions of lean meat smothered in a piquant sauce, served with tiny buttered potatoes and hearts of artichoke.

"Dreamy," she said appreciatively.

"Shall we go to the *fado* later?"

Melissa lifted a cautious eyebrow. "Okay, I'll buy it. What's the *fado?*"

"A local form of entertainment. You'll like it."

"Another of your intuitions about me?"

"Have I been wrong yet? Trust me, Melissa."

Looking at him across the table she knew, helplessly, that she could easily trust him with her life. She instructed her brain to hold on to a few doubts, a few cautions. But doubt and caution were dissolved away somewhere in the dark, dark depths of those velvet brown eyes.

"Tell me about this *fado*." She implied, without a shred of truth, that she was keeping her options open.

"It's something you really must experience if you hope to understand Portugal and the Portuguese. It is part of us, part of our very heart and soul. The throbbing pulse of this nation."

"My word, that sounds high-flown for a form of entertainment."

Phil's quick smile held a hint of apology. "The *fado* is more than just entertainment, though. It's a vibrant, living art form to which the Portuguese are addicted. Roughly translated, the word means 'fate.' In a sense, I suppose, it could be called folk music, but that, too, is a gross understatement. The *fado* is heavily linked with the past, the glorious past when Portugal played a leading role on the world stage. We think about those long-gone days with a nostalgic sadness that eats into us. It's called *saudade,* which is a word that couldn't possibly be translated, but it's always there in the songs the *fadistas* sing. They tell of unrequited love, of sorrow and jealousy, and behind the story line is a hopeless yearning for past greatness, a regret that it will never return. *Saudade.* An acceptance of our destiny, of the heavy hand of fate, which nothing can ever change. Understand that, Melissa, and you will understand the Portuguese."

She gave Phil a wondering look, surprised by the vehemence of his tone. "Do you really believe that . . . about the heavy hand of fate that nothing can change?"

"I'm Portuguese, aren't I?"

"So how do you explain the success of Caves da Silva Cunha under your direction? I've read a lot about you in the trade press, all of it praising your drive and initiative."

"Put that down to the fifty percent of me that's American," he said with a lopsided grin.

"Maybe. But what I'm seeing all around me here isn't a

nation accepting the heavy hand of fate with resignation. It seems to me that Lisbon is a lovely city filled with people who are determined to live gracious, meaningful lives."

"It seems to me," he returned, holding her gaze, "as if you're beginning to like us already, Melissa."

She swallowed. "I'm not having to try very hard."

The waiter came to pour more wine for them, but Melissa quickly put a hand over her glass to stop him from refilling it. The evening promised to be a long one, and she was determined to keep her wits about her.

"So it's agreed that we go to the *fado?*" Phil queried.

"After that buildup you gave it, how could I refuse?"

The entrance to the *fado* club, a heavy studded door that was firmly closed, was sandwiched between a pharmacy and a bookshop. When the door opened to Phil's ring they were inspected carefully before being admitted. A bit, Melissa thought with an inward giggle, like an old-time speakeasy; the impression was reinforced when they were led down a flight of worn stone steps at the foot of which the host drew aside a heavy curtain. They were in a sort of crypt, the ceiling arching overhead, with candlelit tables dotted all around. In the center a space had been left clear, with chairs set out for the musicians. A few people were eating, but mostly they sat with just a bottle of wine before them, talking animatedly. The place seemed full to capacity, but magically a table was found for them in a good position.

"Champagne again?" Phil asked her as they sat down.

"I'm not sure that I should have any more to drink."

"The things one shouldn't do are usually the most interesting," he said, giving his order to the waiter.

"And usually the most dangerous." Melissa glanced around her. "I like it here. There's a special sort of atmosphere."

"It's Lisbon's in place just now."

"Do you come often?"

Phil lifted his shoulders. "Much of the time I'm not in the

city. When I am, the *fado* is just one of the many things I like to fit in. But I've managed a few memorable evenings here."

With a woman, of course. The same woman? Or a different one each time? Moodily Melissa munched a salted almond from the bowl the waiter had left them.

The room lights dimmed, and a spotlight shone. There was movement through a pair of curtains at the back, and three musicians emerged. All men, all dressed somberly in black suits. Two were thickset and one thin and gaunt—an improbable trio, Melissa thought. Yet their playing, two on guitars that seemed to have an unusually large number of strings, and one on a sort of large mandolin, was sheer delight as their dexterous fingers plucked out a wistful rhythm. All conversation instantly hushed as a fourth figure appeared, a woman this time, again in black, a long-fringed shawl draped across her fine shoulders. She struck a dramatic posture, hands lodged on her voluptuous hips, head thrown back to display a length of sculpted throat that was creamy white against the raven black of her severely drawn-back hair. The sound that emerged from deep within her breast was harsh, almost strident, yet it possessed a strange, soulful beauty that captured Melissa in an instant, though she couldn't translate a single word of the song. It was a story of lost love, a lover who had gone, never to return, an unhappy ballad of jealousy and despair and vanished hope. *Saudade,* Phil had called it.

Melissa felt her eyes pricking with tears, and was then embarrassed to find Phil's gaze upon her. When the song came to a vibrant end he leaned toward her and whispered, "Why, Melissa, you're not a hardheaded businesswoman at all. You're soft and vulnerable."

She laughed shakily. "Who wouldn't be, exposed to this heady, emotional stuff?"

"I'm glad," he said. Glad about what? It was too late to discover, because another song had commenced. Absently

Melissa reached for her glass of champagne to moisten the taut dryness in her throat.

The evening wore on as in a dream. The singers changed, an older woman, a younger one, and then the first one again, all pouring forth their beautiful, poignant songs. And in the breaks she and Phil talked and flirted, smiling into one another's eyes. Melissa loved every moment of it, but she kept reminding herself that it had nothing to do with reality. Her life in England, her home, her job, even her two children seemed part of a separate existence. . . .

At one point, looking at Phil's hand where it rested on the table, letting her eyes feast upon those lean, strong fingers, Melissa suddenly noticed the dial of his wristwatch. She gave a startled exclamation. "Two-thirty! Surely that can't be right!"

"I'm afraid it is," he said. "I suppose we *had* better think of leaving. Otherwise you'll be accusing me of tiring you out on your first evening here so that you're not fit for the clash of wills."

"The clash of wills?"

"Business discussions commence in the morning," he reminded her.

"Oh, yes." Melissa sighed, wishing she didn't have to think about business. "And you have a reputation for being such a tough negotiator."

Phil lifted his eyebrows, looking amused. "Who told you that?"

"Oh, the word gets around," she countered lightly, but she was vexed with herself for having let that remark slip out.

"I suppose it was your brother-in-law," Phil persisted. "Did he deliver a solemn warning that I was a tricky character to handle?"

"Of course not. It was just a matter of . . . well, praising your business acumen." Curse it, she felt the telltale warmth of color rising to her cheeks. What a ridiculous position to have put herself in, as if Colville's were a timid little outfit scared of the harsh realities of the commercial world. "You ought to be flattered," she added.

"Why flattered? It's no more than my due."

"My word, aren't we modest again?" she flipped.

Phil signaled the waiter, then initialed the check. Turning to give Melissa a strange, long look across the table, he said, "I wouldn't expect you to be flattered if I called you a beautiful woman. Gratified, perhaps, but not flattered."

"What makes you think I'd even be gratified?"

His slow smile somehow managed to convey a great deal. "Shall we go, then, before they start another *fado* session?"

Melissa was aware, and the knowledge gave her pleasure, that the eyes of many of the women present followed them out, admiring Phil, envying her. She was not aware, though, that Phil felt equally pleased about her effect on the men present.

Outside, the air felt pleasantly cool on her face, with intriguing, unfamiliar scents wafted to her on the night breeze.

"Do you feel like walking?" Phil asked. "Ten minutes to the guesthouse, I'd guess."

"I'd love to walk, but what about your car?"

"I can collect it later."

They seemed to have the city to themselves as they strolled together along the waterfront. Phil laid his arm lightly across Melissa's shoulders, and she let it remain there, loving the feel of his masculine warmth and closeness. This evening she had laughed from pure happiness and been stirred to tears by poignant singing, and it was a very long time since either of those things had happened. It seemed that the tight-wound control she'd carefully kept on her emotions was easing, beginning to uncoil. Suddenly she was conscious of the beauty of the world, the joy of living, the sensation that there were a million exciting things to be discovered. It scared her, and yet she felt wonderfully thrilled.

In recent years she had refused to think of the future because it seemed to hold no chance of happiness for her beyond the maternal joy she experienced with Jenny and Mark. She had lived through each passing moment, never looking ahead. Even now, even on this momentous evening of her rebirth, she wasn't looking ahead. But there was a quality about her pleasure in the present moment that was different from anything she had known before. Each second seemed jewel-bright and precious. The future was some-thing else; the future was reality. This—walking with Phil in the darkness, his arm warmly about her shoulder, his thigh sensuously against her hip—was sufficient in itself. A beau-tiful dream.

It had to end, of course; every dream had to end. They turned away from the waterside and climbed the short hill to the guesthouse. The lower street doors had been left open for latecomers.

"Thanks for a lovely evening, Phil," she said. "I've really enjoyed myself."

"Me, too."

"Er . . . what time should I be at your office in the morning?"

"Whenever it suits you. But I'll come up with you now and see you safely inside."

Melissa felt pleased; it would delay their parting for a few more precious moments. They walked side by side up the two flights of shallow steps, concealed lights making a fairyland arbor of the trailing ivy. The upper courtyard was in darkness, but a glimmer showed from behind the glass of the entrance door. She went to ring for the night porter, but Phil's hand came up to restrain her. As she turned slowly and went into his waiting arms she discovered that the dream still hadn't quite ended. He held her close, his lips resting lightly on her hair, and Melissa reveled in the pulsing life of his strong male body. She felt deliciously weightless, floating freely among the stars that glittered brightly be-tween the lacing branches of the courtyard trees. In the

seeming silence there were night sounds . . . the faint
strains of a radio somewhere, a car swishing past. Far off,
the siren of a departing ship; near to, the restless rustling of
a bird in the creeper that clad the ancient walls. But the
loudest sound in her ears was the hammering of her own
heartbeat as Phil drew her still closer.

"You're a remarkable person, Melissa," he murmured.

"You're . . . pretty special yourself." Her tone, intended
to be lighthearted, emerged as thin and husky.

"I'm glad it was you who came, and not your brother-in-
law."

She forced a laugh. "Hadn't you better wait and see
before you say that? I might be a whole lot tougher than you
bargained for."

"I can't believe it."

"You'd better believe it."

But, and they both knew it, they were only spinning out
the lovely moments of anticipation before the inevitable,
before Phil's mouth came down to meet hers. His lips were
cool and soft, then suddenly warm and demanding. Melissa
felt herself drowning in a great wave of sensual excitement,
but somehow she clung to a shred of sanity. Twisting in his
arms, she freed a hand and reached out to press the bell.

"That's enough, Phil," she said raggedly.

For several moments longer he still held her, his lips
trailing across the satiny skin of her cheek. Then, as the
heavy door rattled and swung open, he reluctantly let her
go.

"I can't imagine ever having enough of you," he whispered.

Melissa slipped inside without answering him because she
didn't trust her voice, or her emotions. But as the porter
was closing the door again, she heard Phil give a soft
chuckle.

Ascending the stairs was like coming out of a swirling fog.
Her head began to clear, and a niggling inner voice challenged her. Was she being an utter fool? How much of this

evening had been just a softening-up process on Phil's part for the coming business negotiations? Had she been conned by a smart operator? Surely not, she couldn't really believe that.

Upstairs in her room she didn't put a light on but stood at the open window, gazing out at the rippling reflections on the dark waters of the estuary. From the street below she heard a faint sound of receding footsteps. Could it still be Phil, or was it some other late walker?

With a sigh Melissa turned away and found a light switch, then drew the curtains. It was a symbolic gesture, as if she were coming back to her normal self. She felt no anger or resentment against Phil, just a sadness that this evening hadn't been for real. She would have to watch Phil Maxwell with rather more care in future, she warned herself, and not be so easily swayed by his devastating charismatic charm.

But it had truly been a beautiful evening.

Chapter Three

$\mathcal{I}$n the morning Melissa took a refreshing shower and pondered what to wear for the day ahead. The right image was essential. She needed to look confident, relaxed and efficient. Not glamorous. Definitely not sexy. Last night had been last night, but this morning she was meeting Phil Maxwell to do a job.

She allowed herself the luxury of thinking about Phil while she ate the breakfast of croissants and apricot preserves that had been brought to her room by a young maid. She was sitting on one of the broad window seats from where she could look out across red rooftops at the morning-bright waters of the Tagus estuary. He was an incredibly attractive man, and she couldn't help responding to him—wouldn't any woman? There was a look of dynamic strength in his hard, loose-limbed body, a sensation of leashed power. She liked the way he held his head, relaxed but attentive, and there was such intelligence in his strongly marked features. Phil didn't give his feelings away, so it wasn't easy to guess what he was thinking, but she couldn't doubt that his feelings went deep. He was a superb companion with the ability to make the woman he was with feel important. Obviously he was accustomed to escorting women around; Melissa didn't fool herself into thinking that meeting her had been of any great significance in his life. And yet . . . there had been a warm look in those compelling dark eyes of his that thrilled her even now as she remembered it. His good-night kiss had been shattering, awakening emotional needs in her that she had believed were gone forever.

While drinking her second cup of coffee Melissa decided to call home. Allowing for the time difference, she calculated that there was about a half hour before Pauline would be setting out to drive the children to the pre-school they attended, Mark for mornings only.

"Hi, Pauline," she greeted her sister-in-law. "It's me."

"Good morning, Melissa." The tone was cool, almost as if Pauline resented the fact of her phoning. Yet her sister-in-law would have been equally critical if she'd neglected to show concern about Jenny and Mark while she was away.

"I thought I'd call before you got tied up today. Is everything okay?"

"Naturally."

"Yes, of course. Er . . . could I have a word with the children?"

"One moment, I'll fetch them to the phone." Pauline unbent enough to inquire, "Is your trip going according to plan?"

"Yes, fine thanks. You might tell Selwyn if he calls from Germany that I've already made contact with Senhor Maxwell, and we've chatted about things in general terms. I'm meeting him at his office this morning to get down to formal discussions."

"You seem to be making fast progress." There was a grudging undertone in Pauline's voice. Did she ever regret, Melissa wondered, not for the first time, that she had limited her activities to the running of Pendlehurst and hadn't directly involved herself in Colville's? But the direction of Pauline's thoughts became clear when she added, "You mustn't try to rush things, Melissa. Selwyn wouldn't be at all pleased if you reached a hasty, ill-judged agreement with Caves da Silva Cunha, just because you wanted to hurry back to Jenny and Mark."

Translating this as "I hope you won't come back too soon, because I'm thoroughly enjoying having total charge of your children," Melissa said tactfully, "I promise I won't do that, Pauline. I fully realize how important this deal is to us at Colville's." It was nice, she thought impishly, that she was being actively encouraged to prolong her stay in Lisbon.

"Ah, here are the children," Pauline said. "Jenny . . . Mark, your mother is on the telephone, all the way from Portugal. You may speak to her for just a minute, and then you must get ready for school."

Melissa heard them squabbling over who should be first, then they were both chattering at her together. "Mummy, Mummy, I runned fastest in the whole class yesterday," said Mark, and Jenny piped in with, "Miss Searle put my picture of Kimbo on the wall." Melissa talked to them for a few minutes; then, anticipating Pauline, she brought the call to an end. "It's lovely here in Lisbon," she told them. "I must bring you both one day." The idea suddenly seemed very attractive. "Goodbye, darlings."

Thirty minutes later Melissa had made up her face, fixed her hair in a french knot and finally decided to wear her cream linen suit matched with a silky emerald blouse. She was giving her appearance a last look in the mirror when there was a knock at her door. It was the maid bringing her a large bouquet of yellow rosebuds. A white card inscribed in a bold, flowing hand read, *"Thank you for a perfect evening. I look forward to seeing you again this morning at my office. Phil."*

Melissa let out a long sigh of pleasure. It was years since she'd been given flowers, not since her first wedding anniversary. The following year Toby entirely forgot the date, and after that such a romantic gesture wasn't part of their relationship. But her pleasure was shadowed by a feeling of ruefulness. She'd vowed last night—despite knowing how difficult it would be—not to let Phil Maxwell sweep her off her feet. His gift of roses threatened to erode her resolve completely.

A white pottery vase used as a shelf ornament was just the right size, so she arranged them in that, fetching water from her bathroom. The display of roses made a beautiful focal point on the antique writing desk, and their delicate fragrance pervaded the room.

The Caves da Silva Cunha offices, Phil had explained to her the previous evening, were in the commercial district not far from the guesthouse, so it wouldn't take her long to get there. But Melissa felt impatient to be out and about on such a lovely morning. She wanted to explore for a while, to get the feel of Lisbon. The breeze from the river was like silk on her face as she set forth carrying her brown leather document case, a folded street map in her other hand. With an almost childlike feeling of wonder and delight she wandered through the maze of narrow streets which zigzagged in all directions, often rising steeply, then plunging down again. Streetcars clanked past noisily, taxis and delivery vans rushed past her at recklessly high speeds, and the cobbled sidewalks were thronged with people, some of them carrying large packages or bundles of vegetables balanced on their heads. She passed little shops selling fashionable knitwear or smart shoes that were right next door to dark, cavelike grocery stores that had sacks of loose beans and potatoes and dried apricots stacked around the entrance. On almost every corner was a café or winebar, with a shoe-cleaning boy or an old man selling lottery tickets outside.

Eventually Melissa emerged into a huge open square with lots of trees and smart shops and dominated by an impressive statue of a cloaked figure on a tall stone column. On the geometrically patterned black and white cobbles were magazine stands and flower stalls shaded from the sun by gaily striped umbrellas. Among the profusion of exotic blooms Melissa spotted yellow roses, but none so fine, she was pleased to note, as those Phil had sent her. At one end of the square was a magnificent columned building in the Grecian style, which Melissa discovered from her guide-book to be the National Theater. Centrally placed opposite it was a large ornate fountain with allegorical sculptures. She stood for a while watching some children skipping around its stone basin, shrieking with laughter when an occasional breeze sent the spray spattering over them. Smiling, Melissa strolled nearer, intrigued by the way the sunlight struck through the curtains of water, making it sparkle like pale silver gilt. A silver fountain.

The thought made her pause. This fountain possessed the frothy lightness and dancing gaiety of a glass of champagne. Could it be the answer for marketing the new *vinho espumante?* Silver Fountain. It sounded right; it had the feel of effervescence, of romantic imagery. Suddenly excited, she felt impatient to tell Phil. She glanced at her wristwatch and was astonished to see how the time had fled. She ought to hurry. She hailed a passing taxi, and within minutes she was alighting before a modest, four-storied building facaded with the delicately patterned blue and white tiles that seemed to be a feature of so much of Lisbon's architecture.

Inside, Melissa's first impression was of dignified comfort. A courteous receptionist on the second floor greeted her in English and invited her to be seated while her arrival was announced to Senhor Maxwell. Within moments Phil appeared through a doorway, a warm smile of welcome dancing in his dark eyes.

"I've been waiting impatiently for you to arrive, Melissa."

As before, he kissed her hand, but this time his lips lingered a moment. She felt a swirl of excitement ripple through her.

"I hope I'm not late," she stammered. "It was such a

lovely morning that I decided to stroll around for a while, and I rather lost track of time."

Phil took hold of her elbow and steered her across the lobby to a flight of stairs at the rear. "If you'd told me you wanted to look around this morning," he said, "I'd have escorted you. Where did you go?"

"I hardly know, the street layout is so confusing. I ended up in a big square . . . Rossio, isn't it?"

"With the statue of Dom Pedro IV on a high column?"

"Yes, and the National Theater."

"Well, on all future excursions," he said reproachfully, "please remember that I shall be your guide. There's a great deal for you to see in and around Lisbon."

"And when are we supposed to discuss business?" she inquired drily. "Slot it in between this church and that museum?"

"I doubt if we shall need to spend very much time in formal negotiations, Melissa."

"You speak as if it's already signed and sealed that Colville's shall represent you in Britain."

Phil opened a door at the head of the stairs and ushered her into a spacious office. "I don't imagine that we're going to find it difficult to reach an agreement, do you? We're both intelligent people, fully aware of the advantages our respective firms can bring each other. I don't anticipate that you'll want to quibble over the terms, Melissa."

"That depends on what you're laying on the table."

Phil laughed, and she shivered at the note of confidence in the sound. He was a man who was very sure of himself, she thought . . . too darn sure of himself. In those first moments she was so acutely aware of him that she paid no attention to her surroundings. He ushered her into a chair, and as she sat down he stood behind her, his hands resting lightly on her shoulders. "What can I offer you to drink? A glass of wine, or would you prefer coffee?"

"Coffee, I think, at this hour of the day."

"Sure." To her relief—and equal regret—Phil removed

his hands and walked to the desk, picking up the phone and speaking in rapid Portuguese. Melissa watched him. He wore a lightweight mid-gray suit that was casually cut yet perfectly molded his lithe, athletic frame. It was teamed with a white shirt and dark blue tie, and once again she was struck by the clean, healthy look of his dark hair. Her fingers itched to tangle themselves into its glossy lushness.

Melissa forced her attention away from him and glanced around the office. It was comfortable and recently re-painted, though she guessed it hadn't been greatly changed since his father's time, as if Phil valued tradition. In that he would be at one with Selwyn, but in no other way was there any similarity between the two men. They had been born in the very same year, but her brother-in-law seemed content to slide gently toward staid middle age, while Phil Maxwell had about him the energetic vitality of a much younger man, plus style and panache, plus . . .

Darn it—her thoughts kept reverting to him. Annoyed with herself, she looked out one of the long windows at the little green oasis of a churchyard below. The click of the replaced phone snapped her back.

"Thank you for the roses, by the way," she said. "They're beautiful." With a light laugh she added, "I hope you don't imagine that a bunch of flowers is going to undermine my bargaining ability."

"If I did," he said, his glance meeting and holding hers, "it would be a case of the biter getting bit."

"Meaning?"

"For a woman to come to talk business in a man's office looking the way you do, Melissa, is taking an unfair advantage. It won't be easy for me to keep my mind on negotiating the terms of a contract."

"Roses first, then flowery compliments. What's your next move, I wonder?"

Phil's mouth curved one-sidedly. "You can't expect me to reveal my campaign strategy so early in the battle."

The arrival of coffee saved Melissa the need to find a

comeback. Not that she'd have had any difficulty. Strangely, despite her rapid pulsebeat, being with Phil gave her a terrific feeling of confidence in herself, as a business executive and as a woman. She was going to enjoy every minute of her stay in Portugal, which didn't mean losing sight of what she was here for. . . . The two things went together.

Phil was pouring from the silver coffee pot into fragile little gold-rimmed cups. "Cream?" he asked.

"Just a dash, please."

"Try one of these cakes," he said, offering her a plate. They looked incredibly tempting, tiny custard-filled pastry shells. Melissa took one and popped it into her mouth, where it melted on her tongue. "Mmm! Delicious."

"The Portuguese," Phil observed, "tend to have a sweet tooth."

She laughed. "I see that I'll have to watch my weight while I'm here."

He subjected her to a long and leisured scrutiny, as if making a critical study of her figure. Melissa began to feel uncomfortable, but she steeled herself not to let it show.

"So where do we start?" she asked briskly.

Phil seemed to come out of a reverie. "I'm sorry . . . ?"

Melissa reached for the document case that she'd propped against her chair leg. "I have a number of general queries to clear up before we can get down to detailed discussions, and I expect the same applies to you."

"Right," he said. "You go first. Fire away."

"Colville's will need solid facts and figures about the size of your operation," she began. "We know from what you've already told us in your letters that you've made a heavy commitment to champagne, Phil, but we have to be satisfied that you can meet the demand that we create for you in Britain. Nothing kills interest in a new product faster than a shortage of supply. If you were manufacturing plastic kitchenware or whatever, Colville's, as selling agents, would only need to insure that you had the factory capacity to step up production at short notice. But with a product like wine, demanding a lengthy process from grape on vine to matured wine in bottle—a product, morever, that is so dependent on year-to-year vintages—it's tricky to get the right balance between demand and the available supply."

Phil eyed her with new respect. "You're not just a pretty face, are you, Melissa?"

"I thought you'd cottoned on to that already," she said with a laugh. "So what assurances can you give me?"

"Plenty. All the facts and figures you could possibly require will be made available to you. And you can take my word for it that it'll be authentic data."

"How about export licensing and so on? Colville's hasn't done all that much trade with Portuguese wine growers so far, but judging from our experience in other countries, officialdom can be a real pain."

"Don't worry, I can handle the bureaucrats," Phil said confidently. "No shipments of my wine are going to be left languishing on a quayside somewhere for lack of proper documentation."

Melissa noted the determined set of his jaw and believed him. "Query number three," she went on, "is quality control. A branded wine, unlike a vintage wine, needs to be standardized in every respect, always reliably the same."

Phil nodded. "When you come to visit the Silva Cunha wineries, I know that you'll be favorably impressed. In matters of hygiene and so on we go a lot further than the minimum standards required by law. And as for producing wine of unvarying quality and flavor, I didn't go in for large-scale production of *vinho espumante* until I was completely satisfied that our blending procedures had been perfected."

Melissa had one or two more initial queries. Then Phil asked some very pertinent questions about Colville's. "You've had a few failures, haven't you?" he said. "I seem to remember that a couple of years ago there was a German wine you couldn't shift. What went wrong?"

She answered him candidly. "Several factors were involved, but the chief error was our misjudgment of the market. The vacant slot we had anticipated for such a sweet wine proved too small to justify the cost of the operation. That particular wine was very expensive, too, which didn't help in a time of recession."

"I like your honesty, Melissa."

"In a business like ours," she said lightly, "if you aren't straightforward you soon come unstuck."

"You'll never convince me that you tell the truth for purely practical, commercial reasons. You tell the truth, Melissa, because you're that kind of woman."

"If it pleases you to think so . . ."

"*Know* so," he corrected. "Now, I think it's time for a tasting so you can judge my honesty in awarding my *vinho espumante* nine and a half marks out of ten."

A couple of minutes later, in response to Phil's instruction, an elderly man appeared bearing a tray with a gold-capped, green-tinged bottle in an ice bucket, and two champagne flutes. After placing everything on the desk he bowed and withdrew. Phil lifted the bottle and wrapped it in a white napkin; then he expertly dealt with the cork and filled the two glasses with foaming liquid. Melissa accepted the one he handed her and held it up to the light, watching the stream of tiny pinpoint bubbles rising from the bottom and springing to the surface with a faint hiss.

"Last night," she reminded him, "we were talking about finding a suitable name to market this under."

"Have you been giving it some thought?"

"Not seriously. But an idea struck me on the way here this morning." She felt strangely nervous as she tried her inspiration on him. It really mattered a lot to her that he should like it. "I was wondering what you'd think of calling it Silver Fountain."

Phil didn't speak for a few moments, savoring the shape of the name. Then he murmured, "Fonte de Prata."

"Is that what it would be in Portuguese?"

"Yes. It sounds good in both languages, don't you think?

Yes, I like it." He gave her a wide, approving smile. "We seem to have found the answer, Melissa."

"It's only a first thought," she said, with sudden qualms. "Shouldn't we make a list of possible names before we decide?"

"First thought, last thought—if it's right, it's right." He looked at her intently, and the caressing expression that made her skin tingle was there again in his eyes. "I'm a great believer in first impressions, Melissa. Now, what do you think of the wine?"

She sipped slowly, appreciatively, and felt the bubbles prick deliciously against her palate, then suddenly fountain through her with an exhilarating glow. "It's exactly as I expected, really first class. Perfectly balanced, with a faint hint of acidity. You categorize it as a *seco*, don't you? And it's certainly just the right degree of dryness for the British palate." She tasted again. "Yes, I think it's very good indeed."

"So you foresee a bright future in Britain for Silver Fountain?"

"I certainly do."

"Let's celebrate over lunch."

"Celebrate what, exactly? There's no contract even drafted yet."

"So we'll anticipate a little. Come on."

They walked to the restaurant, which was just a short distance away. Like the *fado* club, it had an unimposing entrance off a narrow, cobbled street. Yet when they entered the dining room it was utterly charming, with a fine oriental carpet on the floor, antique carved chairs and tables set with white napery and glinting silver and crystal. It overlooked a small, sunlit garden, and they were escorted to a table beside an open window with some kind of clinging vine trailing around it. Melissa caught the honey-sweet scent of blossoms blending with the appetizing aroma of food.

"What a delightful place!" she said enthusiastically. "No stranger would ever suspect it was here."

Phil grinned. "We like to keep a few secrets from the tourists." He glanced at the menu and said, "Fine. I was hoping they'd have sea bass today. Last night's catch was specially good."

"How do you know that? You don't own fishing boats as a sideline, do you?"

"If you live in Lisbon, you know what the boats bring in day by day. In the same way, it's not only the wine growers in Portugal who know the state of the vintage, not only the farmers who keep abreast of how the maize crop is coming along, and the olives and the oranges."

"It sounds to me," Melissa said slowly, "as if the Portuguese have their priorities right."

He ordered sea bass for them both, discussing with the waiter the salad that would accompany the fish. When the man had departed Phil asked, "And what are your priorities in life, Melissa? Your personal priorities?"

She shrugged with a dismissive smile. "About the same as most people's, I guess. To have the basic necessities, plus the occasional luxury. Good health, of course, contentment . . ."

"And tell me," he said softly, "have you achieved those modest aspirations?"

"More than my fair share, in some ways. I have two lovely children, and a standard of living that's beyond mere comfort."

"But . . . ?"

Oh, damn him, Melissa thought forlornly, could he see right through to her soul? She gave him a defiant glance. "Of course there are buts. No woman expects her life to be perfect. Do men?"

"Some men do," he said. "Some don't."

Melissa thought about him as she broke off a piece of the crisp roll. At thirty-eight he was still unmarried, yet she hadn't a doubt that women rated as highly important in his life. Was there, she wondered with a curious pang, one woman who counted above all others?

"Which category do you fit into?" she queried.

"I don't fit into categories."

"So you're unique. Perhaps you find your career totally fulfilling?"

"When I'm at the office, or out in the vineyards, I get great satisfaction from it. But there's more to life than just work. I'm sure we're agreed about that, Melissa."

While he spoke Phil studied her profile, silhouetted against the sunlight. Melissa was gazing through the open window and appeared to be watching a yellow butterfly as it flitted from bloom to bloom gathering nectar. She seemed unaware of the graceful picture she made. Perhaps it was this unconscious beauty of hers that appealed to him so much. He had known many beautiful women, but none who carried their feminine charm so effortlessly. Each of her features was delicately molded, and every movement she made had a natural grace. Her smile when it came was enchanting, her laugh even more bewitching. But she didn't laugh easily, and there was a sadness behind her smile. Phil wanted her, wanted her so much that he felt feverishly impatient; she would be in Portugal for such a short time. Yet he knew with certainty that Melissa Colville was not a woman to be rushed.

How much had she suffered, he wondered, as a result of losing her husband? Or had his death been a happy release for her? From gossip in the wine trade he'd gathered that the crippled Toby Colville had been a hellishly difficult man, seeming to take pleasure in venting his bad temper on those around him. Had Melissa stayed in love with the man she'd married right to the end? Had she remained faithful to him? Somehow Phil felt sure that she had, which must have been tough on her. He knew instinctively that Melissa was a passionate woman.

Sooner or later she would have to start living a normal life again; a passionate woman's instincts and needs couldn't remain thwarted forever. A love affair at this stage would undoubtedly be a good thing for her, so there was no reason for him to hold back. Yet he sensed a vulnerability behind Melissa's outward assurance and air of brisk competence. Her emotions were fragile, and she could easily be hurt. So he must go gently with her, Phil told himself, and not try to bulldoze her into anything.

Their fish came, smothered in aromatic herbs and butter. He allowed a few moments to pass in silence, content to observe Melissa's pleasure in the food. She became aware of his gaze and looked up. They smiled at one another across the table, and he noted the faint flushing of her cheeks.

"On the subject of work," he said, "I think we put in a good morning, don't you? So let's play hookey this afternoon, and I'll show you something of Lisbon."

"But—"

"Stifle that overdeveloped conscience of yours, Melissa, and say yes." He watched temptation flit across her face and felt pleased. "You can't visit Portugal without doing some sightseeing."

"I'm planning to see as much as I can possibly fit in," she protested.

"I'm glad to hear it. So think how much more efficiently you'll cover the ground with someone who knows his way around. Besides," he added after a momentary pause, "I shall be terribly disappointed if you turn me down."

Melissa knew that he was referring to more than just accepting him as an escort. She had no intention of allowing herself to be swept into something she didn't want, that much was certain; but she was still undecided what she did want from Phil. She wasn't a free agent. She had two children to think of and a duty to her dead husband's family. But here, a thousand miles from home, did the same rules apply?

"I won't promise never to disappoint you," she said with a laugh, "but your logic on the subject of sightseeing this afternoon can't be faulted."

"Great! We'll do a whirl around some of the main tourist

attractions and finish up along the coast at Estoril for dinner."

"Hey, I didn't agree to dinner," she protested.

"Give me one good reason why you shouldn't dine with me this evening."

The only reason was one that Melissa couldn't possibly voice. While she hesitated Phil said triumphantly, "So, we dine at Estoril."

She ought to refuse, a cautious inner voice warned her. Having determined not to let Phil sweep her off her feet, she was permitting him to do just that. But another inner voice was coaxing her to give way, and that was the voice she heeded.

"We're still eating lunch, for heaven's sake, and you're already talking about dinner," she grumbled. "I shall have no appetite."

"Then you'll present all the greater challenge to the skill of the chef."

The matter seemed to be settled.

Chapter Four

The crag-perched palace of Pena was cloaked in mist as they approached the little town of Sintra in Phil's car, having left Lisbon half an hour earlier at the end of another day of business discussions in his office.

"It's too bad, Melissa, that you can't see Pena," he said. "Up there was a crazy site to build a royal palace, considering that half the time it's lost in the clouds. But then Pena is a crazy palace, a conglomeration of mock-Arab minarets and Gothic turrets and heaven knows what else. On a fine day it looks like something straight out of Hans Christian Andersen, and you certainly get a fabulous view from up top. If it's clearer tomorrow I'll take you up there."

"I've read about Pena in my guidebook," Melissa told him, "and I'm longing to see it."

"And I'm longing to show it to you." He flashed her a quick grin that made her heart jolt. "I guess I just like being with you."

Businesswise, she and Phil had made steady, satisfactory

progress, but their private relationship was moving forward at a speed that dismayed her. He was a fantastically attractive man, no one could deny that, but her sensual response to him was scary. She tried to console herself that it was all very understandable in the circumstances. For the first time since Toby's death she was free, or relatively free, of the restraints of home. She was a normal, healthy woman, and Philip Maxwell had a dynamic charisma about him, so naturally she found herself attracted to him.

They'd spent the previous afternoon sightseeing in Lisbon, followed by another splendid dinner at a seafront hotel in Estoril. What Melissa remembered, though, far more than the places they'd visited and the superb food they'd eaten, was the touch of Phil's broad, strong fingers when he'd taken her elbow to steer her; the desirous look in his eyes each time their glances had met; the clean, spicy masculine tang of him. At the Castle of St. George, perched high on one of Lisbon's seven hills, he had stood right behind her to point out landmarks over her shoulder, and Melissa had shivered at the slight warm pressure of his body against her back, the roughness of his sleeve against her earlobe.

At the picturesque Gothic ruins of the Carmo Monastery, devastated like half of Lisbon in the terrible earthquake of 1755, Phil had momentarily held her by the shoulders as she turned to face him with a question. They had stood like statues for an instant before she broke away, her heart hammering and her voice unsteady as she babbled about the Carmo's archaeological exhibits, trying to pretend that nothing significant had happened.

Okay, Melissa said to herself now, endeavoring to be totally honest, Phil's a sexy man, and I admit that I'm tempted by the thought of making love with him, of being held in his arms and coaxed to passion by his kisses and caresses. But that doesn't mean that I'm going to let him charm me into bed, as he obviously wants to do. I'd be crazy to let myself get involved in a relationship that could only last a few days. I couldn't just forget about Phil when I got back home, or—as he himself would doubtless do—tuck the episode away in a corner of my mind as a pleasant but unimportant interlude. I'm certainly not about to put my emotional happiness at risk for the sake of a brief affair, however rapturous.

And yet, when she returned to England after their business was completed, would she bitterly regret the lost opportunity and call herself a fool?

Phil's invitation to visit the Silva Cunha vineyards and wineries was something that Melissa had anticipated. It was necessary if she was to obtain a full picture of the firm's operation. But subtly the weekend at the Quinta das Andorinhas had seemed to change from its original purpose; it was turning into a social visit with a bit of business thrown in, rather than the other way around. She was grateful, at least, that Phil's grandmother would be there. Dona Carlota's presence would keep down the emotional temperature between them.

The route Phil took out of Sintra—what he called the old road—was sheer delight. Almost devoid of traffic, the narrow highway wound between ancient stone walls thickly encrusted with tawny-colored lichen and overhung with lush green creepers. Now and again Melissa had tempting glimpses through a gateway of a gracious villa set in a leafy garden, of sunlit terraces and shady arbors.

"It's very lovely around here, Phil."

"Have you ever read *Childe Harold*?" he asked.

"I can't say I have."

"You should one day. Byron went into raptures about Sintra. I think that you'll fall for the Quinta das Andorinhas in a big way, Melissa. The house was a wreck when my father took it over, and the Silva Cunha vineyards were run down and unproductive. He worked damned hard to lick it all into shape again. Unfortunately, though, he had a fatal heart attack before he could achieve everything he'd hoped for, which was to build Caves da Silva Cunha into one of the major wine houses of Portugal."

"But you've continued what your father started. How old were you when he died?"

"Twenty-two. It was lucky, I suppose, that I'd just finished at Harvard. At that time my mother was still alive, and she was able to help me."

"Wine making must be immensely satisfying," Melissa said. "I know that it's a constant battle against the weather and disease and pests, but you're creating something that brings a lot of enjoyment to a lot of people."

"You're in the wine trade, too," Phil pointed out. "You help to bring people enjoyment."

"Yes, but marketing a product isn't quite the same as creating it."

"I guess you're right. Still, your own creative urge is satisfied by your children, isn't it?"

"That's true to some extent," Melissa acknowledged. "But the concept of maternal fulfillment is a sly argument that male chauvinists use to keep women down. Men have a hand in creating children too, don't forget. And women just as much as men need to express their personalities in ways beyond home building and domesticity. That's why most women these days want to have careers, as well, even if they don't actually need the cash."

"It's beginning to happen in Portugal, too," Phil commented. "More and more young women are looking for careers."

"Bully for them!"

The road descended into a village of pretty, pastel-colored houses, most of them garlanded with colorful climbing plants and trails of greenery. The mellow chime of a church clock broke the early evening hush, and a cloud of pigeons fluttered skyward. A bent old woman in long black skirts hobbled on a stick, carrying a basket of vegetables, while a teenage girl with bare legs and boldly made-up eyes whizzed past her on a moped. To Melissa, it typified the old and the new order in Portugal.

Beyond the village the Silva Cunha vineyards began, long rows of lush, regularly spaced vines just coming into flower. A cluster of low buildings marked the winery, white stone walls turned to glowing gold in the early evening sunlight.

"That's where it all happens," said Phil with a flourishing gesture of his hand. "The transformation of grapes into the magic of wine."

Melissa was impressed by the neatness of everything. "It all looks so immaculate, Phil. I can't see a weed anywhere."

He laughed. "I've declared weeds illegal. Why should they have water and nutrients that belong to my vines?"

They came to a point where a high stone wall ran beside the road, and Phil slowed the car. A moment later he swung in through an impressive entrance marked by two tall gate piers crowned with sculpted eagles. A smooth graveled driveway led between an avenue of cypress trees to a large pink-and-white mansion that had a central Grecian pediment and a balustraded wing on either side. The window embrasures were decorated with elaborately carved stonework and most of them had their louvered shutters closed against the bright sunlight. Just before the driveway reached the house it divided to skirt an ornate circular fountain with prancing nymphs and satyrs. The dancing jets were flung high into the air, and Melissa was reminded of her sudden inspiration for the name of Phil's champagne. It delighted her that he had been so enthusiastic about her suggestion.

The car scrunched to a halt before an apron of wide, shallow stone steps. At the same instant the double entrance doors opened and a white-jacketed manservant emerged.

"This is Manoel, our house steward," Phil told her as they climbed out. He spoke with the man in Portuguese, then went on, "Manoel says that your room is all ready for you, Melissa. Would you care to go up to it straight away?"

"Thanks. I'd like to freshen up a bit."

As they mounted the steps together Phil continued, "Ask the maid for anything you want . . . tea or whatever. Maria speaks enough English for you to make yourself understood. We'll be dining at eight, but do come down before then . . . whenever you like. I'll be around."

A shy, darkly pretty girl led Melissa across the spacious hall to a white marble staircase. Columns of rose pink marble rose to support the lofty vaulted ceiling, from which painted cupids gazed down against a background of cerulean blue. At a turn in the staircase she glanced back and saw that Phil was standing where she'd left him, watching her ascend. The look of admiration in his eyes was unmistakable, and her heart gave a little skip of pleasure.

An hour or so later, as Melissa was going downstairs, she saw Phil just entering the hallway below from one of the side rooms. His dark eyes followed her progress, glowing with appreciation.

"I'm glad you decided to come down early," he said, moving forward to meet her. "You look ravishing in that dress, Melissa. The coppery fabric matches your eyes; it mimics the way they keep changing color according to your mood."

"My eyes," she corrected, "are a very ordinary pale brown."

"I beg to differ, Melissa. Your eyes are . . ." He broke off with a laugh. "I guess I'd better not start waxing poetic so early in the evening. Come into the salon for an aperitif."

He led her into a large, rectangular room which was decorated in green and gold with touches of lilac. The ceiling was deeply coved and exquisitely painted with formalized designs. There were three scrolled sofas and several easy chairs ranged around, all covered in sage green velvet, and the drapes were of a darker shade of green. An enormous Chinese washed-silk carpet covered the floor.

Between two of the long windows stood a fine grand piano in beautifully grained rosewood.

"What would you like?" Phil inquired, crossing to the cocktail buffet.

"A glass of white wine, please. One of your own," she stipulated. "I do like this room, Phil. It is cool and tranquil."

"A little old-fashioned?"

"But that's right for a lovely old house like this. Any modern treatment would be criminal."

"A sensible observation." The voice from the doorway was firm and assured, so when Melissa turned she was astonished to see such a diminutive figure entering the room. The old lady was slim and straight, walking with her head held proudly. She was elegantly dressed in black silk, with no touch of color except for the diamonds that sparkled at her throat. Her hair, nearer white than gray, was swept up in a severe style.

She turned her head to stare at Phil. "Well, Felipe, aren't you going to introduce me to your guest?" Though her English was excellent, she pronounced his name in the Portuguese manner—and her tone was challenging in a way that reminded Melissa of Pauline.

"Give me a chance, Grandmama," Phil said good-humoredly. "This is Mrs. Colville, who has come from London to discuss marketing our new champagne in Britain. Melissa, this is my grandmother, Senhora Dona Carlota da Silva Cunha."

"I bid you good evening, Mrs. Colville," said the old lady, whose keen black eyes had glinted at Phil's casual use of Melissa's first name.

Having read in her guidebook that the Portuguese were a highly formal people, Melissa replied carefully, "I am very pleased to meet you, Senhora Dona Carlota. Your grandson has spoken of you to me in terms of the warmest admiration and affection."

She saw from Phil's swift glance at her that she'd struck the right note. He went forward to his grandmother, and she took his arm to be escorted to one of the sofas.

"I was just pouring drinks, Grandmama," he said. "May I fix one for you?"

She said something briefly in Portuguese, then turned to indicate with a regal gesture of her hand that Melissa should join her on the sofa. "In your opinion, Mrs. Colville, is there a good market for the new *vinho espumante* in Great Britain?"

"I'm convinced of it, Senhora Dona Carlota. A champagne-style wine is always popular, and the competitive price at which we can offer this one should insure it a wide sale. I sampled some yesterday at your grandson's office, and I thought it was outstanding."

"As are all the Caves da Silva Cunha wines." The hint of reproof in the old lady's voice reminded Melissa again of Pauline. Amused, she said soothingly, "I'm sure they are, Senhora Dona Carlota. Caves da Silva Cunha has a fine reputation. I was merely speaking of the wine I have so far tasted."

Phil brought them both their drinks. "You'll be glad to know, Grandmama, that Melissa has thought of a wonderful name for the champagne. Fonte de Prata . . . Silver Fountain, in English."

"Silver Fountain?" Dona Carlota frowned elegantly. "The name has a certain aptness, I grant you, Felipe. But as a Portuguese wine it should surely be Fonte de Prata wherever it is sold."

"Melissa has convinced me otherwise," Phil said. "It's a matter of customer psychology. People will be kept from asking for it in the stores if they feel uncertain of pronouncing the name correctly."

The thin lips were pursed in distaste. "It is a very different world from the one I'm familiar with, when one is obliged to pander to the ill-educated."

"It's the world we're living in, Grandmama," he rebuked

her gently. "The world that provides us with our income. Now, aren't you going to ask Melissa how she's enjoying her first visit to Portugal?"

The conversation was far from easy. Melissa hoped that her enthusiastic comments about Lisbon would earn the old lady's approval, but she could elicit no warmth from her hostess. Her inquiry as to whether Dona Carlota knew England was answered with a brusque, "Of course, I have visited England on several occasions." But the comments that followed, delivered with a great weight of authority, dealt with a lifestyle that Melissa failed to recognize, and it turned out that Dona Carlota's memories dated from before World War II. She'd be terribly shocked, Melissa thought, to see how democratic London has become since those days.

When dinner was announced Phil squired the two ladies across the hall, one on either side of him. Keeping to Dona Carlota's slow pace made it a stately procession. To Melissa there was a feeling of unreality about the *quinta,* a beautiful mansion absurdly underoccupied by just two persons—and Phil was only there for part of his time. This is a family house, she thought, and it needs more people to make it come alive . . . the presence of children, their playthings left around, their happy laughter breaking the hushed silence.

Dinner was a formal affair. The table was circular; otherwise, Melissa thought with wry amusement, Dona Carlota and Phil would have been seated at either end of something long and imposing, and she herself placed somewhere in the middle. She couldn't fault the food, though. They were served from chased silver platters, first with grilled fresh sardines, then fillets of chicken in a subtly flavored cream sauce with a selection of fresh vegetables. And for dessert there was a light-as-a-feather orange soufflé accompanied by bite-size shapes of almond-flavored pastry.

Since Melissa's praise of the food earned her no more than a negligent shrug, she searched her mind for a subject that might strike a responsive chord in Dona Carlota.

Tentatively she mentioned the fine piano she'd seen in the salon. "My father told me once that my mother, who died when I was very small, had always longed for a full-size concert grand, but our house just wasn't big enough."

"Your mother was a musician?" There was a spark of interest in Dona Carlota's eyes.

"Daddy called her a very talented amateur."

"And you have inherited the gift from her?"

"I'm afraid not. I had lessons for a few months, but I hated them, and Daddy didn't press me to continue."

"How extremely remiss of him!" The slight display of interest was instantly gone, seeming to have evaporated in a puff of contempt.

"Grandmama considers it a crime not to develop musical potential to the full," Phil explained. "Her monthly soirées here are quite famous. It's considered an honor to be invited to play at the Quinta das Andorinhas—by amateurs and professionals alike."

"It must be a very wonderful thing to possess a special talent in one of the arts," said Melissa with a smile. "I envy anyone who does."

But it was clear that Dona Carlota was in no mood to be won over so easily. It came as a relief to Melissa when, as soon as they'd finished eating, the old lady announced that she felt a little tired and would retire to her room.

"Let me show you the rest of the house," Phil suggested when they were alone.

"Wouldn't it be better tomorrow, in daylight?" Melissa felt suddenly nervous, unready for his next move in their relationship.

"You can see it all over again then. But after dark there's a special quality about the *quinta* that I'm sure you'll appreciate, Melissa." His smile was coaxing, tempting. "With moonlight slanting in through the windows, it's very romantic."

Romantic. A shiver rippled over Melissa's skin. She was a

fool, she chided herself, to be so edgy. What on earth was there to be anxious about?

"You'd better lead the way, then," she said lightly. "And I shall expect an informative running commentary about the house."

Phil took her first to the formal dining room, larger than the more intimate family dining room they had used. Adopting the flat tone of a professional guide, he began, "This chamber has recently been restored to a near approximation of its appearance when the *quinta* was first completed in 1742. It will be observed that the design of acanthus leaves on the dado is echoed in the ceiling painting. The furniture is mostly English, or copies thereof, as is the chandelier. The small painting between the windows is of interest, being of the founder of the vineyard which adjoins this site. If you will kindly follow me, you may see the display of Chelsea porcelain, presented to the family by Albert, Prince Consort of England, to mark his appreciation of the superb Colares wines sent as a wedding gift on the occasion of his marriage to Queen Victoria, and . . ."

"Idiot!" said Melissa, laughing.

"We will now proceed to the library, which comprises no less than ten thousand volumes, accumulated by the family over the years."

The library was a long room, with bookshelves ranged high on all sides. Glancing along a row of titles, Melissa saw that many were in English and dealt with various aspects of viticulture and wine production.

"I'm impressed," she said.

"That was the general idea. Now," Phil went on, walking back to the door, "we'll see if the ghost will oblige us by walking tonight."

"Ghost?" Before Melissa could ask for details Phil had flicked off the light switch, plunging the room into darkness. "Hey, what did you do that for?"

"The apparition only walks in the dark . . . or in moonlight. She's timid, I guess."

"She?"

"A cousin by marriage of the Silva Cunha family. Her lover was killed in the Peninsular War against Napoleon. According to legend the poor girl died a few weeks later of a broken heart. She walks the library because that's where they last met, in a poignant parting before he went off to fight, and she hopes that his spirit will return to join hers."

"How sad."

The pale shafts of moonlight striking through the shutters filled the room with an eerie light. Phil moved to stand behind her, and she felt his hands come to rest lightly on her shoulders. For long moments she stood frozen into stillness, her heart thudding. Her flesh seemed to be burning where his fingers touched her through the fabric of her dress, and all her nerve endings were acutely sensitive to him. Very slowly Phil turned her to face him, and Melissa didn't attempt to resist. She saw the glint of his eyes in the moonglow before he bent his head and brought his lips to feather against hers; then he strengthened the pressure and she was lost in his drowning kiss. His arms slid around her, and he drew her close against the length of his tall frame. She felt beautifully warm and weak, her body fluid, her senses swirling. It was as though she were in a trance, yet at the same time she felt more intensely alive than she could ever remember.

When the passionate embrace ended Phil's lips began a tender exploration of her face, bestowing kisses everywhere, skimming across her cheek and outlining the delicate arch of each eyebrow. He kissed her closed lids and the pulse points at her temples, then caught the lobe of one ear between his teeth, nibbling at it erotically. Her flesh flamed where his mouth touched; her body throbbed against his warm pulsing strength, and the musky male scent of him was dizzying. When his lips slid down the curving line of her jaw to caress the petal-tender skin of her throat, Melissa threw back her head and moaned with the sheer delight of it.

Phil murmured something huskily in Portuguese that she

couldn't understand, then he whispered in English, "Melissa, sweet Melissa. You're so lovely. So soft and feminine, so utterly desirable."

She sighed softly in response, no longer able to doubt that she wanted his lovemaking. As Phil's lips found hers once more her hands came up to slide over his shoulders, then clasped about his neck, and she pressed herself closer against him. . . .

There was a faint click of the latch and the double doors swung open, allowing a shaft of bright light from the hallway to shine directly upon them. With a gasp of dismay Melissa drew back, and Phil let her go. Etched against the brilliance was the tiny figure of Dona Carlota.

She spoke in Portuguese, her voice harsh and chilling. Her meaning became clear when Phil replied in English, his tone coolly courteous. "I'll be with you in a few moments, Grandmama. Wait in the salon, if you please."

"I said now!" It was a brusque command.

"In a few moments." Though Phil still addressed her gently, there was a steely ring to his voice.

The battle of wills was brief, and easily won, it seemed, by Phil. The old lady reluctantly turned away. "Do not keep me waiting long."

"I think I'll go up to bed now," Melissa said uneasily as she watched the diminutive figure retreating across the hall.

"There's no need for—"

"I want to," she cut across him. "I'm rather tired. Besides, your grandmother might keep you some time."

"No, it won't take long," Phil replied confidently. He moved to the door and switched on the lights. "While you're waiting for me, why not take a look at the books, Melissa? You'll find something to interest you."

"I might look for a book to take up with me." When Phil didn't immediately depart, she added, "You'd better go to Dona Carlota now."

"Not if you're going to walk out on me while I'm gone," he objected.

"This . . . it shouldn't have happened, Phil."

"How can you say that?" he protested with a spark of anger. "It's been inevitable since the moment we met."

"No!" Melissa went to walk past him, and when he caught her wrist she shook him off forcefully. "Good night, Phil. I'll see you in the morning."

Chapter Five

*W*hat was being said downstairs in the salon? Melissa wondered as she prepared for bed. It was obvious that Dona Carlota was angry with Phil about something. But what, for heaven's sake? It couldn't be, she thought with a nervous giggle, that his grandmother was reproaching him for taking advantage of a houseguest. The old lady would have seen in a single glance that there was nothing one-sided about the embrace she had witnessed in the library. Still, all things considered, Melissa decided, the interruption had been for the best. Her relationship with Phil had threatened to get out of control.

Melissa slid into bed between the cool white linen sheets and opened her book to read for a while. Somehow, though, she found that she couldn't concentrate on the emotional conflict of the heroine; her own emotional conflict was too intrusive. She kept thinking about that kiss, reliving the sensual imprint of Phil's lips on hers, feeling again the exciting pressure of his lean flesh against her own. But soon her wayward thoughts deserted reality and she began to fantasize. In her fantasy she imagined that Phil lay with her in the large canopied bed . . . he was naked beside her, and she was naked too, their bodies responding to one another in a crescendo of desire.

Shocked and angry with herself, Melissa switched off the bedside lamp. But sleep was impossible as she tossed and turned restlessly, her mind swamped with erotic images. Despairingly she tried to tell herself that this was no more than the natural response of a woman who had for so long been deprived of sexual fulfillment. The needs of her body had been dormant, sternly suppressed during the years of Toby's incapacity and in the months since his death. Her reawakening *had* to come sometime, she rationalized, and any man with half Phil's potent masculinity would have caused it to happen.

But she was kidding herself. This was no reawakening of something dormant; it was the birth of something she had never before experienced. Not even in those happy early months of her marriage had she felt such a keen desire for lovemaking.

Suppose, just suppose, that she succumbed to the urges that seethed within her. Who would she be hurting? She was thirty-two years old, and surely she had the right to snatch at a little happiness. Wasn't she mature enough to acknowledge the fact that she possessed a normal woman's sexuality? She wanted Phil, and he wanted her . . . that was obvious. So why not accept with gratitude what fate seemed to have brought her? A brief, beautiful romance with Phil, then home to family and duty and the acceptance of whatever the future held.

But a suspicious voice still managed to retain a foothold in her mind. Was Philip Maxwell merely softening her up for tactical reasons? So far in their negotiations, though she'd seen that he truly was a tough negotiator, as Selwyn had warned her, Phil had appeared to be fair, completely on the level. Or was it that her critical faculties were being jammed by the magnetic force of his personality? Suppose she returned to London with precious memories of a passionate love affair but a less-than-satisfactory contract? What would Selwyn think? She'd never be able to explain how she'd let him and the family firm down. And how would she live with her conscience afterward?

Restlessly Melissa threw back the covers and padded to the french window, which opened onto a balcony. As she stepped outside the terra-cotta tiles were cool to her bare feet. The moon, striking through the gently swaying fronds of a tall palm tree, dappled her with its silvery light. There was a faint chill in the sweetly scented night air, but it did nothing to cool her fever of wanting. She stood on the balcony's edge, her hands resting on the stone coping, her eyes closed, and her breathing shallow and fast. Heavens, she thought with a forced inner laugh, if I go on like this I'll be falling in love with the man. But the attempt to regain common sense was a total failure. In her heart, Melissa knew that she was already in love with Phil . . . she'd been in love with him since heaven knew when in the past couple of days. One way or another she faced heartbreak over him; there was no escaping it.

"Melissa!" Phil's voice came drifting up to her from the fragrant darkness below. In the first startled moments she thought that she must be hallucinating. But her name had sounded so real, spoken in that vibrant deep baritone that was uniquely his. Her pulses racing, she peered down into the shadows, trying to see if he was truly there. Then she heard the sound of a footfall on the flagged terrace, and Phil's tall figure appeared in a pool of moonlight.

"Can't you sleep either, Melissa?" he called softly.

She had to clear her throat of its huskiness. "I . . . it's rather a sultry night, and . . ."

"It's not the sultriness that's making *me* wakeful. My grandmother interrupted us at one hell of a bad moment. You should have waited for me in the library. I was only gone a few minutes."

"I think that Dona Carlota's entrance was extremely well timed."

"You don't mean that, Melissa."

"I most certainly do." It was as well, she thought, that he couldn't see her trembling.

Phil laughed. "Brave words, when we're separated by a twenty-foot wall. I wonder if you'd dare repeat them if I were up there with you."

"It's an academic question," she parried. "My bedroom door is locked, and I intend to keep it locked."

"You think that's enough to deter me? I'll be forced to risk my life and limb climbing up to your balcony, relying on footholds that might give way under my weight."

"For heaven's sake, don't," Melissa cried in genuine alarm when she saw him prepare to climb.

"So anxious? What for, I wonder? Your reputation, or my safety?"

"Naturally I wouldn't want you to break your neck on my account."

"I'm relieved to hear it. So I'll not play Romeo tonight, but come up by the less romantic but far safer means of the staircase."

"I presume that you'll have to use the staircase to get to your own bedroom, but certainly not to mine." Melissa realized that she was enjoying this flirtatious wordplay with Phil. But where was it getting her? She could fend him off for the moment, perhaps, at the cost of a sleepless night. But what would she have gained? Tomorrow, or the day after, she would succumb . . . succumb not to his skillful wooing but to her own desire. Her yearning body would never forgive her for throwing away a chance at blissful happiness, however fleeting. She would burn with the misery of unfulfilled passion, as she was burning now. The decision was in her hands, and so easy when every cell in her body dictated only one course of action.

Phil's voice reached her again from the darkness. "I've had an idea, Melissa. If you don't want me to come up to your room, why not come down to join me? It's so beautiful here in the garden, and quite warm. There are fireflies flitting around, and the moon is turning everything to silver."

"It . . . it sounds very attractive."

"It would be a lot more attractive if you were down here too. Do come, Melissa. We'll go for a stroll."

She still hesitated, but the battle was already lost. "Very well," she said, "for just a little while. Give me a couple of minutes to get some clothes on."

Melissa retreated into her room and switched on a light. Quickly she slipped off her robe and nightdress and in their place dragged on jeans and a cotton top. She ran a comb through her silky hair, but didn't bother with makeup. In next to no time she was hurrying along the silent, dimly lit corridor. She paused at the head of the stairs when she saw Phil standing in the hallway below waiting for her.

"Hi," he called in a muted voice. "I highly approve of a woman who doesn't need a full hour to get herself ready."

Melissa hadn't bargained for his seeing her in anything but moonlight, and as she descended the staircase she did a quick mental check of her appearance. She wished now that she'd delayed long enough to put on a little makeup.

As if Phil could read her doubts, when she joined him at the foot of the stairs he took both her hands in his and stood back admiringly. "You look very lovely," he said without a trace of teasing. Swiftly he leaned forward and touched his lips to hers. It was over in a moment; then they were walking toward a rear door with his hand holding hers. Yet Melissa felt light-headed from that brief kiss, and her heart was thudding at an absurd rate. A few rational cells in her brain were demanding to know what on earth she was doing there. But to the rest of her mind and body the question was irrelevant. To be walking in the moonlit gardens with Phil would be a joy; to have him pause and hold her close and kiss her again as he had kissed her in the library would be sheer bliss; to go beyond a kiss into realms that her imagination hardly dared envisage . . . She shivered, and Phil noticed.

"You're not cold, are you?" he asked solicitously as they stepped outside and he pulled the door closed behind them.

"Heavens no. I . . ."

Thankfully he didn't tease her. "Shall we go down to the lake?"

"You have a lake?"

"And a couple of fishponds. There are extensive grounds at the Quinta das Andorinhas. At the last count we had a hundred and sixty kinds of trees growing here, and innumerable different species of plants. We have rose pergolas and an arbor of clipped yews, romantic paths that wend their way through woodland glades and ferny glens. And statues everywhere."

"How gorgeous! It's a shame that a lot of the time there's almost no one to appreciate it all."

"There is now."

"But I meant—" Melissa broke off and started again. "How large are the grounds? How many acres?"

"This," he reprimanded her, "is not the moment for boring statistics."

"But I'm interested," she protested untruthfully. Competent though she was with figures concerning business, other sorts of numbers didn't coalesce in her brain. To Melissa right then the gardens of the Quinta das Andorinhas were a magical fairyland of moonlight and shadow.

Phil laughed and started giving her a stream of information. Melissa didn't trouble to follow what he was saying, happy just to listen to the rich vibrancy of his voice, happy to concentrate on the sensation of his strong fingers intertwined with hers. She could feel little waves of pleasure spreading through her body with a honey-sweet flow.

At the lake a slight breeze was blowing across the water, raising tiny ripples which splintered the moon's reflection into a thousand glittering diamonds. Phil drew her closer against his hip, sliding his hand about her slender waist and turning to touch his lips to the silken cloud of her hair. Melissa let her head fall to rest on his shoulder, abandoning any pretense of hiding her response to him. She was exquisitely conscious of Phil's subtle masculine aroma and the warmth of his flesh, the quickened rise and fall of his breathing. Halting, he turned and cupped her face between his hands. With his thumbs he caressed her throat slowly, sensuously; then he put his lips to hers in a long, breath-robbing kiss.

After a timeless age when she floated halfway to heaven Phil drew back a little and looked at her lingeringly in the pale moonglow. His voice was shaky and very deep as he whispered her name. "Melissa?" It was an unspoken question, and her mouth went suddenly dry. While she struggled to find an answer Phil said urgently, "Please don't say no to me, Melissa darling. It will be wonderful, *querida;* I promise you. Wonderful beyond belief."

Melissa didn't dispute that. But for her there would be a cost to count: the cost of tearing herself away from the man she loved and returning home to England in desolation.

"You make it sound so simple," she said with a deep sigh.

"It *is* simple. I want you, you want me. There's nothing to prevent us, and all the opportunity we could wish for. A routine business trip for you has turned into something exciting that neither of us will forget in a hurry."

Phil laid his mouth to hers again, coaxing her lips apart and enticing her to flirt with his tongue. With his palms he began a slow, sensuous circling against her nipples. Hard already, they responded with a stab of ecstasy.

"Oh, Melissa . . . sweet, lovely Melissa. You're such an enchanting woman. Since the moment I first saw you at the airport two days ago I've thought about you continuously— thought about you and wanted you. I felt desperate this evening when my grandmother interrupted us in the library and you refused to wait for me. I wondered how I was going to get through the night without losing my sanity. It was like an answer to a prayer when you came out onto the balcony."

"I . . . I didn't realize that you were there," she said faintly.

"I know you didn't. Fate was dealing in my favor. Thank you, darling, for coming down to me. We have so little time together before you'll have to go back to England that I couldn't bear to waste any of it when we could be making love."

Melissa shivered at his words. Phil was rushing her, taking far too much for granted. Yet hadn't her decision already been made back on her balcony when she'd agreed to join him in the garden?

His arms cradling her, Phil buried his face in her hair, and they stood with their bodies pressed close for several long moments. Melissa knew that he was giving her time to get herself together. She was grateful, and yet, though only a second before she'd been blaming him for hurrying her, now she wanted to be swept off her feet and carried quickly beyond the point of no return.

It was as if Phil were acutely tuned-in to her swiftly changing mood. His lips came to meet hers again, and the kiss was deeper and more intense, with a kind of savage tenderness. Melissa felt the velvety rasp of his tongue against hers, erotically driving in and lifting her to a high peak of arousal. Her own tongue curled and quivered, tasting and savoring the sweetness of his mouth and the smooth ivory perfection of his teeth. Phil's hands were moving over her, making erotic patterns across her back. He lost patience with the barrier of her cotton shirt and tugged it up so he could touch her heated skin. When he discovered that she wore no bra to bar his way, he groaned with satisfaction and his hands came round to cradle the two soft globes of her breasts.

"You're magnificent," he murmured. "Darling Melissa, I want to make love to you now, right here."

"*Here?*"

"Why not? It isn't a bit cold. The whole household will be in bed by now, and no one else will come this way."

"Phil, this is crazy . . ."

"Crazy-wonderful, yes. People ought to do crazy things more often."

"But you don't understand," she said huskily. "I . . . I haven't . . . not since Toby's accident. I'm not sure that—"

"Hush, *querida,* there's nothing to be afraid of." His lips wandered around the curve of her jawline and fastened on the petal-soft lobe of her ear. "You can't pretend that you aren't aroused," he went on with a gentle laugh, "when I have evidence to the contrary. As you do about me. Don't worry about anything. Just let it happen."

Why am I stalling? Melissa asked herself impatiently. Why do I hesitate as if I haven't quite made up my mind? I made my decision before I even left the house, and nothing has made me change it. There's no reason why I shouldn't go through with this. In fact, she realized as a sudden flood tide of desire surged through her, she couldn't stop herself now if she tried. With a sigh of surrender she reached up and twined her slender arms around his neck, pulling his head down to hers and capturing his mouth with her kiss. She felt light-headed, enveloped in a haze of love and longing.

As the kiss ended, Melissa pushed back from him slightly and felt Phil's protest until he understood that she was fumbling to find the buttons of his shirt. When she had undone it to his waist she pushed the thin fabric aside to lay her palms on the smooth hot skin of his chest, riding the firmly molded contours, brushing the small male nipples and feeling them tauten under her touch. Phil gave a gasp of pleasure and in a single fluid movement pulled Melissa's shirt up over her head, casting it aside heedlessly. With her breasts freed she leaned against him, delighting in the feel of her softness pressed against his hard body. His hands dropped to the waistband of her jeans, unclipped the fastener and slid the zipper open. Then without pause he was pushing the denim down across her hips, down to a crumpled heap around her ankles, dragging it free of her feet; then her panties were treated likewise. He remained on his heels, gazing up at her, his dark eyes glittering in the moonlight. Slowly, reverently, he passed his hands over her feminine shape as if committing it to memory.

"You're exquisite," he whispered in a passion-roughened voice. "Every man's dream of womanly perfection."

"Phil, please . . ." She urged him to rise, feeling embarrassed to be gazed at so worshipfully. She needed the sensuous intoxication of his warm flesh against hers, his strong arms holding her captive; she needed to be swept along by the heat of his passion. When Phil rose to his feet he paused a moment to throw off his own clothes . . . first his shirt, dragging the still-buttoned cuffs over his hands, then kicking off his shoes while he dragged down the slacks he wore. She glimpsed white briefs against the dark tan of his skin; then they, too, were gone and he clasped her to the full length of his naked body, thrusting his hips against hers. They stood rocking together, gasping with excitement and pleasure, murmuring soft lovewords. She said his name over and over again, as he did hers, as if the very sound of it was a wonderful newfound joy to him.

After a few moments Phil lifted her off her feet, holding her clasped in his arms as if she were a feather. Melissa gripped him around the shoulders, feeling the bunched hardness of his muscles as he carried her. Then, gently, he laid her down on a patch of moss-soft turf and stretched himself beside her. His hands began a leisurely exploration, weaving gossamer patterns everywhere, across her hips and down the soft flesh of her thighs, lingering at her knees to mold their shape, then moving round to the sensitive skin behind the knees, down her calves to brush over her feet.

Mistily she could see his lithe, muscular torso gleaming in the moonlight, the wide, powerfully contoured chest narrowing to a taut waist and lean hips. She could see the evidence of his desire, and without conscious thought she found her hands going forward to touch him. Phil groaned, then reached for her urgently, pulling her to him and kissing her in a hot fever of need.

"Oh, Melissa . . . sweet love, do you know what you're doing to me? You're so beautiful."

"You, too," she whispered huskily. "You have such a fine body."

"I want you to like it, to enjoy it. I long to give you pleasure, darling."

"You do, you do!"

He moved to take the soft weight of her breasts in his hands. Though she could feel him trembling, his caresses were restrained, fondling her nipples with an almost lazy circling motion that sent shafts of desire throbbing through her body. She grasped him more feverishly, rejoicing in his shuddering reaction. Then, as one of his hands left her breast to slide purposefully across the curve of her abdomen, she lost awareness of Phil's response in the violence of her own. Her hips rose involuntarily as she arched her back, twisting and turning as the sweet sensations of ecstasy burned at her core, rippling outward in widening echoes throughout her whole being.

Overhead the moon seemed to swell against the velvet sky, dazzling her eyes with its silvery light. In her ears there was a clamor of sound . . . the hammering of her heartbeat, her gasping breath and the moans and little cries wrung from her throat by the delight of Phil's relentless torture.

"Yes," she sobbed. "Oh yes, yes . . ."

In a frenzy of wanting she clung to him and dragged him closer. She exulted to feel his trembling delight as he entered her and began to move in a slow rhythm. She could guess the discipline he was exerting to match his pace to hers. Desire curled and lapped within her, screaming for release. And when release did at last come in a great burst of glory, it was as if the moon had shattered in some cosmic upheaval and was raining down glittering crystals of silver.

"You were wonderful, Melissa," he murmured, his body finally quiescent.

"And you, Phil . . . it was incredible."

For a long while they remained lying together, cradled in each other's arms while tiny echoes of the rapture Melissa had known danced and shimmered in a long, slow descent. Both of them must have dozed, slipping away into a dreamworld where there was only delight and deep contentment. She roused to find Phil kissing her again, touching his lips to her closed eyelids, then feathering them down the side of her nose. With his tongue he lightly traced the curving shape of her mouth.

"Are you happy, *querida?*"

She smiled. "Gloriously happy."

She felt Phil's muscles tighten as his desire stirred again, and in moments she was once more being swept along on a rhapsodic journey. His hands and lips were everywhere, coaxing and arousing her, electrifying her flesh and making her senses swirl deliciously till the sweet tension building within her finally exploded again in a great fulfilling enchantment.

Long minutes later, after they had rested together in silent harmony, Phil gave a low, throaty chuckle. "I think that we'd better have a dip to cool my ardor."

"In the lake, you mean? Won't it be cold?"

"Let's find out." Crouching beside her on one knee, he lifted her into his arms, then stood up. Without pausing he turned and began to wade into the water. Melissa wriggled protestingly, laughing; then as they went deeper and her toes touched the water, she gave an excited giggle. "For pity's sake, it's freezing."

"Nonsense. It's just pleasantly cool."

"Listen," she ordered, "you're to put me down at once. At once, do you hear?"

"Whatever you say." Unceremoniously Phil dumped her into three feet of water.

Melissa surfaced, spluttering. Though the water wasn't

really cold, the shock of it against her naked body made her gasp for breath. Yet it felt wonderfully exhilarating.

"You beast!" she cried, laughing. "You hateful beast."

"You weren't calling me names like that a few minutes ago," Phil observed calmly, still standing with the water lapping around his middle.

An imp of devilry possessed her. Standing quickly, she placed her two palms against Phil's chest and pushed with all her strength. He was taken by surprise and toppled backward into the water with a shout of protest.

In a flash, Melissa turned and struck out toward the center of the lake. She had gained a slight advantage, but within moments she knew that she wasn't going to escape him. Phil was racing after her, cutting through the water, it seemed to her, like a streamlined torpedo. With another shout, of triumph this time, he reached her and grasped her waist with both hands. Melissa struggled wildly, but somehow their two bodies became ever more closely entangled. As they sank down into the now much deeper water his lips found hers and she was suddenly still, clinging to him. Slowly, dreamily, they floated back to the surface, and Phil trod water to keep them there. His arms were tightly around her.

"My male dignity has been affronted," he claimed, "and I need my revenge. What shall I do to you?"

"Pushing you over was just getting my own back," she protested. "We're quits now."

"No way. Now, let me see . . . I could duck you a few times."

"Don't you dare!"

"Maybe I will, maybe I won't. I'll make you wait to find out. How do you like swimming in the nude, Melissa? It's especially good, don't you think?"

"I wouldn't call this swimming," she said evasively. "Why don't you let go of me?"

"I'll let go of you when I'm good and ready."

She wriggled in his arms, and Phil half released her for a

moment to change his grip. Seizing this chance, Melissa scooped up a handful of water and threw it in his face, then darted away, though she knew he'd be able to catch her again. They gamboled like children, laughing and splashing one another.

Phil watched her twisting and turning, sinking and rising, and likened her in his mind to a beautiful mermaid with her silken hair floating fanlike around her shoulders. It's been a long time, he thought with sure conviction, since she has laughed like this from sheer high spirits. Just as it's been a long time since she last made love with a man. But these carefree moments were fragile. Nothing he said or did must cast a shadow across her happiness.

"Let's make some coffee," he suggested.

"It sounds great," she said. "But won't we wake the household?"

"There's a changing hut a bit further along the bank," Phil explained. "There'll be towels there, too. If we're lucky, we might even find a packet of cookies."

After emerging from the water they collected their cast-off clothes and ran together to the hut. Within seconds Melissa enveloped herself in a huge fluffy towel, and used another to dry her hair. Phil pulled on his slacks, but left his torso bare. In the oblique light from an overhead lamp she noted his graceful musculature and the fact that his skin gleamed like bronze.

While Phil set about making coffee she hastily pulled on her clothes. When he brought over a tray set with blue china mugs and an earthenware coffee pot, she said apologetically, "I don't have a comb, so I'm afraid my hair looks a mess."

"It looks fetchingly tousled," he said. "Look, I've found some almond macaroons."

"Scrumptious!" She took a couple and started munching. "Swimming certainly gives one an appetite."

"Swimming?"

Her cheeks colored faintly, deliciously. Phil felt a sudden

tightening around his heart. Already he desired her again. It would be wonderful to spend the rest of the night in her bed, but something warned him that it would be a mistake to suggest that. Melissa wouldn't care to be taken for granted.

"Tomorrow morning," he said in a practical voice, "we'd better make an early start. There's a great deal for you to see on the estate, and I'd like to keep the afternoon free for taking you up to Pena Palace."

"Right," she said, thankful to be back on a level of conversation that she felt able to handle.

As they walked back to the silent house, Phil's arm around her shoulders, they were too preoccupied to notice a diminutive robed figure standing at an upper window. Dona Carlota gazed down at the couple strolling across the lawns, passing into the dense shadow of a giant magnolia tree and emerging into the moonlight again. She stood watching until they had reached the terrace and passed from her sight. Only then did she let the curtain fall back into place.

Chapter Six

*M*elissa stretched her awakening over long, delicious, languorous moments. She clung to a dreamy semiconscious state, feeling that to let herself become fully alert would be to shatter her cocoon of joy.

She allowed thoughts to enter her mind very slowly, one by one. The bed was warm and soft, the room large and lofty, filled with a rich golden radiance from the morning sun. The ceiling was vaulted, and the paneled walls had circular insets, each depicting a sylvan scene. The large bed on which she lay was canopied with a striped satin fabric in green and ivory. On a carved wooden chest stood a large vase of white lilies which scented the air with their subtle fragrance.

Beyond her room was the rest of the beautiful Quinta das Andorinhas, and outside were the extensive gardens, and then the vineyards and wineries she had come here to see. Phil . . . suddenly he was there in her mind, dominating everything else, the cause of her waking joy. Melissa savored her images of him . . . as she had first seen him at the airport in casual gear; then smart in a business suit; immaculate in a white tuxedo; then—giving her a stab of erotic excitement—naked in the moonlight the previous night, his body gleaming in its muscled perfection. She basked in the beautiful memories of his lovemaking, resisting as long as she could the advent of wide-awake consciousness that would mar her wonderful mood.

But it couldn't be held at bay for long—the bleak awareness that her present happiness was only fleeting. Its end was already fixed. The day she left Portugal her affair with Phil would be over. There was no escaping that somber fact. If she had been foolish ever to let herself get involved with him, it was too late for regrets now. She was utterly committed. It was no more in her power to break with Phil at this moment than to flap her arms and fly like a bird. Don't think about it, Melissa told herself sternly. Just take each of these precious days as it comes and enjoy it to the full.

After throwing back the bedcovers, she went to the adjoining bathroom to run herself a bath. As she lay back in the deep, scented water she whispered to herself, "Today is a wonderful day, and I'm going to be happy." The silky water seemed to caress her body until it felt deliciously voluptuous. Each small movement she made caused a swirling around the two soft mounds of her breasts, almost like the remembered brushing of Phil's fingertips. Flushing, she sat up and started soaping herself, turning her thoughts away from Phil with fierce determination.

She would phone home again after she'd had breakfast. She marshaled little stories in her mind about the places that Senhor Maxwell had taken her to see in Lisbon . . . the ancient Castle of St. George perched high on its hill overlooking the city and the wide river estuary. She would mention the quaint little funicular tramway that had taken them up there. Then the famous Tower of Belem, built in the early sixteenth century to mark the spot from which many of Portugal's famous navigators had set sail for the unknown. Mark would have loved exploring Belem with its drawbridge and crenellated walls. Much more to Jenny's taste was the fabulous coach museum nearby, filled with magnificent carriages—each and every one of them resplendent enough to have taken Cinderella to the ball. Melissa recalled suddenly that while she had been admiring a beautifully painted Spanish coach Phil had come to stand close behind her, resting his hands on her shoulders, and she had felt his warm breath gently ruffling her hair. It had been so difficult to concentrate on what the guide had been saying. All she had been able to think about was Phil. Phil had filled her thoughts that whole afternoon of sightseeing . . . and every moment since then.

Melissa stepped out of the bath, then dressed in navy slacks and a blue cotton sweater. Downstairs she was directed by one of the maids, a pretty dark-haired girl with shy eyes, to a small breakfast parlor. Melissa's heart jolted as she saw that Phil was already there, seated at the table with a cup of coffee before him.

"Hi, there!" he greeted her with an easy smile, rising to his feet. "How did you sleep?"

"Very well, thank you." Melissa knew that her answer sounded ridiculously formal and stilted, but she couldn't help it. Though she'd been expecting to meet Phil at breakfast, she suddenly felt totally unnerved at coming face to face with him after what had happened between them only a few short hours before. She mustn't let Phil see her fall apart; she had to adopt his cheerful, matter-of-fact attitude as her own: So we made love last night and it was good, and we'll probably do it again. No big deal. She steeled herself to act composed as she accepted the white-painted chair he pulled out for her, steeled herself not to shiver as his hands lightly caressed her shoulders.

"There's fruit, hot rolls and coffee," said Phil, resuming his own seat. He leaned forward and poured a cup of coffee for her, adding, "Please say if you'd like an English breakfast instead."

"No, what's here will be fine." Melissa sipped the coffee nervously and babbled, "Mmm! That's good, just what I needed. I'm really looking forward to the vineyard tour this morning, Phil. I've read a good deal on wine production, of course, but my education is somewhat lacking on the practical side." She took a roll from the basket, broke it and dabbed on butter and cherry conserve.

Phil studied her covertly. It surprised him that she was so cool and collected. He'd been prepared for a certain amount of embarrassment from her, but to all appearances Melissa was taking last night's episode at the lakeside in her stride. She'd told him that he'd been her first lover since her husband's incapacitating accident. He was forced to wonder if that was really true.

What the hell? he thought dismissively. She's a fantastic woman, and I'd be a fool to waste time worrying over the possibility that she might be a bit tougher than I first took her to be. If she was, it suited him all the better, didn't it? He'd had more than one sticky experience with a woman who read too much into something that he'd never intended to be more than a casual liaison. No danger of that sort of misunderstanding with Melissa, it seemed. Oddly, though, what should have been a comforting thought left him with a vague feeling of depression.

Melissa found that it was very warm out in the vineyards. The sun blazed down from a clear blue sky, penetrating even into the leafy tunnels formed by the rows of tall vines that were trained pergola-fashion on wires.

"This district has always been renowned for its red wines," Phil explained to her. "Its white wines, by and large, are nothing very special."

"So what gave you the idea of producing champagne here?" she asked. "Most of the best *vinhos espumantes* come from further north, don't they?"

"That's true," Phil said, "but various circumstances made me think that champagne would be a good bet here. First, the soil in this immediate locality has the right chemical balance for growing Chardonnay-type grapes; then, owing to the configuration of the land on the Silva Cunha estate, we have an ideal microclimate. And finally, the estate already possessed extensive *caves*—cellarage, if you like— which are necessary for the lengthy process of producing a sparkling wine by natural fermentation.''

As they strolled on together Phil constantly exchanged greetings with the men working among the vines, who were mostly engaged on spring pruning. He seemed to be on very good terms with them all, addressing each man by name. Melissa was surprised at how many workers there were.

"You seem to be quite labor intensive here," she remarked.

"I try to strike a happy medium," Phil explained. "For some processes I'm forced to use modern machinery if I'm to sell at a competitive price. With other processes, though, there's really nothing that will ever fully replace human skill. Besides, the men around here depend on the Silva Cunha vineyards for a livelihood, as their fathers and grandfathers did before them."

Melissa smiled. "I suspected before that you're a believer in tradition, Phil."

"Sure I am. There's a natural rhythm to life in wine-growing country. As each season comes around there are the old, familiar routines to be carried out, which bring with them the satisfaction of a job well done . . . ploughing and pruning, fertilization, spraying the grapes with fungicide and so on. But nothing equals the thrill of the harvest in September. That's something really worth seeing. Perhaps," he added, turning suddenly to face Melissa, "you could come back to Portugal then, and stay longer."

What on earth, Phil wondered instantly, had made him say that? He waited with some anxiety for her reply, and felt relief wash through him when Melissa said quickly, "No, I don't think that would be possible."

Even if it were possible, she reflected, it would certainly

be unwise. The height of lunacy, in fact. Either their affair would begin all over again, with the inevitable heartache to follow, or, far more likely, she would find that Phil was involved with another woman and no longer interested in her. This was just a springtime interlude for both of them. A few days stolen out of time, never to be repeated.

Inside the winery it was chilly by contrast, and Melissa was glad to have the warm jacket that Phil had advised her to bring. He took it and draped it over her shoulders, and allowed his hands to rest on her for a few moments longer than necessary. Melissa tensed in electric response to his touch. She was thankful that the presence of the workers forced her to remain composed.

Phil showed her the machinery for removing stalks from the hand-gathered bunches of grapes. Then they moved on to the crushers, which applied just enough pressure to release the juice without at the same time breaking the pips, which would give a bitter flavor to the wine. The crushed flesh and juice were then transferred to wooden butts holding fifty to sixty gallons apiece. After fermentation the resulting wine was racked and clarified, then carefully blended to obtain a uniform product. By that time the wine was ready for bottling, and then the special champagne processes which put the sparkle into a still wine began. Phil explained this to her as they went through to one of the bottling lines, which at this season of the year was in full swing.

"Before the bottles are corked," he said, "a tiny quantity of a solution containing sugar and yeast is added to each one. This causes a secondary fermentation, and because the resulting gas can't escape from the bottle it remains dissolved in the wine. So far, so good. But the problem is, of course, that whenever any degree of fermentation takes place there's always a sediment formed, and naturally we have to get rid of that. I'll show you how it's done when we get downstairs."

As she descended with him to the cellars, Melissa was

amazed at their sheer size. Lining one wall, stretching as far as the eye could see, were thousands and thousands of bottles set in specially tilted racks. Phil explained the purpose of these racks, which he called *pupitres*.

"You'll notice that each bottle is resting in an oval-shaped slot. This is so that the angle can be changed very gradually from horizontal to vertical, bottom up. Every day, for as long as six months, a man gives each bottle a little shake and upends it slightly more until all the sediment is resting right behind the cork. My best men can handle up to thirty thousand bottles daily."

"It must be monotonous work," Melissa commented.

"Actually, the skill involved saves it from being monotonous. There's the comforting knowledge that no machine has ever been invented to do this particular job half as well as the human hand."

"And then you're faced with the tricky business of getting the sediment out of the bottle without losing half the wine, too. And all those lovely bubbles."

"That's right. It used to be a lot trickier for champagne producers in the old days, but, as I expect you know, the method now is to freeze the neck of the bottle, remove the cork plus the sediment, then top up with spare wine and recork. Then the bottles come back to the cellars for aging before being labeled and crated, ready for shipping."

"I'm very impressed with your whole operation," Melissa told him.

"Which is exactly what I hoped you would be."

"Did you have any doubt on that score?"

He raised an eyebrow. "A man can never be sure how a woman will react to anything."

"That sounds suspiciously like a male chauvinist remark," she chided him.

"No chauvinism intended. It's just that women have a disconcerting habit of seeing right through the outer trappings of a situation and coming up with awkward questions."

"Does that mean you have something to hide, Phil?"

"Lots of things. Doesn't everyone?"

"So what are your dreadful secrets, I wonder?"

He grinned. "For instance, I wouldn't want some of my competitors to know how financially stretched I am at the moment. My investment program over the past few years has been heavy."

"No one would ever guess, judging from the way you've maintained the *quinta,* that you have a cash flow problem."

"No one is supposed to guess," he said, with a twisted smile.

"You've been deliberately putting on the style, have you?"

"Sort of."

"So why are you spilling the beans to me?"

Phil laughed. "Now that's exactly the kind of awkward question a man gets from a woman. Come on, let's go back to the house and get changed. I'm taking you out to lunch."

"Great. Where are we going?"

"Wait and see."

They left the vineyards and entered the grounds by a trellised gate that was overhung with starry-flowered clematis. The path dipped through a grove of rhododendrons and azaleas, brilliant in color and with a heady fragrance that floated on the soft, warm air. Then it rose again to a ridge crested with larches and mimosa trees. When they reached that point they could glimpse the house through the breeze-stirred foliage, and beyond the house, away to the left, the lake. Melissa was at once swept back to those wild moments the previous night when Phil had made passionate love to her on the grassy bank, and to the abandoned gaiety of their naked swim in the water afterward.

Phil must have been remembering too. He said her name huskily; then she was in his arms. Without hesitation she opened her lips to his kiss and responded to the thrust of his tongue, and she was instantly uplifted to a high peak of joy. As he pulled her closer Melissa's hands moved lovingly across his back, where the thin cotton of his shirt was stretched tight over his corded muscles, then moved lower to the lean firmness of his buttocks.

At length Phil drew back a little, and she felt the warm breath of his sigh against her temple.

"Oh, Melissa . . . we have so little time."

She was gripped by a sudden sense of chill. She'd forced herself to accept, at least in the rational part of her brain, that this love affair with Phil would be as fleeting as a shooting star, over almost as soon as it had begun. But did he have to keep reminding her?

Phil sensed her sudden change of mood as she eased herself out of his arms and turned to walk on. How changeable she was, how unpredictable . . . just like all women, he thought. But the comparison with other women jarred in his mind. There was something very special about Melissa. He wished to heaven that her stay in Portugal weren't so brief. If only she were there for a few weeks instead of just a few days, what a wonderful summer it would be. Her imminent departure hung over him like a dark cloud.

Phil gave himself a mental shake. He was getting overly sentimental. There had been one or two of his past affairs which had lasted as long as a whole summer through, but many of them had held together only for a week or so. Never before had he fretted about the approaching end, counting as infinitely precious what little time they had left. It ought to be enough to enjoy Melissa's fascinating company while he could, he chided himself, and then say goodbye to her without any regrets. What had possessed him, earlier on, to talk of her returning to Portugal? A relationship that never quite ended could bring a load of trouble.

Their approach was watched from the front terrace by Dona Carlota. She was sitting in a basketwork chair under the scented shade of a walnut tree. A bottle of white wine rested in a silver ice bucket on the small table beside her.

"Come and join me," she called when they had drawn

near, and she reached out her hand to tinkle a little porcelain bell. Almost before Melissa and Phil were seated a maidservant had appeared from the house. Dona Carlota spoke to her briefly in Portuguese, clearly ordering more glasses to be brought.

"You approve what you have seen of the Silva Cunha vineyards, Mrs. Colville?"

"I'm most impressed, Senhora Dona Carlota. You and Phil have every reason to feel proud."

The old lady inclined her head as if regally accepting what was no more than her due. "Felipe has done well here," she declared, "as did his father before him. Possibly an injection of foreign blood in a family once in a while can prove to be a good thing, however regrettable it seems at the time. Though I must confess that it continues to grieve me that the present head of an ancient Portuguese family should bear a foreign surname. I have to be grateful that, apart from his name, Felipe is truly Portuguese in every other respect."

Phil grinned amiably at his grandmother, and a look passed between them that Melissa couldn't interpret.

"I'm taking Melissa up to Pena this afternoon," he said. "I thought that we'd stop off for lunch at the Seteais Palace."

Dona Carlota pursed her lips in vexation. "Manoel mentioned that you wouldn't be lunching at home. I fail to see why not."

"I think a meal at Seteais is an experience that no visitor to Sintra should miss," Phil said evenly.

The maid returned with two glasses on a silver tray, and Phil poured the wine. Dona Carlota refused any more for herself. "Kindly insure that you are not back late from Pena, Felipe. I have invited some guests for dinner this evening."

"Guests?" Now it was Phil who didn't look pleased. "Who's coming?"

"Just a few friends." The old lady listed half a dozen names.

"I wish you had discussed this with me first, Grand-mama."

Her eyes sparked coldly. "I did imagine, Felipe, that I was free to invite people to the house without first seeking your approval."

"You knew that I didn't want anything formal arranged for this weekend," he protested.

"Having my friends to dinner is hardly formal, Felipe. All the same, it would be discourteous if you were not here to greet them on arrival. Mrs. Colville, may I enlist your support? I think you should be back here by six-thirty. Felipe can at times be . . . forgetful."

"You surprise me, Senhora Dona Carlota. I've gained a very different impression."

She was awarded a frown of displeasure, but Phil looked amused.

After they'd finished their wine Melissa went up to her room to change, choosing a crisp pleated cotton dress in white and kingfisher blue. As they were heading toward Sintra in Phil's car she asked, "What was that all about with your grandmother?"

"What was what all about?"

"I detected something in the air. She seemed to be making a point of some kind."

"My grandmother rarely opens her mouth without making a point of some kind," he said with a rueful laugh. "She's of the old world, with a strong sense of family tradition, and she's swimming against the tide. She deplores the fact that both my sisters have married American men and consequently produced offspring whose blood is only twenty-five percent Portuguese. She doesn't want that to happen with her one and only grandson. To Grandmama it's imperative that I marry a Portuguese girl."

"And what about you?" The words came out faintly, and Melissa found herself gripping the edge of the leather seat with tight fingers while she waited for Phil's answer.

"Marriage doesn't feature in my thinking. I guess I owe it to the family to produce an heir one day, but not for quite a while. I've been far too busy these past few years to voluntarily take on any extra responsibilities."

"Is that how you view marriage?"

"Isn't that how it always is—for men, anyway? And women too, sometimes," he added, giving Melissa a quick sideways glance. "You must have found that."

She chose her words with care. "An acceptance of responsibility is a necessary part of any marriage. I'm all for standing by one's vows to take each other for richer for poorer, in sickness and in health. But it seems to me a terrible outlook to enter into marriage as if it's putting chains around one's neck."

"You, I suppose, take the romantic view?"

"Yes, I do," she said unashamedly.

Phil appeared to choke back a hasty retort, then said, "We in Portugal—at least among the landed families—take a more practical view. To us, marriage is for the continuation of the line."

"So anyone will do as a wife when the time comes?" Melissa didn't attempt to conceal the scorn she felt.

"By no means! The selection process is long and arduous. My grandmother is constantly producing likely candidates."

"You'd let your grandmother select a wife for you?"

"Good Lord, no! I'll pick my own wife. Still," he added with a sigh, "it might make for a more peaceful life if our choices were to coincide." In silence Phil steered the car around several more bends, then said, "I don't know how we got onto this gloomy subject."

Melissa injected a note of humor into her tone. "Neither do I. Let's drop it."

"Agreed." He flashed her a smile. "You and I have far more interesting things to talk about, Melissa."

She felt sick at heart. Yet nothing that Phil had said changed their relationship, she told herself fiercely. She would only be here with him for just a few more days . . . a short segment of time out of her life, a beautiful memory she would carry home in her heart.

Phil slowed and turned in between tall gates onto a curving driveway which led to a white mansion of palatial elegance. Inside, Seteais proved to be even more splendid. They entered a long, galleried hallway furnished with superb tapestries and antiques.

"It's more like an art gallery than a hotel," said Melissa, gazing around in awed admiration.

"Just wait till you see the drawing room; that's really fantastic. Let's take a look now, then we'll go and eat."

"This place wasn't built as a hotel, surely? How old is it?"

"Not so very old. Late eighteenth century, I think. It was built by a Dutchman who'd made his fortune out of gold and precious stones. Since it was turned into a hotel, though, just about everyone who ever rated has stayed here. The guest book reads like an international Who's Who."

"In that case, will they deign to serve us ordinary mortals?"

Phil's dark gaze rested on her. "You, Melissa, are just about as far removed from an ordinary mortal as it's possible to be. You're a very, very special person."

"You're not exactly an *un*special person yourself, Phil."

He smiled into her eyes. "So we two are well suited, aren't we?"

Suited for a short fling, he meant. How comfortable it must be for a man—able to enjoy an uncomplicated, carefree love life, plunging into a new affair whenever the fancy took him. Why had she been born a woman, destined to endure this feeling of deep commitment in what should be just a lighthearted episode? Melissa's sense of grievance lasted no more than a second. She would ten times rather endure the pain and heartache of a deeply felt love affair, however brief, than indulge in a series of casual encounters. A hundred times rather. Were there any men, anywhere, she wondered gloomily, who could feel committed to a woman for a lifetime through?

She must have given an audible sigh, for Phil said with concern, "Don't you like this place? Do you think it's a bit overdone?"

"Heavens no! It's absolutely perfect."

Everything was perfect. The beautiful dining room, the tables sparkling with glassware and silver and graced with fresh flowers, the attentive but unobtrusive service. The food was out of this world . . . She and Phil both chose turbot in a rich cream sauce served with leaf spinach, and the dessert trolley was wickedly tempting. Most of all, her companion was perfect.

Afterward they drove up the winding road to the royal palace of Pena, perched on its lofty crag. There were no clouds, and the views in all directions were breathtaking. Near at hand, on another lofty crag, were the romantic ruins of an old Moorish castle, and below them lay all the picturesque buildings of Sintra. Phil pointed out the chimneys of the Quinta das Andorinhas a little distance away, and the Silva Cunha vineyards adjoining it. Farther off in another direction Lisbon could be seen, and on a distant, sunlit plain the majestic monastery of Mafra. And then there was the ocean, the glittering blue Atlantic.

"It was from this spot, back in the fifteenth century, that King Manoel the Fortunate, while hunting in the forest, spotted Vasco da Gama's fleet arriving home from India. In thankfulness he built a monastery right here."

"What about the palace? It's such a mix-up of architectural styles. I can't begin to guess when it was built."

Phil laughed. "I'm not surprised that you're puzzled. It was the brainchild of Maria the Second's consort, Dom Fernando, who incidentally was a first cousin of both Queen Victoria and her husband, Prince Albert. Fernando built Pena as a summer palace for the queen, incorporating the former monastery."

"Lucky queen!"

"Not so lucky queen. Her first husband died after only four months of marriage, and she herself died in childbirth when she was thirty-five. Her descendants were doomed, too. Her son and heir, Dom Pedro, and two of his brothers all died of cholera within a week."

"How tragic."

"It didn't stop there. The new king was a fourth brother, Luis, whose reign lasted nearly thirty years. But his heir, Carlos, was assassinated while driving in his carriage in Lisbon, together with the crown prince. Two years later, in 1910, Portugal became a republic."

They strolled through ornate reception rooms, some of them showing Chinese or Indian influence. In a vaulted bedroom with a large, canopied four-poster Phil paused and asked her with a grin, "How would you like to live up here, cut off from the rest of the world?"

Melissa allowed her answer to trip off her tongue uncensored. "That would entirely depend who with."

"I can think of someone."

To live with Phil up here in this magical fantasy world! To live with him anywhere! She had to settle for just a few days, and the minutes and the hours were fast ticking away.

Before returning to the car they wandered through the surrounding park, catching dramatic vistas through gaps in the lush greenery. Beside a pool of dark, still water where black swans glided, Phil paused and turned her to face him, folding his arms around her. His lips brushed across her cheek with tender passion.

"Last night was wonderful, Melissa."

"Yes, Phil," she said huskily. "Oh, yes!" No pretense, there wasn't time for pretense.

She gave herself up to the swirling pleasure of his kiss, feeling soft and weak as his hands slid over her caressingly. She folded her arms about his neck and pressed herself against him, thrilling to feel his matching desire. Nuzzling her face into his shoulder, she kissed the warm pulsepoints of his throat while Phil's tongue made a sensuous exploration of her left ear. His hands found entry to the silken warmth of her skin, and his fingers crept with slow haste to cup her breasts, teasing the nipples to blissful peaks of joy.

It was a long time before they finally broke apart, Phil saying with a soft, shaky laugh, "To be continued later."

As they strolled on she happened to catch sight of the clock on the palace tower. Where had the time flown? "We ought to be leaving," she said. "Your grandmother asked us to be back by six-thirty."

"There's no hurry. It'll only take five minutes to get to the car, and then it's barely a fifteen-minute drive."

When they arrived at the *quinta* there was a sense of anticipation in the air. Servants were hurrying about, moving chairs, fixing large displays of flowers in the hall and main reception rooms. This was no casual gathering of a few family friends, Melissa realized, and was thankful that she'd brought a dress that was suitable for such an occasion.

She and Phil parted at the head of the stairs. In her room, Melissa luxuriated in a warm, scented bath and spent time on her hair and face. Stepping back for a final full-length view of herself, she felt pretty good. The gold-printed black taffeta dress molded her breasts and swirled softly about her knees as she walked. She'd hold her own with most women, she decided, then acknowledged ruefully that holding her own with other women wasn't the real object of the exercise. She wanted to look entrancing to Phil. She wanted him to think her by far the most attractive woman in the gathering. She wanted him to think she looked so sexy and desirable that he could hardly wait to make love to her again.

When she entered the salon a few minutes later she saw from the expression glowing in his eyes that she'd achieved her aim. Phil himself was wearing a black tuxedo with a pale blue dress shirt, and she realized breathlessly that she had never seen a man to equal him, not just in the clean hard lines of his face and those compelling dark brown eyes, but in his entire charismatic personality. He broke away from a couple of early arrivals and came across to her.

"Melissa, you look wonderful. Absolutely stunning." He lowered his voice and added, "It's simply not fair to expect me to spend the evening performing social niceties when you're doing your damnedest to make me throw social niceties to the wind and carry you off to the nearest bed."

"I'm doing nothing of the kind," she protested untruthfully.

"Aren't you? Look me straight in the eye and deny that you carefully calculated the effect that dress would have on me."

Melissa colored and glanced away. "You're neglecting your duties as host, Phil," she reminded him. Fortunately, his grandmother entered the room at that moment with four more guests.

"Come and be introduced," he said, taking Melissa's hand.

The newcomers were all of one family. The two stolid, plumply built women were twin sisters, one of them married to the middle-aged man who accompanied them. He carried his short stature with pompous dignity. The fourth member of the party was their daughter, Josepha. In her mid-twenties, she had even white teeth, and her hair was the rich glossy brown so often seen in Portugal. She wasn't bad looking, and might even have been attractive if only she'd taken the slightest trouble with her appearance. As it was, Josepha Carreiro wore her hair scooped back lankly behind her ears and had put on crimson lipstick that clashed terribly with the scarlet poppies on her fussily draped crepe dress.

"Josepha is so interested in the champagne process, Felipe," said Dona Carlota, condescending for Melissa's benefit to speak in English. "I told her that you would be delighted to give her an escorted tour of the wineries."

Phil inclined his head with unenthusiastic courtesy. "Of course. Any time."

When Melissa next happened to be alone with him, she

said skeptically, "So Josepha is keen to learn about the champagne-making process."

Phil grinned. "Haven't you guessed? Josepha is currently being considered by Grandmama as a possible wife for me. She has all the right qualifications."

"All?"

"All that are required in a wife. Good health, moderately good looks, and she comes from a solid, respectable family which could be persuaded to provide her with an excellent dowry. The Carreiros are into citrus fruits and olives in a big way."

"So why don't you snatch up Josepha plus her fat dowry before someone beats you to it?"

Phil gave an easy laugh. "Wasn't it Oscar Wilde who warned that all women grow to resemble their mothers? Can you imagine me in twenty years' time married to a replica of the good Senhora Dona Isabella?"

"It's nice to know," she teased, "that your choice of wife won't be wholly guided by mercenary considerations."

"Don't look at me like that, Melissa."

"Like what?"

"With fire in your eyes. It excites me."

"Go and talk to Josepha, then. That should cool you down." She moved away from him and was promptly joined by a middle-aged man who told her in careful, precise English that he owned several hotels. He was gray haired, with a military precision about him, and he showed great admiration for Melissa's grasp of the wine trade.

"My cellars, I am proud to boast, are among the finest in all Portugal."

"Will you be stocking the new Silva Cunha champagne, Senhor Baltazar?"

"But of course. It is very good, no?"

"It's very good, yes!"

His first startled response to her quip changed to a smile. To judge from his wife, who at that moment was conversing with Dona Carlota, he would be accustomed to women coming in neat packages labeled *Subdued, Obedient, Colorless*. He seemed to appreciate the new variety that Melissa Colville represented. It chanced that they were seated together at the table, so they continued chatting throughout dinner.

When everyone returned to the salon to be served with liqueurs, Phil joined her again.

"You seemed very friendly with Carlos Baltazar." It was said with a hint of accusation.

"He's a very agreeable and interesting man."

"I warn you, he's at a dangerous age."

"Is there a non-dangerous age for men?"

He brushed that aside. "Carlos will go home and fantasize about you while his wife is snoring beside him."

"He can fantasize about me to his heart's content. That's harmless enough."

"Shall I tell you some of *my* fantasies, Melissa?"

"That depends," she said cautiously.

"They concern an Englishwoman I met the other day, a fascinating creature with beautiful hair, and eyes that mysteriously change color with her mood. She has a fabulous, sexy figure and a complexion that must drive Portuguese woman mad with envy."

"She sounds," Melissa commented in a dry tone, managing to keep herself from smiling, "almost too good to be true."

"That's what I'm afraid of," Phil said somberly. "But she's so real and vivid in my mind that I tell myself she cannot possibly be just a figment of an overactive imagination. She looks like a Greek goddess, and makes love like one, too."

"Like a marble statue, you mean?"

"Like a warm, vibrant Aphrodite who's come down from Mount Olympus especially to enchant me."

Her lips twitching, she said, "So you cast yourself in the role of Adonis, eh?"

"That, I hope, is how she sees me in *her* fantasy."

Melissa became aware that they were being watched from across the room. Dona Carlota, seated on a scrolled sofa with another elderly woman, was observing their laughing intimacy with angry eyes.

"Your grandmother doesn't look any too happy," she said uneasily. "Perhaps we ought to break it up."

"For heaven's sake, why? You're my guest . . . and a V.I.P. where the vineyard is concerned. It's only right that I should give you my attention this evening."

"I think it's the nature of the attention you're giving me that's bothering Dona Carlota."

Phil chuckled. "She's annoyed because her little plan has come unstuck. When I phoned to say that I'd be here this weekend to show you the vineyard, she hastily arranged this dinner party as an excuse to get me face to face with Josepha again. I shall have to break the news to Grandmama that this latest scheme of hers hasn't a hope of succeeding."

They were joined by two men, one of them Melissa's companion at the dinner table.

"My dear Senhora Colville," he began, beaming at her, "please give us your valued opinion. Senhor Gomez and I were discussing the best way to please British holiday-makers, and . . ."

Melissa scarcely heard what he was saying. She felt mystified by Dona Carlota's hostile attitude toward her. It was understandable this evening, when the old lady wanted Phil to pay court to Josepha, that she objected to his flirting with someone else. But the hostility went deeper than that; it was on a more personal level. Melissa had been conscious of it from the first moment she'd arrived at the Quinta das Andorinhas. Was Dona Carlota shrewd enough to have guessed that the Englishwoman had fallen in love with her grandson? Did she fear a serious entanglement that would threaten her plans for him? If she only knew, Melissa thought forlornly, that I represent no more danger to Phil's emotions than any of his other women have done.

She rallied her fragmented attention. "It's safe to say,

Senhor Baltazar, that the British people are much more ready to experiment with food and wine than they once were. I don't think you need pander too much to our likes and dislikes, but just provide whatever you consider is the best."

Phil nodded in agreement, and said with a secret wink at her, "You can trust Melissa's judgment, Carlos. She has excellent taste—in all things."

Chapter Seven

*W*hen all the guests had departed Melissa said good night to Phil and his grandmother and went upstairs to her room. She did not, as on the previous night, turn the key in the lock. She knew that Phil would be coming to her, and she scorned the pretense of being taken by surprise. In such an ephemeral relationship as theirs was doomed to be there was no place—and no time—for anything but honesty between them. Though not *complete* honesty. She could never admit to Phil that she felt for him a great deal more than he felt for her, that she loved him. For her pride's sake she had to make him believe that she was as ready for a brief affair as he was himself. If that made her seem a hard-bitten woman it couldn't be helped. If Phil were to suspect how deeply she felt about him, he'd probably groan inwardly and take steps at once to cool things with her. So she had to put on an act for his benefit. She could show passion, but not loving tenderness; tenderness would reveal far too much of what she felt in her heart. She could reveal her keen desire for him as long as she was careful to conceal the sense of commitment that was an essential element of that desire.

Later, when the house was still and silent, his tap came at her door. Melissa arranged a smiling welcome on her face, holding back the poignant tears that pricked behind her eyelids. Phil took her straight into his arms and released a shuddering sigh.

"I thought those people would never leave," he said. "I've been so impatient to be with you."

They kissed for long, passionate moments, and afterward she clung to him fiercely, with a kind of desperation.

"Phil . . ."

"What is it, *querida?*"

How could she tell him when she didn't even know herself what she'd been about to say? That she loved him? No, she had to banish that thought totally from her mind—especially when Phil was with her, in case she let it slip in an unguarded moment of high emotion. She *wanted* him, just as he wanted her . . . that was the word he would use.

Pressed close against him, she could feel Phil's body pulsing with desire. But he didn't hurry, didn't take anything for granted. He treated her with gentleness, almost as if she were fragile, letting his fingertips move over her face with a butterfly touch, stroking the creamy length of her throat and caressing her shoulders.

The previous evening she had frolicked with him naked in the lake and made love with him in passionate abandonment. Yet now, as he touched her breast, she shivered nervously. When Phil, becoming impatient with the flimsy barrier of her nightdress, loosened the ribbons at the neck and made to remove it, she instinctively tensed. He didn't persist at once, but gave her a moment, brushing his lips against the silkiness of her hair and running his questing hands down the length of her spine before again tugging at the ribbons. This time the pale apricot silk shimmered to the floor, and she stood naked before him.

"You're so lovely," he murmured huskily. "So perfect!"

Suddenly Melissa's own impatience overtook her. Her fingers fumbled with the buttons of his shirt, then dragged it free of his waistband. She slid her hands up across the heated skin of his chest and twined them around his neck, laying her cheek against his shoulder. There was a jumbled thudding in her ears as her own racing heartbeat mingled with his.

"Darling Melissa?" he whispered, and left a question mark hanging.

"Yes," she answered him. "Oh, yes, Phil . . . yes, yes."

He held her a moment longer and kissed her on the lips in soft promise. Then he released her long enough to throw off his clothes, his shirt and trousers joining her nightdress on the floor. His body, in the mellow light of the bedside lamp, gleamed with the deep richness of bronze.

As if effortlessly, Phil lifted her in his arms and carried her to the bed, then lay her down on the quilted velvet cover. He knelt beside her, gazing at her reverently.

"You're beautiful," he said softly. "All day long I've been wondering if my memory could have tricked me. Was it possible that any woman's body could be so perfectly formed as I remembered yours?"

She felt herself flushing under the intensity of his regard, and reached to turn off the bedside lamp.

"No, leave the light on, *querida*. Last night I had only the moon to see you by. Tonight I want to see your every wonderful detail." He bent and kissed her throat, and his lips seemed to burn their imprint on her flesh. With one hand he inscribed a slow, sensuous line across the satin smoothness of her stomach to the valley between her breasts, then paused to circle them, savoring their shape and form. When he bent again it was to touch his lips to the rosy center of each breast in turn, causing Melissa to moan softly and writhe beneath him.

"Your nipples look like rubies set in milk white marble,"

he murmured. "But rubies and marble are both cold stone, and your body is beautifully warm flesh. More than just warm, you're on fire for me, aren't you, darling?"

"Oh, yes." Melissa reached up, wanting to draw him down to her, to feel his thrilling weight. But Phil resisted, smiling tenderly.

"We have all night before us," he said. "Hour after incredible hour. Tonight is going to be a memorable one, for us both."

Memorable for how long on his side? she wondered. Just until after I've gone back to England and he's found another woman? But the tiny bud of bitterness was nipped off before it could grow as his fingers continued their erotic exploration of her body, blazing a trail for his lips to follow.

Phil lingered at her navel, probing the soft indentation, tasting it with his tongue. "Like honey," he whispered. "Like nectar in a flower. What makes you smell and taste so delicious and intoxicating?"

She moved sinuously under the sweet torment. "Oh, Phil, I . . ."

His fingers splayed open to shape her thighs, then slid round beneath her to grip the soft flesh of her buttocks while his questing mouth moved upward to capture the coral pink peak of one breast. His tongue became a velvet rasp which teased the nipple into swollen hardness.

"Phil, Phil . . . oh, please . . ."

She could feel the tremors that racked his whole body, evidence of the cost of his iron self-control. She gasped in thankfulness as he stretched out beside her. Yet still Phil held back. One arm encircled her, and with his other hand he drew lazy, sensuous circles on the curve of her abdomen until Melissa was almost shrieking aloud at the waiting, wanting torture of it. And then the torture was over as his fingers reached their destination and the ecstasy began, mounting higher, wave upon wave, each one seeming almost more than she could bear until her body was thrashing wildly and she burned with molten heat. Yet still she climbed from brink to brink, until at last the tension burst in a great flooding torrent of liquid gold that left her feeling weak and helpless and gloriously, wonderfully happy.

I love you, Phil. No, don't say it, just think it. Just bask in the secret knowledge, and hold at bay the dreadful parting that looms so terribly soon.

She reached for Phil, clutching him in a fever as she guided him between her thighs, needing now the reassurance of this total intimacy. It was the beginning for Melissa of another ascent toward heaven, this time in unison with Phil, onward and upward until the mattress beneath her had no more substance than a gossamer summer cloud. The glow of the bedside lamp became the heart of the sun, pouring out its warmth and radiance until they were engulfed in a final blaze of glory, their bodies moving together in the ultimate rapture. She cried his name, and he moaned hers on a long, shuddering breath, and then they both lay still and spent.

Presently, Melissa opened her eyes and watched him, his face relaxed and his long dark lashes lying peacefully upon his cheek. The skin of his shoulders gleamed with the cooling sweat of his passion. They had so little time, Phil had said. Exactly how much time was up to her to decide. There had been no fixed date for her departure; her stay in Portugal was to last until their negotiations were complete. And what remained to be done? There were a few loose ends to tie up, a little horse trading over the odd percentage point, perhaps a discussion with Phil's lawyer about the actual wording of the contract.

She had to face the fact that there was no earthly reason to extend her stay beyond a couple more days . . . say Wednesday. And a couple of days with Phil seemed like no time at all. A flurry of panic made her shiver.

Phil stirred, his muscles firming as he held her more

tightly to him and kissed her with tender gratitude. "That was so wonderful, Melissa. What a fantastic woman you are."

Locked in one another's arms they drifted slowly toward sleep, cocooned in the deep silence of the countryside. And Melissa slept sweetly, wrapped in golden dreams of timeless eternity spent with Phil. . . .

When she awoke the early morning sun was slanting into the room. A vague shape loomed above her, and she brought it into focus. Phil was propped up on one elbow, gazing down at her fondly. He touched a finger to the tip of her nose.

"Hi! Did anyone ever tell you that you look especially cute when you're asleep?"

"I'm not sure that 'cute' is flattering to a woman of thirty-two."

"Then I'll say it in Portuguese." He did so, at considerable length.

"What was all that?"

Phil pressed the tip of her nose again, reprovingly. "Fishing for compliments?"

"For all I know it might have been highly *un*flattering."

"Likely, isn't it?" he scoffed. "After last night. And this," he added, thrusting himself hard against her. Melissa felt the throb of desire in his naked body, and a great wave of love and longing surged through her.

"Phil," she said uneasily, "you ought to go now."

"Go?" He sounded incredulous. "It's barely six A.M. Besides—"

"There'll be servants about soon," she pointed out.

"So what?"

"I suppose," she said on a sudden wave of bitterness, "that they're accustomed to you and your affairs by now."

He gave a reproachful shake of his head. "Let's confine ourselves to you and me, Melissa." Pushing back the sheet that covered them, he began to weave swirling patterns on the softness of her stomach. "Your skin is so white, almost translucent. It fascinates me."

"Phil—," she began uneasily.

He pressed a silencing finger to her lips. "If you were going to say something more about my leaving, I'm not listening." He let his fingers play around her mouth, skimming along the lower lip. Then he took away his hand and replaced it with his mouth, beginning with light, feathery kisses that became more and more demanding. Melissa's protests were forgotten; she was suddenly, urgently, hungry for his lovemaking. Her arms went up and twined around his neck, drawing him closer.

There was a feverishness about their passion. So little time, so little time . . . those words of his seemed to mock Melissa. She would have to tell him soon of her decision to leave on Wednesday. Meanwhile, she thrust the thought away.

He was a magician with his hands and lips, lifting her from peak to higher peak toward the final ecstasy. When he pressed his open mouth to her breast and she felt the grainy texture of his tongue on the pointed nipple she moaned with pleasure, rocking from side to side in an agony of delight.

"Please, Phil . . . oh, please!"

He felt a swift thrill of excitement, delighting in her uninhibited response, proud of making her want him like this. She was fantastic in bed, almost wanton in her eagerness yet always tender and considerate of his own needs. To judge from the intensity of his desire for her right now he might have been sex starved, the long night behind them might never have happened. Phil was stunned by the overwhelming strength of his feelings for her, and one part of his mind resented Melissa for having him so totally within her power. Never before had a woman affected him like this. With others he had desired, then quickly satisfied his desire. With Melissa, he wondered if it would ever be possible to have enough of her.

The tips of his fingers appreciatively caressed her silken skin, tracing the delicate bone structure of her face, moving over the lovely slender shoulders and graceful arms. He lingered for an indulgent moment on the voluptuous softness of her breasts, then moved on across the slim waist to the velvety plane of her abdomen and slid round to grip her yielding buttocks before smoothing down the long lengths of her thighs, making an exquisitely sensuous trail. Then upward again, remorselessly teasing and tormenting, willing her to want him all the more.

"Phil . . . oh, Phil!"

Melissa could feel his body shuddering from repressed passion, and she could stand it no longer. She reached for him and urged him to her, shuddering in her turn as he slid into her. Ecstasy beckoned from its lofty peak, yet she surged toward it confidently, knowing that with Phil it was so easily attained. Enveloped in the gilded radiance of morning sunshine pouring through the windows, they reached the summit together, and their soft cries of gladness mingled with the chorus of birdsong coming from the jacaranda trees outside.

"I suggest," Phil said when they were having breakfast, "that we meander back to Lisbon today. We can take in the royal palace of Queluz on the way."

She had to tell him of her decision to leave on Wednesday. "Phil . . ."

"Don't you like the idea?"

"Er . . . oh, yes . . . it sounds lovely." Somehow the moment had gone by. Here in his family home she felt that she couldn't cope with any argument from him. Back in Lisbon would be better. The atmosphere there would seem more businesslike. "Tell me about Queluz," she said, putting on an interested smile.

"It's a fabulous rococo palace, built a couple of hundred years ago. It's reputed to have been inspired by the French palace of Versailles. And there's a good restaurant in what used to be the kitchens."

She laughed. "You seem to think of nothing but food."

Phil looked deep into her eyes. "How wrong can you be!"

"Pour me some more coffee," she said, feeling a warm flush creeping up her cheeks. "Make it black this time. I shall put on pounds if you insist on feeding me huge, delicious meals."

"A few big meals aren't going to harm a figure like yours, Melissa, and I want your visit to Portugal to be one you won't forget."

No danger of that! She smiled back at him, but said nothing.

They left around midmorning. Dona Carlota's farewell was coldly polite, with no wish expressed to see Melissa again at the Quinta das Andorinhas. You needn't worry, Melissa thought, I won't be coming again. Yet as they swept down the driveway to the tall entrance gates she couldn't resist looking back at the lovely house set amid its tranquil gardens. She had taken one or two snapshots earlier on, but she'd need no pictures to remind her. The beauty of the Quinta das Andorinhas would remain with her forever in every vivid detail.

At Queluz they toured a series of ornate rooms, Phil translating the guide's patter for her. Afterward they lunched splendidly in the restaurant, then spent a while wandering hand in hand through the topiary gardens. Phil told her scandalous stories about the virago queen, Carlota Joaquina, her lovers and her plots against her poor husband, Dom Joao. So much, Melissa thought wryly, for the romantic Spanish princess who had come to Lisbon in a beautifully painted coach when she'd married her prince.

As they stood under an orange tree Phil reached up and plucked a ripe fruit, peeled it deftly and broke it apart.

"Open your mouth, Melissa," he instructed, and slipped a juicy segment between her lips.

"I've never eaten an orange within a minute of its being picked," she said between swallows as he continued to feed her and himself. "It tastes delicious, Phil . . . so sharp and tangy."

"You, too, are delicious," he said, his dark eyes devouring her.

"Not sharp and tangy?"

"Sharp as a knife, at times. And you definitely leave a lingering aftertaste." He impatiently tossed away the remainder of the orange and took her into his arms. "You're the sort of woman who makes a man greedy. Last night seems an age away, and waiting for tonight is like having to wait forever."

He's taking me for granted, was Melissa's drowning thought as he kissed her. And then her mind was submerged in the delight of feeling his body pressed against hers.

"We'll spend the night at my apartment, Melissa," Phil said later, in the car.

"No!" Her rejection was quick, instinctive. Phil glanced at her in surprise. "Why not?"

She couldn't really explain her feelings, not in a way that would make sense to him. She would go with him to his apartment and they would make love there. But later she intended to return to the guesthouse. She just said firmly, "I won't stay the night, Phil."

He shrugged, his expression registering perplexity at the mysterious workings of a woman's mind.

Reaching Lisbon, they were soon immersed in the city's Sunday evening whirl of traffic. As on that first day, when Phil had driven her from the airport, he skillfully avoided the worst of the holdups. His apartment turned out to be in a quiet street of gracious old houses with delicate ironwork balconies at the upper windows. He led Melissa up two flights of stairs that had an ornately carved banister. The hallway inside Phil's front door was slightly cramped, but when he ushered her into the living room Melissa gave a gasp of astonished delight. What she hadn't appreciated from the street was that the houses had been built on a steep hillside. The ground at their rear sloped away, and from the three tall windows of his living room there was a fantastic view over the city to the Tagus and the distant hills beyond. The view was even more breathtaking when Phil opened a french door and they stepped out onto a pretty, creeper-clad balcony.

"It's fabulous, Phil," she said excitedly. "And so unexpected. I never guessed you'd have a view like this."

"That's Lisbon for you. It's a labyrinth of narrow, twisted cobbled streets and tiny courtyards, with the houses all built cheek-by-jowl, leaning on one another and with stairways to nowhere . . . then, bingo! you suddenly get a view across the entire city."

There had been a note of pride in his voice, and she turned to smile at him. "You love Lisbon, don't you?"

"I guess I do, at that. I'll tell you something, though . . . showing you around, I've seen it all through fresh eyes. I've noticed things that I've never really noticed before. And there's masses more for you to see. I have quite an itinerary scheduled for the coming week."

The time had come to tell him, no dodging it. "Phil . . ."

"Why the voice of doom, *querida?*"

"Well . . . we shall have everything wrapped up by tomorrow, or Tuesday at the latest. So I've decided to take the morning flight to London on Wednesday."

He looked shocked, appalled. "But you can't. That's much too soon."

"I came to Portugal to do a job, Phil. When that job is completed I shall have no excuse for staying on."

"Aren't I a good enough excuse?" he asked reproachfully. He gripped her shoulders and pulled her to face him. "Melissa, listen—"

"No, you listen, Phil. Okay, I'm not pretending it hasn't

been good between us . . . more than good. And we'll still have until Wednesday. But not any longer than that. I'd feel cheap, inventing reasons for staying on that don't exist."

He scowled at her. "Surely, as a senior executive of your firm you don't have to *invent* excuses to anyone?"

"You don't understand a thing, do you?" Her voice held a note of anger. "I'd *feel* cheap; can't you get that into your head? Me, myself, *I'd* feel cheap."

"I don't see why you should."

"But you're not a woman, are you? As a man you can happily grab at any chance of casual sex that comes your way without . . ." Melissa skidded to a halt. Whenever she spoke impulsively, whenever she stopped weighing her words, she was in danger of revealing too much about her feelings for him.

"Without what?" he prompted, his eyes accusing.

"What's the use of trying to explain?" she answered evasively. "You'd never see the point. I'm just telling you, Phil, that when our business deal is wrapped up, so is our personal relationship."

"Personal relationship!" he echoed in disgust. "How very cold-blooded you make it sound. Don't forget that I'm the man who's held you in his arms these past few days and felt you—"

"If you'd prefer it," she retorted challengingly, "we can end things right here and now. That's fine by me. I'll leave at once, and we'll confine future meetings to your office."

"No, Melissa, you can't go. I won't let you." Phil dragged her back to face him, and his eyes were blazing. Then she watched him make an effort to control his fury, and he said in a quieter, strained voice, "Why are you doing this to me, Melissa?"

Because I love you. No, she mustn't say it, mustn't even think it. Yet how could she avoid thinking it when every cell in her body, awake and asleep, sang with the joy of loving him?

"I'm merely trying to be practical, Phil," she said, and hoped that he didn't notice the trembling of her voice.

"Are you such a hard-boiled woman that you won't allow your heart to rule your head once in a while?" he burst out accusingly. "Won't you let your emotional needs take precedence over hard calculation?"

Melissa closed her eyes against the pain. He knew how to hurt her, all right. "Please, Phil," she said weakly, "can't we . . . I hate quarreling with you like this."

"Do you imagine that I enjoy it?" he challenged. But his tone was subtly different, softer, with a note of pleading. "Melissa, let's talk later about when you're going to leave. All day I've been waiting impatiently for the moment when we'd be alone together again. Let's not spoil it."

She looked back at him in helpless despair. She knew that this was no solution, to let their bodies resolve what argument couldn't. But it was going to happen that way. The instant he kissed her all her resistance would melt like a summer morning mist before the heat of the sun. They would make love now as surely as night followed day. It was inevitable, and they both knew it.

"Oh, Phil . . . ," she gasped with a stifled sob.

They stood there on his balcony, locked tight in one another's arms, oblivious to the pink-and-white city spread below them. When at last they moved, they moved in harmony, in perfect agreement that the moment had come. Inside, with the french doors still wide open, Phil peeled off her clothes slowly and savoringly. Naked, Melissa could hardly contain her impatience as she tugged at his buttons, his zipper, more hindrance than help to him, until he too stood in all his nude splendor. For one pulsing second—two, three—they were frozen in time gazing at one another in reverent appreciation; then they sank together to the softness of the carpet.

At first they made love leisurely, lingeringly, with the entire evening stretching before them. But as their passion built their languorous movements became urgent ones. Their hands caressed, searched, clutched and kneaded. Phil's hungry lips seared trails of heat across her already molten skin, and his thrusting tongue invaded her mouth with tender savagery until she was frantic with delight. And when the frenzied excitement couldn't be borne for an instant more, she parted her legs in invitation, urging him to bring her the fulfillment she so desperately craved. Their bodies moved sweetly and rhythmically in mounting rapture until the final bliss came in a great convulsive shudder.

"Oh, Melissa . . . you wonderful, wonderful woman," she heard him whisper as she drifted down from the summit.

She opened her eyes to be dazzled by an angled shaft of evening sunlight. Phil's face was in shadow, his eyes gleaming softly like two dark pools in which she would willingly drown. No amount of heartache later would be too great a cost for this supreme experience.

"Melissa! You can't possibly go on Wednesday."

"But I must."

Phil shook his head. "No, it would be too cruel . . . for both of us. Stay another week, darling. Just a few days longer. Please."

"No, I can't," she said stubbornly. "There'd be no point, Phil." But she didn't really mean that. Her objections were mere tokens, raised only to be swept aside.

"You told me the day you arrived," Phil reminded her, "that your sister-in-law was tickled pink to have your children all to herself for a while. And you said that the kids themselves would be having a ball, and probably getting spoiled rotten. So you have no excuse. I've had a great idea, darling," he went on enthusiastically. "There's a small seaside chalet on the west coast that belongs to my family. It's a beautiful spot, and very remote. How about you and me going there, say on Tuesday afternoon, and staying for a few days?"

"Phil—"

He laid his hand across her lips. They were still lying on the rug where they had made love. Neither had any inclination to move, unwilling to risk breaking the spell of enchantment that enveloped them. "You'll love it there, Melissa darling. There's a fantastic feeling of cleanness and space, with nothing but three thousand miles of ocean between it and the next chunk of land—America. The nearest habitation is three miles away, and then it's only a small farmhouse."

It sounded like heaven. A few days alone with Phil in joyous isolation. Wasn't she entitled to that much?

"Just for a day or two?" she queried hesitantly.

"If that's all you'll give me, yes. You say till when."

Melissa considered for a moment. For the sake of her own self-respect she had to stay in control of the situation . . . to some extent, at least. "We'll come back Friday," she stipulated. "I'll need to pack my things, pay my bill at the guesthouse. I'll get a plane home Saturday morning."

"Great!" Phil felt triumphant. He had the reprieve he'd asked for, and Saturday was a long way off. Strange, he mused, how vital it had been for him to keep her for just a little while longer. Another couple of days would help to get her out of his system. He wouldn't forget Melissa Colville, ever; she was someone extra special. But when they'd had a chance to spend a bit more time together he'd be better able to get her in perspective.

Sliding his arm under her shoulders, he drew her close against him and pressed his lips to her smooth, cool forehead. Yes, Saturday was still a long way off.

Chapter Eight

$\mathcal{M}$elissa was enchanted with the chalet. It was an old fisherman's cottage, really, that had been skillfully converted, and it stood on the rocks above a little crescent-shaped beach of soft yellow sand. Stumpy, wind-bent trees nearby were mute evidence of savage winter gales, but the scene that morning was utterly peaceful as she and Phil lay sunbathing beneath a cloudless sky. Not another soul had come by all morning to disturb their privacy.

They had arrived from Lisbon at dusk the previous evening, bringing cartons of food and several bottles of wine. After unpacking she and Phil had set about preparing dinner. From a fishing hamlet along the coast they'd purchased newly caught sole, and this Melissa fried in butter and covered with roasted almonds, while Phil fixed a salad of lettuce and tomatoes with a tangy, herb-flavored dressing. There had been a lovely warm intimacy as they worked together in the tiny kitchen, then carried the food through to the low-ceilinged living room. They sat at a little circular table with only the pool of muted light from an overhanging brass oil lantern. For dessert they had eaten fresh fruit, and Phil had laughingly fed her grapes, slipping them between her lips one by one.

Afterward they had wandered outside and descended to the sandy beach by three short flights of wooden steps. The moon had not yet risen, but there was a phosphorescent glow upon the water as they strolled together, arms entwined. They stopped to kiss, and then, suddenly caught by rising passion, they had shed their clothes and collapsed together on the sand. For Melissa there was something especially joyous and free about making love with Phil in the open air, as on that first magical evening at the *quinta*.

"Oh, Phil," she had moaned, clinging to him.

"Melissa . . . wonderful Melissa."

When they'd roused, stirring from a delicious languor, they found that the moon had risen, resting like a silver ball upon the clifftop. After gathering up their scattered clothes they'd wended their way back to the chalet with the moon shadowing them, giving light enough to guide them upstairs to the low-ceilinged bedroom dominated by a large, old-fashioned bed. They'd fallen upon the white counterpane and made love again, leisurely, with an age of time before them in which to think of nothing but each other. They had slept at last, exhausted, waking to find the sun high in the sky. It was past ten o'clock.

"What a way to spend a glorious morning," Melissa had exclaimed in dismay. At home she was invariably up by seven.

"Why sound so shocked?" Phil smiled an enticing smile. "I can't think of a better way of spending a glorious morning, can you?"

"Oh, no, you don't!" She made to leap from the bed, but he caught her by the wrist and held her easily, dragging her back into the captivity of his arms.

When they had finally risen it was for a brunch of

scrambled eggs and toast, slices of cool melon and mugs of hot strong coffee. And then down to the beach again, Melissa in a yellow bikini that she'd purchased in Lisbon, and Phil in skintight navy briefs.

Melissa was watching him now as he lay on his back, stretched out full length with his eyes closed against the brightness of the sun. His body was the perfect example of male beauty, his skin glistening like bronze over the hard bone and rippling musculature. Phil stirred restlessly, as if conscious of her intent scrutiny, then rolled over onto his stomach and lay propped on his elbows, studying her with a look that melted her insides.

"What shall we do this afternoon?" Melissa inquired hastily.

He raised a scathing eyebrow as if she'd asked the most stupid question, and she added, "I'd like to see something of the countryside around here while I've got the chance."

"If you must. But on one condition."

"What's that?"

"We'll have dinner out somewhere, then come back here for a midnight swim."

Melissa grinned at him. "It's a deal, *senhor.*"

He took her to Mafra, a huge monastery and palace modeled on the Escorial in Spain. As they wandered through the labyrinth of fabulous rooms—nearly nine hundred of them in all, she was amazed to learn—Phil sketched in its history for her.

They made their way back to the coast through quiet byroads, reaching a tiny fishing village in time to see the boats returning with the day's catch. In the absence of any kind of harbor these had to be hauled up onto the beach, which was done by means of oxen yoked to long chains.

"What a charming scene it makes," said Melissa.

"Charming to us," Phil observed soberly, "but it's a hard life for them. Dangerous, too."

Melissa gazed thoughtfully at the black-shawled women

who waited for their menfolk, ready to clean the fish for market. One evening perhaps they would wait in vain for the men they loved to return from the ocean . . . the cruel ocean that at this moment looked so deceptively calm, a sheet of hammered bronze in the brilliance of the setting sun. The wistful sadness of eventide caught her as she and Phil made their way up the narrow stepped street to the inn where they were to dine.

It was a simple place, but spotlessly clean. A smiling girl in a colorful embroidered blouse showed them to a scrubbed table, serving them at once with a large flagon of red wine. The food Phil ordered turned out to be fresh-caught hake in an herb sauce. Red wine with fish? So much for convention, Melissa thought wryly. Yet it was a perfect blend, along with coarse, crusty bread. She ate with zest, and Phil watched her approvingly.

"I'm glad you like it here," he said. "I hoped that you would."

Melissa smiled. "You should have known that I would."

"There's so much about you that I *don't* know, though. What were you thinking just now when we walked up from the beach? You looked so pensive."

She bit her lip. The hard lot of the fishermen's wives had only been the trigger to her mood of melancholy, making her brood upon how fragile happiness was. Giving him a cheeky grin, she lied, "I was thinking about food, actually. Lunch seemed such a long time ago."

"How terribly prosaic," Phil grumbled. "When I'm with you, *querida,* I can only think of you."

And when you're not with me, she thought, what then? Will I be promptly forgotten, or relegated to a limbo of pleasant memories? I'm getting maudlin, Melissa rebuked herself sharply, and switched on a bright smile.

"You weren't so lost in admiration yesterday at your office," she reminded Phil, "as to let me slip in that penalty clause in our contract."

"I admired you for trying," he said, and went to refill her glass.

"No more wine for me, or I'll be drunk."

"I'm drunk already just from looking at you. Come on, don't dawdle over that fish. I want to get you home."

Back to the chalet, then down to the beach . . . it was a repetition of the previous evening, only even more wonderful. Their lovemaking was like a slow-motion dream sequence until, as their mutual passion became more ardent, more urgent, the tempo quickened in a final frenzy of desire.

Afterward, rousing from a contented half doze on the soft warm sand, they ran into the foaming breakers and splashed around like children, naked and free. Melissa lay back and let herself float, luxuriating in the steady rise and fall of the waves beneath her while she watched the moon riding a mackerel sky. She was alerted by a sudden cry and struggled up to see Phil being washed ashore, a dark hump on the crest of a breaker. Her heart thudding in alarm, she struck out strongly toward him. He lay on his back, spread-eagled on the sand, the surf foaming and hissing around his ankles. As she knelt beside him, she saw the glint of his eyes in the moonlight, and he said with a chuckle, "Quick, I need mouth to mouth resuscitation."

Melissa felt quite dizzy as relief washed through her, and there was a bitter taste of fear in her mouth. But she refused to let him see how panic-stricken she had been.

"Huh!" she muttered as she went to stand up. "It looks to me as if resuscitation is the last thing you need."

Phil reached up and caught her while she was still off-balance, then dragged her down on top of him. His hands slid over her wet skin and his mouth locked once again onto hers.

Dawn was streaking the sky with skeins of apricot and rose when she awoke from a deep, contented sleep. Phil was awake, too. She turned to see his dark head on the pillow beside her, his eyes looking into hers.

"I like watching you wake," he said, "with your hair all tumbled across the pillow like a cloud of silk."

He slid his arms about her, moving to press his body hard against her, and Melissa gasped at the electric speed with which he could rouse her to desire. She could hardly trust herself to speak, and just whispered his name tremblingly.

Phil teased her face with his tongue, tracing the arching lines of her eyebrows, the soft curve of her cheek. "I had you really worried last night, didn't I, pretending to have passed out?"

A sudden shaft of anger pierced her as she recalled her sick panic, and all for nothing. She burst out furiously, "Don't you ever do anything like that to me again, do you hear?"

He looked contrite. "I'm sorry; it was just meant as a joke."

A stupid joke, Phil told himself angrily. Whatever had come over him to have acted in such an infantile way? At the time he'd had some crazy idea of wanting to test Melissa's feelings for him, as if in some way her reaction would be an indication of how much he meant to her. Last night she'd been quite jokey about the incident; he knew now that she'd been really upset. But what did that prove, for heaven's sake? Of course she'd been upset. . . . She must have been terrified, stuck in the middle of nowhere with a man who seemed to be unconscious, and without the slightest idea of how to summon help.

"Okay, you've every right to be angry," he went on, "but don't keep me in the doghouse, *querida*. We've so little time together."

She gave him a silent nod.

"You know, Melissa," he said thoughtfully, "we don't need to say a final goodbye when you return to England. I shall be in London from time to time, and between us we can think up reasons for you to come to Lisbon again."

"No!" she jerked out. "I don't want that."

"You mean you'll have had enough of me by then?"

"That's not fair, Phil. I didn't mean that at all, but—"

"But what?" he challenged.

She hesitated before answering, wanting to tell him that saying goodbye would be like tearing out her heart. Instead she said lightly, "It's just not on. What we've shared, it's been good—very good. But we never did see it as more than a short-term thing, did we? So let's keep it short and sweet, not try to drag it out until we're heartily sick of one another."

There was a long pause, then Phil gave a shrug. "Okay, whatever the lady says." He raised his arm to look at his wristwatch. "By my calculations we have exactly fifty-one hours until you catch your plane. I vote that we make the most of them."

They arrived back in Lisbon at the height of the Friday afternoon rush hour. Phil wanted to look in at his office, so he dropped Melissa off at the guesthouse on his way through the city. She was going to collect the rest of her belongings and check out, as they planned to spend their last night together at Phil's apartment. The very first thing she must do, Melissa decided as she climbed the stone steps between ivy-clad walls, was to call Pendlehurst and speak with Mark and Jenny. She had talked to them last on Tuesday afternoon, when she'd told Pauline that she'd be returning home on Saturday. It had been her intention to phone again on Thursday, but somehow the day had drifted by and she'd never quite reached the point of asking Phil to drive her to the nearest phone.

As always, there was an air of deep tranquillity about the one-time convent. It was so easy to imagine black-garbed nuns gliding silently through the long, vaulted corridors. When Melissa approached the reception desk to collect her room key and ask to have her bill prepared she was greeted without the usual bright smile from the clerk. Instead the young woman had a solemn expression on her face.

"Ah, Senhora Colville, I have a message for you. Please telephone Mrs. Drake immediately. The lady has called from England a number of times. She did not believe, I think, that we were unable to reach you," the clerk added a little resentfully, "though I repeatedly told her that you had merely informed us that you would be returning here this afternoon."

Oh God, something must have happened to one of the children. Melissa felt the cold hand of fear along her spine. "Did . . . did Mrs. Drake tell you anything?" she stammered. "Did she say why she wants me to call her?"

"I am sorry, but no. Only that it was imperative that you telephone her at once. I will reach the number now if you wish, and you can take the call in your room."

"Yes . . . oh yes, thank you." Grabbing her key, Melissa hurried upstairs. The phone rang just as she was closing the door, and she snatched it up.

"Pauline, is that you?"

"Melissa, I've been trying to reach you ever since yesterday afternoon." There was unconcealed reproof in her tone. "It really is most inconsiderate of you not to have left word where you could be contacted. I tried the Silva Cunha offices, but they were unable to help me."

"Pauline, for heaven's sake . . . what's wrong? Is it . . . one of the children?"

"There's no need to be hysterical, Melissa. Jenny has had a slight accident and—"

"What happened? Is she badly hurt?"

"No, it's not really serious. She fell off Kimbo at a jump that she'd rigged up in the paddock. In my opinion you encourage that child to take too many risks."

"But what has she done to herself?" Melissa asked frantically.

"There's nothing broken, just bruises and a sprained

ankle. But Doctor Evans insisted on her being admitted to hospital because there was also a slight concussion."

"Concussion? Oh God, is it bad?"

"I said *slight* concussion," Pauline clipped severely. "There's no cause for you to get so worked up, Melissa. Not unnaturally, a girl of Jenny's age, being in the strange surroundings of a hospital, keeps asking for her mother. The poor child feels lost and confused." A note of bitterness crept in as she added, "Even *I* am not a satisfactory substitute, it seems."

"I'll come at once. I'll get the very first flight I can."

"Is your business with the Silva Cunha people concluded?"

"Oh yes, it was finished—" Melissa just stopped herself from blurting out "days ago." She rushed on. "I'll be with you just as soon as I can, Pauline. Give Jenny all my love, and tell her that I'm hurrying to be with her."

She dropped the phone back onto its hook and sank down on the bed, her brain spinning. It took several moments before she could get herself together enough to think, to plan. She felt sick with guilt and remorse that when her small daughter was in the hospital and needed her, she had been away at the chalet with Phil. Taking a few deep, calming breaths, she picked up the phone again and asked the desk clerk to inquire about the first available flight to London. "One of my children has had an accident and—"

"Oh, *senhora,* but how dreadful!"

"It's not too serious, thank heaven. Will it be possible for me to get back to England this evening, do you think?"

"I expect so, *senhora.* Leave it with me, and I will call you back in a few minutes. Meantime, perhaps you would like to get packed in readiness."

"Yes . . . yes, of course."

Hurriedly Melissa gathered her remaining clothes together and stuffed them into her bags, not caring whether she was overlooking anything. Before she'd finished the phone rang.

"You are booked, Senhora Colville, on a flight that leaves in one hour and a half. I have ordered a taxi for the airport in fifteen minutes. Can you be ready by then?"

"Oh, yes, thank you so much. I'll be down shortly to settle my bill."

She had to let Phil know what had happened, but the thought of speaking to him on the phone was more than she could bear. The arrangements they had made for that evening and the night to follow were nothing to her now. Phil was going to buy the ingredients for a meal which they'd planned to prepare and eat together at his apartment, leaving them lots of opportunity to make love. Phil, as keenly as herself, had been anxious not to waste a single minute of their last precious hours together. What had come over her? What had possessed her to think that her responsibilities could be cast to the winds, even for a few short days, without there being a heavy price to pay?

She was tempted to dodge the problem of what to do about Phil by simply leaving Lisbon without a word to him. But that wouldn't be fair. In his own way Phil had been straight with her, and he deserved the courtesy of an explanation.

The porter arrived to collect her luggage. She had only a minute or two before she would have to leave for the airport. She found stationery in a drawer and quickly scribbled a note for Phil. She had no time to consider carefully what she wrote. Just the bare facts . . . Jenny had had an accident and needed her mother urgently. So this was goodbye. "Please," she added, underlining it heavily, "don't write or phone." His contact with Colville's would in future be with her brother-in-law, and there was no reason why their paths should ever cross again.

Melissa quickly sealed and addressed the envelope before she could let her heart add any softening words. Downstairs, when she'd settled her bill, she handed the note to the desk clerk. "Senhor Maxwell will be calling for me later on," she explained. "Please make sure that he's given this."

"But of course, *senhora*. I trust that you will find your daughter recovered when you return."

"Thank you. Goodbye."

In the taxi, as it swung around the great rotunda at the top of the magnificent Avenida da Liberdade, Melissa spared a swift glance over Lisbon's elegant center to the sun-sparkled waters of the Tagus beyond. Her heart lurched in anguish, and then she turned firmly away. She didn't even look down as the plane circled the city before heading northward to England.

Phil ripped open the envelope and scanned the note inside. Jenny . . . an accident! "Did Senhora Colville give you any details?" he demanded.

The young woman behind the desk eyed him curiously. "The accident was not serious, I understand, but the *senhora* felt that she must be with her daughter at this time."

Phil nodded, distraught. "I wish that she'd phoned me. I could have driven her to the airport, tried to comfort her. She must have been very distressed."

"I expect she was too distressed to think clearly, Senhor Maxwell," the desk clerk suggested kindly. "I am sure that she will be in touch with you again soon, from England."

Not according to the note Melissa had left him. She didn't intend to contact him ever again. Their affair was over, finished and dead. The end had been near, of course, she'd made that perfectly clear, and he'd only lost one night with her, but . . . It was odd, Phil thought as he descended the steps to his waiting car, that just one single night with Melissa should now seem so vitally important. It was as if a monumental gap had been left in his life.

Stupid! He'd soon file away the memory of Melissa Colville as another pleasant episode, something he expected to repeat with other women from time to time.

In his car were the cartons of delectable food he'd bought for their last dinner together. The thought of eating any of the stuff alone brought Phil a twinge of nausea. On an impulse he scooped his purchases together and dumped the whole lot into the arms of a surprised doorman. Then he drove off quickly, not knowing where. Just driving.

Chapter Nine

*M*elissa, why don't you go off with the children to the seaside for a couple of weeks?"

It was typical of Selwyn's thoughtful nature that he should suggest that, Melissa reflected as she shook her head. "No, really, Selwyn, there isn't any need."

"But you've earned a vacation, my dear—no question about that. You did brilliantly on your trip to Lisbon—better, probably, than I could have done myself. I can see that it's left you tired, though, and Jenny having an accident while you were away was naturally very upsetting. So wouldn't it be a good idea to take the children away somewhere and have a complete rest?"

Melissa sighed. It was true that she did feel tired . . . or rather, emotionally drained, but all she wanted now that her concern about Jenny was over was to become deeply immersed in work to stop herself from thinking. "I've already been away from the office nearly two weeks," she pointed out. "There'll be a stack of work waiting for me by now."

Unusually for him, Selwyn adopted a teasing tone. "Brilliant though you may be, Melissa, you're not totally indispensable to Colville's. Now that I've sorted out that trouble in Germany, I shan't need to go away myself for a while, so I daresay that we'll totter along without you for a couple more weeks."

"Okay, then," she agreed, resigned to the inevitable. "I suppose it *would* be sensible to get away for a bit with the children. Jenny has had the all clear from Doctor Evans now, but after such a shake-up I expect she could do with some convalescence."

Besides which, Melissa told herself, trying to look at the positive side, a holiday away from Pendlehurst would give her the chance to devote all her attention to Jenny and Mark. It might help to alleviate the heavy burden of guilt she bore for not being available when one of her children had needed her. No amount of reasoning that Jenny's fall from the pony could have happened whether she'd been there or not was any consolation to her. The indisputable fact was that she hadn't been on the spot to comfort and care for her small daughter . . . she hadn't even been reachable. Not sparing a thought for her children, she had stayed on in Portugal to indulge in a tempestuous love affair, and she'd been so wrapped up in her own selfish pleasure that she'd even forgotten to telephone home to see how the children were. If only she had remembered to phone that Thursday, she couldn't stop lamenting, then she would have learned almost at once about Jenny's fall. But, unforgivably, her children had been pushed to one side in her thoughts as she and Phil had lazed through the sun-filled hours before another long night of lovemaking.

Lovemaking? It didn't deserve to be called that, she thought disgustedly. There had been no love involved, not on his side, at least. She had to stop thinking of him.

Yet every hour of every day thoughts of Phil swamped her mind. And the long, lonely nights were made a torture by her body's memories and longings. In Portugal she had rationalized that it would be better to return home with wonderful, unforgettable memories, no matter how much heartache would follow, rather than be burdened with regrets and recriminations for having denied herself a supreme joy. But she hadn't bargained for this terrible feeling of shame . . . shame because, despite her remorse, she still yearned for the embraces of a man she should utterly despise, a man who seemed incapable of love.

Melissa settled on taking Jenny and Mark to Hastings. As the family rose from the dinner table the evening before she was due to set out, Selwyn made the suggestion that the two of them should stroll together to the village pub for a drink. When Melissa hesitated Pauline remarked tartly, "You can't watch over your children day and night for the rest of their lives, Melissa. They're in bed and asleep, and they'll be perfectly safe." Noticing the look that passed between Pauline and Selwyn, Melissa half wondered if he'd been prodded by his sister into issuing the invitation. It was Pauline's sort of strategy. Perhaps her sister-in-law had calculated that having a quiet drink together might nudge their relationship forward.

At the Coach and Horses Selwyn leaned back in his chair and smiled at Melissa across the rim of his whiskey glass.

"This is nice, isn't it?" he said. "We ought to do it more often, Melissa."

She smiled back at him vaguely, making a noncommittal sound. Selwyn was never a man to rush his fences, and she guessed that it would still be a while before he openly raised the subject of marriage. She could hardly turn him down until he declared himself to her, so she would just have to wait it out and meantime try to avoid giving him the least encouragement.

Selwyn took another sip of whiskey and soda, then set the glass down squarely on the small oaken table at his elbow. "I've been thinking, Melissa; you did so well in Lisbon handling Senhor Maxwell that I feel it would be a good idea for you to keep up the contact."

"Keep up the contact?" she gasped, feeling the color drain from her face. "What exactly do you mean, Selwyn?"

"Well, even though you originally went to Lisbon as my stand-in, there's no reason why you shouldn't regard him henceforth as *your* client rather than mine. It's a good idea that you should start to take on some of that side of things. So, assuming that there are no hitches with the contract, as I'm sure there won't be, when the time comes around for Colville's to pay the usual courtesy call on Silva Cunhas in Lisbon, then you can go instead of me."

"No!" she said emphatically, fear clawing her insides.

"But why not?" Selwyn's tone was reproachful, as if she were rejecting a gift. "For myself, I've always found these jaunts abroad a very enjoyable part of the job." Pausing a moment, he added tentatively, "As an alternative, Melissa, we could make the trip together next year. How do you like that idea?"

Another little hint from Selwyn of his interest in her! He was carefully laying the foundation for the proposal that she knew would come eventually. Melissa wished, in a way, that he would hurry up and say something definite. Then she could gently refuse him, and it would clear the air between them. As it was, she had to stamp on Selwyn's suggestion that she might make further trips to Portugal . . . with or without him.

"There's never been any question before of my maintaining contact with the clients, Selwyn. That's your department, and I'm not cut out for it. Going to Lisbon that once, with the German emergency on our hands, was different. But I don't want to do any more of that sort of thing."

"How can you say that you're not cut out for it," he protested, "when you did so brilliantly? I've carefully checked through that first draft of the contract you prepared, and it's solid and watertight. The only queries I have are very minor ones. I couldn't have done better myself. Nobody could have."

She tried to divert him with a joke. "Flattery will get you nowhere."

"This isn't flattery," Selwyn insisted. "It's plain and simple fact. You're a tremendous asset to the firm, Melissa. It would be wonderful to think that one day you'll . . ." Veering away from any risk of getting too intimate, he continued, "I don't understand your objections to handling the Silva Cunha account personally. Is it something to do with Philip Maxwell? He didn't . . . well, make a pass or anything?"

Melissa made herself give an incredulous laugh. "Good heavens, whatever put such an idea into your head, Selwyn?"

"Well, that's a relief." He looked a little embarrassed. "It was just a thought, knowing what some of those Latin types can be like with women. Though Maxwell isn't really a Latin, is he? Only half. You didn't say much about what he's like."

Melissa wished to heaven that she'd never agreed to come out for a drink with Selwyn. She could feel her cheeks growing warm, and she was afraid that she might betray something of her feelings concerning Phil. Looking down at her green skirt and brushing away an imaginary fleck, she said with forced casualness, "There's nothing much to say, really. He was very pleasant, very courteous and hospitable, and he really seems to know his stuff." She took a shaky breath and continued. "He's an astute man when it comes to business, but also fair, in my opinion. I don't think that he would try to pull a fast one."

He hadn't pulled a fast one, even with her, Melissa acknowledged bleakly. According to the Phil Maxwell philosophy of life, he'd played it quite straight. They had been two people thrown together by circumstances, who'd found each other extremely attractive. So it would have been senseless, crazy, Phil would have reasoned, not to do something about it.

Listening to her, Selwyn nodded his head and made no

comment. He wouldn't pursue the issue right now. It was obvious that in some way the subject of Portugal and Philip Maxwell had upset Melissa, though the precise reason escaped him. Something to do, he supposed, with the fact that she had been a thousand miles away when Jenny had had that spill from her pony, and poor Melissa consequently felt guilty. Ah well, it was understandable that a mother should feel like that, however irrational her reasoning. If anything, it increased his already high opinion of Melissa.

"Another glass of wine?" he asked.

"No, nothing more, thanks. If you don't mind, Selwyn, I'd like to be getting back home. I haven't quite finished my packing for tomorrow."

On the short stroll back to Pendlehurst Selwyn said, "I was thinking, Melissa, how would it be if I popped down to Hastings next weekend? Just for the day, I mean. Sunday, perhaps."

The thought of having Selwyn's company on her vacation scared Melissa. *A nail in my coffin* . . . The words actually formed in her head. Mercifully she remembered something that Selwyn was overlooking.

"You won't have any free time next weekend," she reminded him. "You and Pauline are playing in the tournament at the golf club both Saturday and Sunday."

"Of course! Stupid of me. Oh well, we'll plan an outing together some other time."

With the wind whipping her hair and the raucous shrieks of wheeling sea gulls filling her ears, Melissa stood on the pier watching a catamaran being winched up onto the beach. Her mind was sent winging a thousand miles southward to a tiny village on Portugal's Atlantic coastline. It was such a very different setting from this popular English resort.

She had been taking pains to make this vacation a happy time for the children, despite her own depression. Thankfully, the weather had so far been pretty good, and Jenny and

Mark had been happy to spend long hours on the beach building sand castles and making moats to be filled by the rising tide, while Melissa sat knitting a sweater for Mark. During the past ten days the three of them had taken a couple of boat trips and ridden the cliff elevator to the top of Castle Hill to inspect the ancient ruins. They had toured the sandstone caves, and they'd frequently walked on the pier, where one afternoon they'd had their portraits done by a quick-sketch artist. One gray day, when the beach had looked uninviting, Melissa had driven the children to Battle to view the historic site where in 1066 William the Conqueror from Normandy had defeated King Harold and proclaimed himself king of all England.

Melissa's real misery began each evening when Jenny and Mark were finally tucked in bed for the night and she sat in the adjoining room watching—without taking anything in—the TV. She dreaded going to bed herself, and usually remained slumped in her armchair until exhaustion overtook her.

At last the day came for their return home. It was a Saturday, and Melissa had arranged to be back at Pendlehurst in time for lunch. The drive was uneventful, and on such a lovely morning, with soft puffs of white cloud drifting serenely in a sunny sky, she had no notion of the shock that awaited her at Pendlehurst. She drove right up to the front door to unload their luggage before putting the car away in the garage. The family, having heard their approach, emerged to greet them—Selwyn, Pauline and Edward, and . . . Melissa stared at the fourth figure in horrified disbelief, wondering if she could possibly be hallucinating. It was Phil. He was looking at her with such fixed intensity that his glance seemed to sear her skin.

Detachedly, as if in a dream, Melissa was aware of the children hurrying excitedly from the back of the car to greet their aunt and uncles, unable to wait a single moment before presenting the trinkets they'd so carefully chosen as homecoming gifts. Selwyn came forward and smilingly opened the door for Melissa. She tore her gaze away from Phil and tried to smile back at her brother-in-law, but her mind was racing with frantic thoughts of what Phil's presence at Pendlehurst could mean. Whatever had he said to her family to explain his sudden appearance?

Selwyn's expression, though, was in no way disapproving.

"You see who's here, Melissa?" he said cheerfully. "Senhor Maxwell happened to be in London, so he dropped in at the office to make my acquaintance. I was able to persuade him to come stay with us for the weekend. Isn't that pleasant?"

Melissa nodded mutely. Then, almost dizzy with the effort it cost her, she forced herself to behave as might be expected at a family reunion, kissing Selwyn, Pauline and Edward with a bright smile on her face, before finally turning to greet Phil as a man she had recently met for formal business discussions.

"How nice to see you again, Senhor Maxwell. And so soon."

Phil held his hand out to her so pointedly that Melissa was obliged to offer hers in response. As she'd dreaded, he lifted it to his lips, and the touch of his lips sent tingles of sensual excitement racing through her. But Phil acted with perfect decorum and didn't attempt to retain her hand overlong.

"Such a great pleasure, Mrs. Colville," he said. "And these are your two children? Charming. Please introduce me."

"This is Jenny, and this is Mark. Say hello to Senhor Maxwell, both of you. He's the gentleman I had to talk business with while I was in Lisbon."

Jenny grinned up at Phil a little shyly, but Mark solemnly held out his hand in the way Selwyn would have done. In the absence of a father, his uncle was becoming Mark's role model.

"Hi, there," said Phil easily. "Your mother told me all

about you when she was in Lisbon." He looked at Jenny. "You had a fall from your pony, I hear. Are you okay now?"

"Yes, thank you, it doesn't hurt anymore. I've still got a mark on my elbow, though. You can see it if you like." Instantly she pushed up the sleeve of her red cardigan and held out her arm for his inspection. "There."

Phil gave the fading bruise his serious attention for a moment, then nodded gravely. "Yes, I can see that you must have had a very nasty fall. I'm glad to know that it's no longer hurting you."

They all turned toward the house, the children dashing ahead with whoops of delight, as if arriving home were a big adventure in itself.

"Selwyn and I tried to persuade Senhor Maxwell to join us in a round of golf this afternoon," Pauline said chattily as they entered the hallway. "But he told us that golf isn't his game."

"And I," Phil put in, "have been insisting that, as your brother-in-law was kind enough to invite me to Pendlehurst at such short notice, he and Mrs. Drake should not cancel their plans and stay home on my account. I can find plenty to keep me amused until their return." He spoke in a relaxed, easygoing tone, but to Melissa he seemed to be dropping the heaviest of hints. She glanced anxiously at the others to see if they'd noticed anything.

Obviously not, for Pauline said brightly, "Perhaps Melissa could take you to see some of our local sights. There are some really splendid places to see within easy striking distance of here. Are you interested in stately homes and ancient monuments, Senhor Maxwell?"

"How could I fail to be interested, Mrs. Drake, if I had such a charming guide?"

"I'm sorry," Melissa said in a panic, "but I can't do that. Pauline, you seem to be forgetting about the children."

Her sister-in-law looked pained at the suggestion that she could have overlooked anything whatsoever. "Jenny and

Mark can come to the club with us, Melissa. They always think it's tremendous fun to ride in the golf cart, and we'll give them a cream tea at the clubhouse afterward." Pauline beamed a triumphant smile at yet something else satisfactorily organized. "So it's settled, then."

Perhaps it would be for the best, Melissa told herself wretchedly, that she'd get the chance to talk to Phil in private. She didn't believe his story about *happening* to be in London. If he'd planned to come so soon, why hadn't he mentioned the fact while she was in Lisbon? Was it that Phil's male pride had been dented by her abrupt return home, bringing their affair to a premature end? Did Phil insist on being the one to break off a relationship? If that were the case, she thought rebelliously, whatever ideas he might have about stringing along with her until *he* was ready to call it a day, he was about to discover that this particular affair was very definitely over.

Chapter Ten

To all outward appearances lunch was a pleasant, relaxed meal. Mercifully for Melissa, the other four adults did most of the talking, with Jenny or Mark chipping in now and then when they weren't too busy eating. She herself was only called upon to pass the odd comment, mostly to do with the holiday at Hastings. She was seated between her two children, and serving them and helping them to cut up their food enabled her to hide her acute agitation. Her stomach was fluttering so much that she could hardly eat a thing. All the while she could feel Phil's eyes covertly watching her from across the table.

Coffee was served in the glassed-in conservatory where Pauline kept her choicest plants, and shortly afterward the golfing party went off in Selwyn's car. Edward too departed, to return to his dental office, Saturday being a working day for him.

"Nice relatives you have," Phil observed as soon as they were left alone together. "They've made me very welcome.

And I like Jenny and Mark, too; they're such well-behaved children, natural and friendly."

Impatiently, Melissa shrugged that aside. She had no wish to make polite chitchat with him. "Phil, I must talk to you. It's ridiculous that—"

"I'm looking forward to my guided tour," he interrupted her. "Shall we set out?"

Melissa looked back at him with a feeling of despair. Despite her keen determination to relegate Phil Maxwell to a place in history, despite her anger at him, his sheer physical presence was mesmerizing her and sapping all her strength. Even though the others had left he hadn't moved his seat, and there was a gap of six feet between them. Yet her flesh was quivering as if he were actually caressing it with those strong sensitive fingers.

"For God's sake," she burst out, "why are you here, Phil? What's it all about?"

He gave her a swift, warning glance, and Melissa realized that Freda was coming through the glass doors from the drawing room. "Is it all right for me to take the coffee things now, Mrs. Colville?" she inquired. "Then I can get cleared up in the kitchen."

"Oh, yes, please do. We've had all we want."

Freda was a little deaf, so she couldn't possibly have overheard Melissa's remark to Phil, but the woman's entrance was a timely reminder that Melissa would have to be very careful in what she said to him. Even in the grounds, even on a Saturday afternoon, it wouldn't be safe for them to talk. She couldn't be sure that Tom wouldn't be weeding or digging somewhere behind a hedge. So while Freda was still in the room gathering up the coffee cups, she said briskly to Phil, "Right then, Senhor Maxwell, let's begin our tour. I think you might find the town of Tunbridge Wells interesting to start with."

As she drove off with Phil sitting beside her, Melissa looked straight ahead and kept her lips tightly pressed together. She hoped she was making it clear to him that she wasn't ready to start talking yet. She was in such a nervous, pent-up state that she kept crashing the gears. After a couple of miles she swerved into a lay-by, dragged on the hand brake and shut off the ignition. Rounding on Phil, she said belligerently, "Now I want your explanation."

"Of what?"

"Of why you're here."

"If you mean why I'm staying at Pendlehurst, it's because your brother-in-law invited me."

"I mean why are you in England? And don't tell me that you had business in London, because I won't believe you."

Phil met her gaze with a tender look that melted her bones. "I came, Melissa, because I wanted to see you. I *had* to see you."

"Even though I told you in my note that it was all over between us?"

"That was a very cruel note," he said. "Untypical of you."

"You know why I had to do it that way," she protested. "Jenny—"

"No, I do not know." He reached forward and touched her bare forearm, but when Melissa snatched it away he let her go. "You should have called me at the office. I'd have come at once—you must have known that—and I could have driven you to the airport. Instead you chose to run off furtively."

"It wasn't furtively."

"It was! Why did you treat me like that, Melissa? Are you such a hard-boiled woman that what we had together was nothing more to you than a way of passing your spare time while you were in Portugal? I refuse to believe it. I remember how you responded when I held you in my arms and—"

"Please," she said in a choked voice. "This . . . it just isn't fair."

"And what you did to me . . . that was fair?"

For a few moments she couldn't find words to answer him. Her heart was thudding against her ribs, and she felt hot and breathless, as though she were running a fever. "Phil, what happened between us," she faltered at last, "it was . . . just one of those things. I'm sorry if I acted discourteously when I left—I apologize. But it's done now, and there's no point raking over the ashes of our relationship."

"Ashes are dead, Melissa, the remains of something that's burnt itself out. The fire we lit in one another is far from being burnt out. It certainly isn't for me, and you can't convince me it is for you, either."

She couldn't convince herself, either. Melissa thought of the nights since she'd been back in England, lonely nights at Pendlehurst and at the hotel in Hastings, when she'd lain awake wanting Phil, needing him, longing for him.

"Phil, listen to me. I'm not trying to deny that it was good between us—wonderfully good. One part of me will always treasure the memory of what we had together. But the other side of me, the side that really counts, regrets that it ever happened."

"Regrets?" His voice was heavy with accusation and reproach.

"Yes, that's what I said, Phil. When I was with you in Portugal, it was a kind of dream time that was quite apart from reality. For a brief few days I forgot about the real me."

"No, Melissa, that's not true. In Portugal you *were* the real you. A wonderfully warm, sensitive woman who wasn't afraid of passion. Now, for some reason, you're trying to run away from your true personality."

"You don't understand," she said desperately. "I have responsibilities here to my two children and the family I belong to. That means that I have to behave in a responsible way, not selfishly snatch at short-lived pleasure whenever the chance happens along."

"And that's all our relationship was to you, a short-lived pleasure?"

"What else?" she retorted. "For either of us."

His dark eyes challenged her, but Melissa forced herself to return the challenge, meeting his gaze head on. In the end it was Phil who glanced away.

Reaching for the ignition key to start the car, she paused a moment, then said, "Please, Phil, I want you to do something for me."

"Whatever I can."

"I want you to think up an excuse and leave Pendlehurst right away, this evening."

His eyes widened in query. "Why on earth should I do that, Melissa?"

"Isn't it enough that I'm asking you to, begging you to? Don't you see, every minute that you're around spells danger for me. My relatives haven't the least idea that you and I . . . became close."

"I'm aware of that, Melissa. I've been very careful, haven't I, to take my cue from you? I've said nothing in the presence of other people that might embarrass you."

"Yes, I know, and I appreciate it, Phil. But . . . you must have some idea of . . . of continuing our affair, or you wouldn't have come."

"Naturally I want it to continue. But if you're unwilling to admit to our true relationship, then no one else need ever know."

"There'll be nothing for them *to* know," she said heatedly. "Not from now on. I mean that, Phil. So you might as well leave at once."

Frown lines creased his forehead. "You seem to be forgetting that our firms will in future have a close commercial relationship. I can't just vanish from your life, Melissa. Unless," he added musingly, "you want me to take my business away as well."

Shocked, she asked in a furious voice, "Is that a threat?"

"A threat?"

"Meaning that unless I agree to . . . to your terms, there'll be no contract between Colville's and Silva Cunha?"

Phil pounced on her in such sudden anger that she backed away from him in her seat. "What a foul thing to suggest . . . even to think. Do you imagine that I'm the sort of man who'd use such filthy tactics?"

"I . . . I'm sorry," she stammered. "I . . . I didn't mean . . ."

"Yes, you did mean," he said bitterly. "What I meant, Melissa, was that since you seem so anxious to cut me out of your life, then you might prefer it if there were no business contact between us. Then you could pretend to yourself that Phil Maxwell didn't even exist, didn't even live and breathe —and want you."

Melissa turned away from his accusing gaze. After a moment she heard Phil say in a harsh, cold voice, "You're supposed to be taking me sightseeing, so hadn't we better get on with it? Otherwise I won't be in a position to answer the questions I'm likely to be asked by your precious family this evening."

She closed her eyes, fighting down waves of despair. Since Phil refused to leave Pendlehurst, she had no option but to act out an elaborate charade. They would have to appear to be on the sort of terms the others would expect. Playing her role as an executive of Colville's who was keen to clinch the *vinho espumante* contract, she would have to look eager to entertain their Portuguese guest.

"Okay, then," she said defeatedly as she started the engine, "we'll carry on with the sightseeing bit. But . . . will you promise me not to say anything to make the others suspicious about us?"

"If that's what you want, Melissa, very well. It isn't what I'd hoped for, though. I fail to see any need to conceal my interest in you. There's no shame that we should be attracted to each other." Phil shrugged his broad shoulders, seeming bewildered. "Still, I agree to guard my words in front of other people."

Melissa looked at him uncertainly. Dared she trust Phil? She would have to, though; there was no choice.

She made a shamefully poor guide as she escorted Phil around Tunbridge Wells. Just being with him closed her mind to everything else. Her nostrils were teased by faint snatches of the subtle masculine scent that was uniquely Phil, and she longed to reach out and touch his warm flesh, to run her fingertips lovingly over the planes and angles of his face. She was aware that it would take only one slight sign of weakness from her for Phil to take advantage and sweep her into a renewal of their intimacy. So she kept her manner toward him coolly aloof, and the few scraps of information she managed to dredge up were mainly in answer to Phil's specific queries.

"There wasn't really much here before the seventeenth century," she said when he asked her about the town's early history. "Then the mineral springs were discovered, and the place mushroomed up around them. Beau Nash was a famous master of ceremonies at the pump room."

"Beau Nash? I thought his name was associated with Bath."

"He came here afterward. Or maybe it was the other way around; I can't remember."

Phil said ironically, "You appear to have exhausted your knowledge of Tunbridge Wells. Perhaps we'd better go somewhere else."

"If you like." She just didn't care.

As they returned to the car and drove on, Phil was deeply thoughtful, wondering how to thaw Melissa's barricade of hostility. Despite the note she'd left him in Lisbon, he had felt confident that she'd be pleased to see him again. Naturally Melissa had been very distressed at the news of her child's accident, and it was understandable that she'd scribbled the note to him in haste without really considering what she was saying. But afterward, when she'd found that Jenny wasn't seriously injured, surely she would have started to miss him as much as he'd been missing her? Phil couldn't believe that she had been able to write him out of her life with such apparent ease.

He hadn't intended to come after her, though. She'd insisted in Portugal that she didn't want their affair to continue, and he'd accepted that. He'd even told himself that it was for the best. All good things had to come to an end, didn't they? But as the days had gone by he hadn't been able to get Melissa Colville out of his thoughts. Her beauty and her sweetness, her tender passion when they made love, had wound themselves into his senses, and life had seemed bleak and empty without her. Then one morning, surprising himself, he'd woken with a firm determination to go to England and see her. He'd hastily tied things up at the office and taken a plane that same evening. The next morning he had presented himself at the offices of Colville's Wines on the pretext of paying a courtesy call. It had been a bitter blow to discover that Melissa wasn't there, to learn that she was on vacation with her children. But luckily, with only a minimum of nudging Selwyn Colville had issued an invitation for him to stay the weekend at Pendlehurst.

Now, however, when he'd finally contrived to get Melissa alone, he just couldn't seem to reach her. She'd admitted—as if it needed admitting—that their lovemaking had been wonderfully good, so he couldn't make any sense of her arguments against their continuing for a while, as long as they were both enjoying the affair. Phil felt utterly perplexed, but he wasn't going to be defeated at the first hurdle. He'd be patient, tread warily and give Melissa time to come around. He *had* to believe that she'd see sense, or he'd go mad. It was taking all his self-control to sit beside her in the car and not touch her, but he knew that any attempt at physical contact right then would be fatal. Melissa had too much pride to let herself be stampeded.

"Where is it you're taking me now?" he asked in a pleasant voice.

"Scotney Old Castle."

"I've never heard of it. What's its history?"

She shrugged. "Nothing very dramatic. It's not really a

castle but a fortified manor house, mostly in ruins now. The setting is really spectacular, though. It's in a lovely wooded valley, and there's a moat, and on a sunny day like this the ruins are reflected in the water."

"Sounds most romantic," Phil commented lightly, only to be rewarded by a sharp look from Melissa.

Even in such beautiful surroundings Phil couldn't shake her out of her hostile mood. She answered him briefly, snappily. She was being totally unreasonable, and he felt his anger rising. For heaven's sake, was it worth it? Was any woman worth this sort of hassle? But Melissa was, he thought with a despondent sigh, conceding that he was bewitched by her.

Melissa knew that she was acting badly, being rude and snappish to Phil. Yet she couldn't seem to help it. Part of her was standing back watching herself being childish, just as she sometimes watched Jenny or Mark acting badly for no logical reason.

"The children should be home soon," she said, seizing on a feeble excuse to bring this tension-charged outing to an end. "We might as well head back to Pendlehurst now."

"Whatever you say," Phil agreed, keeping his voice amiable. As they strolled up the steep path to the carpark he said, "Your children mean a great deal to you, don't they?"

"Of course they do." Her tone was defensive. "Would you expect otherwise?"

"No, but it's important to get things in perspective. You have a life of your own, Melissa."

"I should live selfishly, you mean?"

"It strikes me," he said quietly, "that you've been unselfish for long enough. It's time you *took* a little, time you started to shape life the way you want it."

"The way *you* want it, aren't you saying?" There was bitterness in her voice, but something more, too. Something he couldn't interpret.

"I can't see what's wrong," he said cautiously, "in

accepting the chance for a little happiness whenever fate offers it to me."

"A frequent occurrence in your case."

He glanced at her in surprise. "That almost sounded like a jealous woman talking."

"Oh, don't be stupid. Why should I be jealous? What there was between you and me is past and done with. Maybe I was wrong earlier in saying that part of me regrets that it ever happened. I don't, not really. But it was just an episode in both our lives. Circumstances brought our affair about, and those circumstances are now over." She shrugged to convey her total indifference. "Who you happened to be involved with before you met me and who you get involved with in the future is of no concern to me. I'm no more jealous of the other women in your life than I am of . . . of the later girlfriends of the boys I knew in my student days. You, of all people, Phil, ought to be able to accept that life has its phases, and that our phase is finished."

"That was quite a long speech," he said drily.

"I was just trying to make you understand how I feel."

"I don't think you succeeded very well, Melissa." They had reached the car, but Phil paused a moment before getting in. "On the other hand, perhaps you did."

Back home, Melissa took the chance to give Jenny a ride on Kimbo. Fortunately her daughter showed no fear of getting back into the saddle after her tumble. It was Melissa who was fearful, though she worked hard not to betray her anxiety. Every activity had its risks, and she couldn't keep her children wrapped in cotton wool.

Melissa had been happy to leave Phil to be entertained by Selwyn. She could see the two men now, sitting on the veranda with drinks. Pauline would be in the kitchen preparing one of her super dinners. A flash of blue caught her eye—Edward's car. He'd just returned home and was about to garage it in the stable block. Melissa gave him a wave as he drove past the paddock. This is my family, she thought fiercely; this is where I belong. Phil is just an intruder, a threat to the equilibrium of my life.

Putting the children to bed and reading them a story gave her a good excuse to avoid seeing Phil again until they assembled in the dining room for dinner. Pauline had talked of inviting some local friends to join them, but Phil had declared that he wanted no formality on his account. He had said that he would prefer to enjoy the company of the Colville family.

Selwyn, seated at the head of the table, made a little ceremony of carving the fine sirloin of Scotch beef. It proved to be succulently tender; the Yorkshire pudding, cooked in a drip pan beneath the meat, was moistly crisp. The accompanying vegetables were glazed carrots, braised leeks, and cauliflower served with a white sauce. For dessert there was shortcrust apple pie with clotted Devon cream. A simple family meal, Pauline would have called it.

"After staying in your delightful home, Mrs. Drake," said Phil, "I shall never again believe the stories one hears about the poorness of English cooking. This meal is superb."

"How kind of you to say so." Her composed, almost queenly acceptance of the compliment concealed the delight that Melissa knew she was feeling. Her culinary expertise was a matter of great pride to Pauline.

Between them, Melissa acknowledged, Selwyn and his sister made a wonderful host and hostess. They kept the conversation flowing easily, and seemed not to notice that Melissa herself wasn't joining in. But Edward, who was never very talkative, kept glancing from Melissa to Phil with interested eyes. Had he guessed something of the truth? she wondered uneasily. If so, wasn't it only a matter of time before Selwyn and Pauline also cottoned on? She longed for this weekend to be over, but she had to play out the charade till Monday morning, when Selwyn was going to drop Phil at his London hotel on their way to the office in St. James's Street.

"Perhaps, Senhor Maxwell," Selwyn was saying, "you'd care to stroll down to the village pub later. You'll find that our 'local,' the Coach and Horses, is a good example of the typical English country inn."

"Thank you, Mr. Colville. I'd enjoy that."

Selwyn glanced inquiringly at his brother-in-law. "How about you joining us, Edward?"

"Not this evening, if you don't mind." Melissa was vaguely aware of Edward explaining that he had a backlog of technical reading to catch up with.

"I know Pauline won't want to come," Selwyn went on, "but how about you, Melissa?"

Before she could give a refusal, Pauline chipped in. "Good idea, Melissa. Don't worry about me. There's some sewing I want to get on with, and you can help Selwyn entertain Senhor Maxwell."

Melissa felt trapped. She detected a glimmer of amusement in Edward's quiet gray eyes as she reluctantly murmured her assent.

Within a few minutes, though, she bitterly regretted not having flatly said no while she still had the chance. Just as they were finishing the meal Selwyn was called away from the table to take an urgent phone call. He returned looking rueful.

"It's a dashed nuisance, Senhor Maxwell, but I'm afraid we'll have to postpone our visit to the pub. That call was from the chairman of the local conservation society, of which I'm a committee member. He's calling an emergency meeting tonight because there's a threat to a magnificent avenue of beech trees near here, and we've got to hustle through a restraining order before the chain saws get going on Monday morning. I'm really sorry about this, but . . . ."

"Please don't apologize, Mr. Colville," said Phil. "I applaud your public spirit."

"On second thought, Senhor Maxwell, there's no need to call off the visit to the pub. You and Melissa can just as well go there without me," Selwyn said, smiling broadly.

"An excellent suggestion," Phil said.

"Well then, that's fixed. I'll join you later if we get through with the meeting in time."

Melissa glanced pleadingly at Phil, willing him to get her out of this. But she might have known it would be useless. As he returned her gaze blandly she felt her face reddening and had to look away. She met Edward's amused eyes. Perhaps it was as well, she thought with a shiver, that at one time Pauline's husband had needed to rely on her discretion. Now, in rather different circumstances, it was his turn to keep silent. She hoped the glance she gave him conveyed that thought.

Chapter Eleven

$\mathscr{I}$t was not yet dark when Melissa and Phil set out. The western sky was streaked with the gentle afterglow of sunset. The last time she'd walked this leafy lane was with Selwyn, she thought, just before her vacation in Hastings. Selwyn, the man who had long ago wanted to marry her, before she'd met his brother Toby. Suppose she *had* married Selwyn . . . suppose that Jenny and Mark were *his* children? But they wouldn't be, of course. Change one factor in life and everything was changed. Just as, after Portugal and Phil, nothing would ever be the same for her again.

"Sorry, what was that?" Phil had said something, and she hadn't been listening.

"I said, do you really intend to send me back to Portugal like this?"

"Like what?"

She heard Phil catch his breath in anger. He halted abruptly and, gripping her by the shoulders, dragged her round to face him. In the twilight his eyes glittered.

"Don't fool around with me, Melissa. You and I have come too far together for this sort of nonsense."

"But it's over between us, Phil; can't you get that into your head? I told you so in my note, and I spelled it out again this afternoon. I thought you understood how I felt."

"It can't be over," he protested heatedly. "Not just like that, not when we have so much happiness to offer each other. There's no reason why we should break up at this stage. You've explained how you feel about your family, and I'll respect your feelings, even though I don't accept your reasoning. But for heaven's sake, Melissa, now that I'm here in England it would be madness for us not to take advantage of it. Listen, I can easily prolong my stay. If I were to remain in London for another week or two, we could meet there, at my hotel."

"No!"

"Why not? We're adults, not teenage kids. We wouldn't be getting ourselves into anything we couldn't handle." Phil's hands came up to cup her face, and his thumbs sensuously caressed the little hollows beneath her jaw. Melissa felt a wave of longing sweep through her, and she was powerless to move away as he brought his lips to hers in a tentative, coaxing kiss. "You want me, don't you, darling?" he whispered against her cheek. "Admit it."

"Yes." The word was torn from her unwillingly. "But, Phil . . ."

"No buts! You can't take that back, *querida*. So now tell me that you want us to continue together. Say it."

"No, I won't," she gulped, moving away from him, and added miserably, "I . . . I can't."

"Why can't you? What's preventing you? We want one another, and that's all that matters. It's so simple, Melissa."

Dear heaven, what was she going to do? She felt desperate; she realized that she was fast losing control of the situation. Somehow or other she had to convince Phil that she really meant what she said about ending things with him. The only way that she could think of right then was to pretend that there was another man in her life.

"It wouldn't be fair to Selwyn," she blurted, not pausing to consider where that might lead her.

"Selwyn? What in God's name has it to do with him?"

The bigger the lie, the more it needed a basis in truth. "Selwyn was always keen on me," she said, "even before I met and married his brother. As things are now, he's just marking time until he considers that a decent interval has elapsed since Toby's death."

"Are you serious?" Phil demanded incredulously. "Are you telling me that your brother-in-law wants to marry you?"

"Yes." Leave it at that, she warned herself. Don't be tempted to embroider.

"And you'll accept him?"

She shrugged her slender shoulders. "He hasn't asked me yet."

"So how can you be sure that he intends to?"

"Because I know Selwyn. I live under the same roof and work closely with him in business. I know Selwyn Colville very well, Phil. I know the kind of man he is."

"And what kind is that?" There was a faint sneer in Phil's voice.

"A very different kind of man from you."

"You're damned right there! Which is why you mustn't think of marrying him, Melissa. It's a crazy idea. Insane."

"Selwyn is a fine man," she insisted.

"He's also stolid and unimaginative. Can you see yourself being rocketed to the stars with Selwyn, the way you are with me?"

"There's a lot more to life than just . . ." She paused to give the word dramatic emphasis, to throw it at him with contempt. " . . . than just sex."

"I'm not trying to deny that, Melissa. But sex, to any normal person, is a vital ingredient."

"Are you suggesting that Selwyn isn't normal?"

"You tell me."

A woman on a bicycle wobbled into view round a bend. She glanced at them curiously as she rode past, and called a greeting to Melissa. "Good evening, Mrs. Colville."

"Hello, Mrs. Phelps."

They waited in silence until the intruder had vanished round the next bend. It gave Melissa a few moments to collect her thoughts.

"I'll tell you what sort of man Selwyn is," she said belligerently. "He's decent and straightforward, totally honest, and very considerate toward other people."

"But also rather dull."

"I'm not saying that."

"You don't need to say it, Melissa. The fact screams at me when I talk to him. Oh, don't get me wrong . . . I'm not implying that I don't like Selwyn. He's pleasant company, he's intelligent, and he has an excellent grasp of the wine trade. I shall be perfectly happy to leave my British distribution in his hands. We're talking about him as husband material."

"Husband material?" Her tone was scornful. "That's a subject on which you can hardly claim to be an expert."

"What I *can* claim to be an expert about is *you*," Phil countered. "I bet that I know far more about you from our short acquaintance than Selwyn could possibly have learned in . . . however many years it is that you've known him. I know, for instance, that you're a woman with a warm, passionate nature, which means that you need a man to match you in those qualities. A humdrum, slippers-by-the-fire, hot-drink-at-bedtime sort of marriage would never bring you the fulfillment you need, Melissa."

"I have two children," she reminded him. "What I need is a secure home for them and a husband who would be a loving stepfather."

"So for your children's sake you'd marry a man who's totally wrong for you?"

She faced Phil, white with fury. "Yes, I would—if necessary. I'd do almost anything for my children's sake. But you're being unfair about Selwyn. He's right for me . . . right in every way that really matters. Now, for heaven's sake let's get to the pub, or he'll be there before us."

"But, Melissa . . ."

"I'm not listening," she said as she turned to walk on.

They spent a difficult hour in the lounge of the Coach and Horses making polite, stilted conversation that they could safely allow to be overheard by the people at adjoining tables. Melissa was infinitely thankful when, just a few minutes before closing time, Selwyn joined them. He was looking very pleased with himself.

"The meeting reached a unanimous decision to bring all possible pressure on the local authority," he told them. "Among us we pack quite a lot of clout, so I think I can say that the beeches are safe from destruction. Now, can I get you two refills before the landlord calls last orders?"

"No, please, Mr. Colville," said Phil, getting to his feet. "This must be my pleasure, to celebrate your victory."

"That's kind of you, Senhor Maxwell. I'll have a scotch, I think. Just a splash of soda." While Phil went to fetch it from the bar, Selwyn said to Melissa, "Sorry to land you with him like this, but it couldn't be helped. Judging from both your faces when I came in, it seems to have been heavy going."

Was it so terribly obvious? Melissa gave her brother-in-law a bright smile. "Oh, we've been getting along okay. I think we'd just run out of conversation; you know how it is."

He nodded sympathetically. "Don't I just! It's hard work, sometimes, socializing with people when you don't have a lot in common. All part of the job though, my dear."

"I wasn't complaining," she pointed out. "Still, now that you've arrived, you can take over. I've done enough for one evening."

Sitting back in her chair, Melissa studied the two men

reflectively, comparing them. Selwyn really did have a great deal going for him, she argued. He too was good-looking and intelligent, besides which he cared about people and the world around him—as shown, for instance, by the committee meeting he'd attended that evening. Their voices washed over her, Selwyn's level and pleasantly modulated as he framed his sentences clearly and with care. Phil spoke in little rushes of words—humorous one moment, then suddenly quite serious, but always there was a rich, sensual quality to his voice that set chords vibrating within her. It was a voice, heaven help her, to which she had become hopelessly addicted.

"All set?" queried Selwyn, glancing in her direction.

"I'm sorry," she said. "What was that?"

"It's closing time, didn't you hear? I've been trying to explain to Senhor Maxwell the mysteries of the British licensing laws, which say that pubs in this area must close at ten-thirty, whereas two miles up the road it's eleven o'clock."

"These laws must be bad for the liquor trade," Phil commented, as they all three rose to leave.

Selwyn chuckled. "Luckily for us, wine—as opposed to beer and spirits—is mainly consumed at home. Or with food in restaurants, where the same laws don't apply."

"I'm relieved to hear it," said Phil with a little laugh. But his eyes were on Melissa as he spoke, and she realized to her dismay that all the time he'd been chatting with Selwyn and she'd believed herself unobserved, Phil's attention had really been centered on her.

"What do you fancy doing today, Senhor Maxwell?" asked Selwyn over a late breakfast the next morning. It was just the five adults seated around the circular, white-slatted table in the conservatory. Jenny and Mark had been invited to join a neighboring family on a Sunday outing to the zoo, and they had already set out.

"I'm happy to go along with anything you suggest," Phil

replied, dabbing butter and marmalade on a triangle of toast. "I'd quite like to get some horseback riding in while I'm here, to enjoy your beautiful English countryside. Oh, but forgive me, Mr. Colville, I was forgetting. You already told me that you don't care for riding."

"Melissa does, though. She's quite an expert." It was Edward who'd spoken. Glancing at him, Melissa saw only a bland expression on his face, but she wondered if the remark was as innocent as it had sounded.

"Is that so, Mrs. Colville?" Phil was looking at her with apparent new interest.

"I haven't ridden for ages," Melissa said in dismissal.

"All the same, it's a skill that once learned is never forgotten, isn't it?"

"There's a first-class stable in the village," Edward volunteered. "I'm sure they could fix you both up, Senhor Maxwell."

It was almost, Melissa thought wildly, as if the two men were in collusion. The very last thing she wanted was to ride with Phil that morning, but the combined pressure of the others proved too much for her.

"Why don't you call Joy Hatchley at the stables right away?" Selwyn suggested.

Melissa glared back at him. "I shouldn't think there's a hope of her having any horses free on a fine Sunday morning."

"I'll talk to Joy if you like," Pauline offered. "She owes me a favor after I took over her flower arranging at the Women's Institute last week."

"No, thanks," Melissa said, hanging on to her temper. "I'm quite capable of calling Joy myself."

As she'd feared, Joy Hatchley was only too ready to oblige. "I guess I can jiggle things around," she said cheerfully. "The Warrenders made a provisional booking for this morning, but they haven't confirmed yet. I'll phone and tell them to make it this afternoon, instead. They won't mind."

"Thanks, Joy," said Melissa in a voice that masked her disappointment. "That's good of you."

"What are friends for? I'll expect you and your client at eleven-thirty. Suit you?"

"Oh, yes, fine! And by the way, can you fix him up with a hard hat?"

"Sure, no problem."

Melissa trailed back to the breakfast table with the glad tidings. Phil looked delighted—more than delighted, triumphant.

"You really are being most hospitable," he commented, smiling around at the assembled company. Then he added with a light laugh, "You mustn't make me too welcome, you know, or I shall want to visit Pendlehurst again very soon."

"I sincerely hope that you will, Senhor Maxwell," said Selwyn politely.

An hour later Melissa set off with Phil in her car. She wore jeans and a rollneck sweater. Phil wore casual slacks and a checked shirt.

"You maneuvered this, didn't you?" she asked as she turned out of the driveway.

"I seized the opportunity of being alone with you, yes." Though she wasn't looking at him, she could feel the pressure of his intent eyes. "I have things to say to you, Melissa."

"We've said all there is to say," she retorted.

"Oh, no, not by any means."

Joy Hatchley had two mares saddled and ready for them, a chestnut and a lovely blue-roan, which was Melissa's mount. Her name was Kalinda. Joy invited Phil to go to the tack room to fit himself with a hard hat.

"That is one gorgeous man," she remarked to Melissa as Phil strode off, walking with long, easy strides. "Lucky you!"

"I told you, he's a client of the firm."

"Don't I wish that I had a client with his sort of looks. He's got his eye on you, Melissa."

"Oh, rubbish!"

"Scoff as much as you like, but I know I'm right. I have a theory that working with horses gives one a kind of second sight."

"It addles the brain, more likely."

Melissa and Phil set off along a grassy track that followed the riverbank, where clumps of bulrushes grew lushly and weeping willows dipped their fronds into the slow-drifting water. Warblers flitted and sang, and occasionally Melissa saw the emerald-and-cobalt flash of a kingfisher. They passed a few anglers sitting patiently on their stools waiting for a bite, and a couple of teenage boys came walking by with their dog. Presently the track veered away from the river and entered a patch of woodland—silver birch and young oaks, with here and there the dark, shady silhouette of a yew tree. All around them was the drowsy cooing of wood pigeons.

Without warning Phil suddenly leaned across to catch hold of Kalinda's bridle and both mares halted.

"What do you think you're doing?" Melissa demanded angrily.

"We have some talking to do," Phil said, "and I need all your attention."

She gave him a cold stare. "Well?"

"Melissa, you can't marry Selwyn. The thought of it has been haunting me all night. For God's sake, tell me that you have no intention of accepting him when he gets around to asking you."

She glanced away and was silent, letting the smooth leather of the reins run through her nerveless fingers.

"I want the truth, Melissa. I've got a right to know."

She raised her chin defiantly. "Where you and I are concerned, Phil, there's only one truth that you have any right to, which is that we have no future together—not on a personal level."

"You can't throw yourself away on a man like Selwyn Colville," he persisted. "I won't let you."

"Won't let me?" she echoed scornfully. "You can't stop me."

A pigeon flew out of a nearby tree with a great flapping of wings, startling the two horses. When they'd been quieted Phil looked at her with a pleading expression in his dark brown eyes. "For pity's sake, think carefully, Melissa. It's insane to imagine that you'd ever be happy married to Selwyn. He needs someone as conventional and ordinary as himself . . . a woman who doesn't have high expectations for her life and is content to let the months and years go drifting by. As his wife, you wouldn't even have the satisfaction of running your own home—you'd still have to play second fiddle to your sister-in-law."

"I'm not particularly interested in running a household," Melissa retorted, trying to shake off the gloomy picture he was painting of life as Selwyn's wife. "You seem to forget that I have a high-level job at Colville's."

"And you think you'd find that enough for you . . . totally fulfilling?"

"Nobody can have everything in this world."

"So you're admitting that marriage to Selwyn would leave you feeling shortchanged?"

Anger overwhelmed her. "You've no right to talk to me like this. What I choose to do with my life is no business of yours."

Phil's dark eyes burned into her. "Let me hold you in my arms once more, Melissa, and then try to tell me that. Let me kiss you till we're both crazy with desire, then see if you can still pretend that it's no business of mine."

She edged her mare a little away from his. "Don't you touch me."

"You don't dare let me touch you." Phil wasn't asking a question but stating a fact. "You know only too well what your response would be, Melissa. You know you would melt in my arms."

She wanted to shout and rage at him, because his words

were nothing but the truth. Instead she said beseechingly, "Please, Phil . . . be reasonable."

"You can't expect me to let you go without a fight, *querida.*"

Melissa drew a deep, shuddering breath. "You want to force an admission from me? Okay, you can have one. What we had together in Portugal was wonderful. I shall always treasure the memory as something precious. But it couldn't last, Phil; we both knew that. I had to return home . . . return to normal and pick up my life again. I freely admit that it would have been better, more considerate, if I'd called you before I left Lisbon instead of writing you that hasty note. But you have to remember that I was in a state of panic. I'd just learned that my daughter had been hospitalized with a concussion, and I wasn't there to be with her. At the very moment when Jenny had her accident I'd been—" She gulped to a stop, misery and guilt flooding through her yet again.

"You'd been with me," Phil finished for her, his voice gentle but unyielding. "Perhaps we actually had been making love when it occurred, Melissa, but there's nothing to be ashamed of in that. You were in no way to blame for your daughter's accident. It was just unfortunate that she happened to fall from her pony while you were away, out of the country."

"But I should have kept in touch," she said wretchedly. "I'd intended to call home on Thursday, but . . ."

"But you forgot. Is that so terrible? Just because you're a parent, it doesn't automatically equip you with a perfect memory."

"You make it sound as if I forgot to wind my watch, or buy coffee or something," Melissa flung at him bitterly. "We're talking about my children, for heaven's sake."

"You've done a fine job with those children of yours," he said. "That must be obvious to everyone. All this guilt is just inside yourself, Melissa."

"Isn't that where guilt usually is?"

"What I'm trying to tell you," Phil said impatiently, "is that you've got nothing to feel guilty about."

"That's great, coming from you. Very reassuring."

"Meaning that you hold *me* responsible in some way? I'd like to know how you figured that out. For wanting you? For making you want me? That's hardly a crime, Melissa."

"Wanting is one thing," she muttered, "but we didn't stop at wanting."

"So we went to bed together a few times. That's no big deal in itself. It happens all the time, in case you didn't know . . . nothing to get riddled with guilt about."

She flinched as if Phil had struck her, but managed to rally quickly. "I can't imagine why you bothered to come all the way to England in pursuit of something that's no big deal. There are masses of women in Portugal who should suit you just as well as I do."

For long, fraught moments Phil glared at her, his eyes stormy with anger. He's as angry with himself as he is with me, Melissa decided . . . angry because he wants me so much.

"Did you honestly imagine," she asked with biting scorn, "that you could turn up here and find me ready to continue the relationship we had in Portugal . . . for as long or as short a time as you chose? How arrogant you must be to think that I'd let you use me like that. A love affair, just like a novel, has a beginning, a middle and an end, Phil. Trying to carry on with it after the end has come is like turning over a succession of blank pages."

"And you believe that the end has come for us, Melissa?" he demanded.

"Of course it has. I thought you'd be experienced enough in this sort of thing to recognize that and accept it." Melissa could feel her lower lip trembling and was afraid that she might break down. She hastily charged on with all the bitterness she could summon. "The pattern of your life has been laid down for you, Phil. You'll eventually marry a

Portuguese woman who will give you heirs to carry on the family line. Meanwhile—and in all probability *after* your marriage, too—you'll continue with your unimportant, lighthearted affairs. Well, let me tell you, you're not the only one whose life has a pattern laid down. My life does, too . . . and that's caring for my children in the best way I can and repaying the Colvilles, who have been so supportive of me. I'll remind you that it's not so easy for a woman to stray from the conventional path without having to pay for it—even in the 1980s. Portugal was one thing. Those were magical days stolen from reality. Now I'm back to normal, and I've got to look at facts head on. *This* is my life, here at Pendlehurst; this is where my duty lies. And that life doesn't include you, Phil. It can't include you."

Melissa was expecting him to pursue the argument in a torrent of angry words. Instead, after a moment of taut silence he leaped down from the saddle and came forward to grasp her around the waist. Pulled off-balance, she fell into his harsh embrace.

"I won't have you talking like this," he said insistently. "There's nothing noble in sacrificing yourself. Your children's futures don't depend on your marrying Selwyn Colville. And if you owe the man anything, then you're repaying it by doing a damned fine job in the family business. Promise me, Melissa, that you'll never agree to marry Selwyn."

She struggled to get free, but Phil held her locked against him, pinning her arms to her sides. She could feel the rapid, angry beating of his heart, and his breath was hot against her temple.

"I can't . . . I won't say that," she said in a broken voice.

An explosive sound came from deep in Phil's throat and made her tremble with a kind of fear. It was the low growl of a man thwarted, a man driven to extremes. His hands swept rapidly over her body in a feverish search for response, but Melissa steeled herself to remain stiff and motionless. She refused to look at him, keeping her face turned away, but

Phil tilted his head sideways and brought his lips against hers, forcing her to accept his kiss. All her senses reeled under this passionate assault. She had to suppress the urge to arch her body against his; she had to restrain her hands from rising to clasp themselves about his neck. She had to do fierce battle with herself to hold back from returning his kiss, from welcoming the thrusting entry of his tongue. Somehow, incredibly, she conquered her throbbing need of him, and at last Phil pushed her away with a muttered curse.

"Damn you, Melissa, why are you doing this to me? Why are you acting so cold?"

"Get out of my life, Phil," she said in a leaden voice. "I want you to get out of my life."

"I can't begin to understand you. Just," he said distractedly, "promise me that never, under any circumstances, will you throw yourself away on Selwyn Colville."

"I'm not promising you anything. Why should I?"

There was wildness and passion in Phil's dark eyes as he stared at her, and Melissa shivered in fear. It wasn't a fear that Phil would do her bodily violence, but that her fragile thread of resistance would snap. If she didn't remain strong . . . if, as she yearned to do, she were to slip her arms around his neck and seek his lips to renew the kiss, she would never again find the will or the strength to resist him.

"Tell me that you won't marry Selwyn Colville," he repeated, as if his sheer persistence could force a promise from her.

Melissa shook her head slowly in mute refusal.

"You'd be crazy to marry him. You'd never be happy. It would be like condemning yourself to life in prison. Someone like you needs the freedom to fly in the light and fresh air."

"With you, Phil?" she queried with a sad little smile.

"Why not with me?"

"For how long, I wonder? A few more days . . . weeks, months even? And then where would I be? A widow with two children left stranded in an emotional vacuum and having to rebuild my life all over again."

She heard him draw a quick, rasping breath. Then, to her utter astonishment, he said, "It needn't be like that, Melissa. Listen, why don't you and I get married?"

The shock waves pulsed through her entire body. For what seemed an age she could find no voice, but just gazed up at him in disbelief. At length she said in a husky whisper, "You don't mean that, Phil."

"Of course I mean it." There was vehemence in his tone, but also, Melissa detected, a faint note of uncertainty somewhere deep down.

"It's a crazy idea. How could I possibly marry you, Phil?"

"Very easily. Just say yes, darling."

"You'd be taking on two children, too," she pointed out.

"Jenny and Mark would be no problem."

Melissa contradicted him with an impatient shake of her head. "You haven't thought anything out, have you? You've thrown this impetuous proposal at me just because you see no other way of getting me back. You're too accustomed to having your own way, Phil, without any opposition. Up until now you've only had to hold out your arms and the woman of your passing fancy would fall into them. As I did myself, in Portugal. But we reached a stage when I wanted out before you did. It's time, Phil, that you accept the fact that a woman has an equal right to finish things."

"Why are you so determined to finish things, Melissa?" he challenged. "Are you afraid to marry me?"

"Yes," she threw back, "I am afraid . . . afraid of what it would do to my children. I married impulsively once before, because I was madly in love with Toby—or thought I was—and I soon realized it was a mistake. If he hadn't had that accident which turned him into a permanent invalid our marriage would probably have broken up. This time, if I were to marry you, I wouldn't only be taking a chance with my own future, but with my children's, too. Jenny and Mark are settled and happy, with caring relatives who love them, yet you expect me to tear them away from all that, to move to a foreign country and give them a stranger for a stepfather. It would be totally irresponsible of me."

Even while she was speaking so heatedly Melissa was filled with yearning thoughts of what she was deliberately throwing away. To be married to Phil would surely be the ultimate peak of happiness and fulfillment for her. She loved him passionately. She loved him with her whole heart and soul, and always would. Phil didn't love her, though; he just desired her. But perhaps, she thought suddenly with a wild flare of hope, if they were actually married and the knot tied, he would eventually come to love her in return. Or if his basic personality made him incapable of loving, then something akin to it . . . deep affection. Was she being insane to refuse Phil out of hand like this?

Despite these wayward thoughts she continued with what had to be said. It felt almost like signing her own death warrant. "My children come first with me, Phil. For that reason—if for no other—I could never agree to marry you."

His eyes were flint hard, and his fingers bit fiercely into her arm. "I admire you for being a strong-minded woman, Melissa. But I don't admire you for being a stubborn fool."

"For not leaping at the chance of marrying you? God in heaven, what a high opinion you have of yourself."

"I think I can evaluate my own worth," he said curtly. "But that's beside the point. I called you a fool because you're denying yourself the chance for happiness. You must be some kind of masochist."

"That seems to make you a sadist."

His jaw tightened. "Don't try to be clever, Melissa. I'm asking you just one more time. Will you marry me?"

"And I'll answer you one more time. No!"

For just a brief instant she feared physical violence from Phil. His face paled, and his whole frame seemed to shake with rage. But after a tension-filled moment he dropped his hands to his sides and half turned away from her. In the pulsing silence the crack of a twig a short distance along the path could clearly be heard. They both glanced around quickly and saw a man in corduroys and gum boots walking toward them, a black spaniel at his heels. Melissa recognized him as one of the local residents.

"Good morning, Mrs. Colville," he greeted her. "Nice day to be out, isn't it?"

"Yes indeed, Major Baxter. Er . . . may I introduce Senhor Maxwell from Portugal. He's staying at Pendlehurst this weekend."

The two men exchanged courtesies, and Major Baxter glanced from one to the other of them curiously before walking on. Melissa knew that he must have guessed they'd been quarreling furiously, even if he hadn't actually heard them. She felt embarrassed, but in one way she was grateful to the major for having broken up the scene with Phil.

"We'd better be getting on with our ride," she said briskly, and went over to where the two mares had strayed and were happily nibbling tufts of lush grass.

She and Phil completed their ride in almost total silence. Having dreaded that Joy Hatchley might take it into her head to make a few teasing cracks in front of Phil, Melissa was relieved to discover that her daughter, Lucy, was now on duty at the stables.

"Mum's gone in to make some sandwiches for lunch," she explained. "That's all we get on Sundays. Did you have a nice ride, Melissa?"

"Yes, lovely, thanks."

"You must have taken it very gently," Lucy remarked, smoothing the flat of her hand across Kalinda's flank. "Not a trace of sweat."

Melissa thought it best to make no comment on that, so she just smiled at the girl and said goodbye.

On the drive back to Pendlehurst Phil announced shortly, "After lunch I'll invent the need to call my grandmother, and discover from her that my presence is urgently needed at the wineries. I'll leave as soon as I possibly can."

Melissa nodded, knowing that it was the best solution.

By midafternoon Phil was packed and ready to leave the house. Naturally there had been murmurings of concern and regret from Selwyn and Pauline when he'd returned from phoning his grandmother. He'd had smooth answers ready for their sympathetic inquiries and for their offers of help. He had already taken the liberty of calling the airline, Phil explained to them, and had discovered that a flight left Gatwick Airport, which was conveniently near to Pendlehurst, around 6:00 P.M. The instant proposal from Selwyn that he should drive their guest to Gatwick was declined with thanks. "I also found the number of your local taxi service on the list by the phone," Phil said in a politely determined voice, "so I called them. They'll be here shortly to collect me."

"Pity about his having to leave so abruptly," Selwyn remarked as the family returned indoors from waving Phil off. "Still, I'm sure the time he spent here was useful. You put in some good work on him, Melissa."

She caught a glint in Edward's eye and turned away quickly. With a muttered excuse she escaped to her room and sank onto the bed in desolation. But before long she heard the children arriving back from their trip, and she had to descend and put a brave face on things. And that, she concluded wretchedly, would be the pattern of her life from now on. Well, she was accustomed to it, wasn't she?

Chapter Twelve

$\mathcal{I}$t was after dinner on Monday. Selwyn had gone to his study to make some transatlantic calls to clients in California, the eight-hour time difference making evenings most suitable for that. Pauline was presiding over a meeting in the drawing room to discuss plans for a charity fete. Melissa, feeling restless and on edge, had wandered out into the twilit grounds. The warm, sweetly fragrant evening air and the sounds of night birds calling softly brought her a sudden poignant memory of the Quinta das Andorinhas. Her heartache over Phil welled up inside her with a fresh wave of pain.

The buzzing of an electric tool in Edward's workshop adjoining the garages drew Melissa in that direction. Spotting her through the open doorway, Edward promptly threw the switch and laid his work aside.

"Come in, Melissa." He gestured to a stool beside his workbench. "Take a pew."

"I didn't mean to interrupt you," she said apologetically.

"That's okay, I've finished drilling for the time being. I'll be glad of your company."

While Edward glued the piece of wood he'd been shaping they chatted in a desultory way about the small three-legged table he was restoring. Melissa suddenly wondered what she was doing there. Edward was the member of the family with whom she'd had the least contact over the years. Yet, strangely, she'd come to his workshop with the expectation that she'd find a bond of sympathy with Edward in a way that she never could with either Pauline or Selwyn.

"Senhor Maxwell left in an almighty rush yesterday," Edward remarked, glancing up at her from beneath his bushy gray eyebrows.

Melissa managed to keep her tone even. "Yes, he did seem in a hurry to get back to his vineyards."

Edward looked skeptical. "Or maybe he was in a hurry to get away from someone."

Coloring violently, she stood up and began to finger a row of wood chisels in a rack on the wall. From behind her Edward said, "You must be careful, Melissa."

"Careful?" Her heart began to beat a rapid tattoo.

"You might cut yourself. Those chisels are very sharp."

"Oh, yes, I see."

Melissa moved away from the tools and went to stand by the window, where a faint draft of air blew in and felt cool against her cheek.

"It must have been quite a thing," Edward commented in a dry tone, "to bring Maxwell haring all the way to this country."

"He . . . he didn't explain quite what his business here was."

"For the simple reason, I'd guess, that there wasn't any business here." Edward's voice gentled as he went on. "I'm not trying to interfere, but I'm a good listener, and it's obvious to me that you've been badly upset." Melissa spun round in alarm and he added hastily, "Oh, I doubt if the others have noticed anything. It takes someone well versed in concealing their feelings to spot the signs in others. That was quite a little pantomime you two put on. What I don't get is, why all the secrecy? Why couldn't you admit to whatever it is that's going on between you?"

With a sigh Melissa returned to the stool, sitting with her legs crossed and her linked fingers hugging her knee. "It was all so complicated," she said. "So impossible."

"I don't see why." Edward ran his hand lovingly over the satin-smooth top of the cherrywood table he was restoring. "Phil Maxwell seems a decent chap. I can't imagine him treating a woman shabbily."

"What exactly does the term 'decent chap' mean in your vocabulary, Edward?" She didn't even try to hide the criticism in her voice.

He gave her a faint, sad smile. "Touché. But—and I hope you'll believe this, Melissa—I love Pauline."

"Then how can you . . . ?"

"Get involved with other women? But it doesn't really mean anything to me, you see."

"No, I don't see," she retorted. "If, as you say, you still love Pauline—"

"I do still love Pauline. But it isn't that simple, Melissa. When I first met Pauline I was completely bowled over. I thought she was fantastic . . . extraordinarily beautiful, with her fair coloring and Junoesque stature, and I admired her enormously for the way she'd brought up her two younger brothers and kept their home together. That had taken great courage and determination, and only a very strong-minded woman could have succeeded. I was overjoyed when Pauline agreed to marry me. It came as a big disappointment to find that she had no intention of starting married life in our own home, but I was prepared to be patient. Both Selwyn and Toby were still young and unmarried, and I understood her feelings about wanting to keep Pendlehurst as a base for them." Edward gave a deep sigh. "If Pauline and I had been blessed with children, maybe that would have made a difference. Only it wasn't to be. I don't really mind for myself, but it's been a great sadness for her, and I truly believe that if we'd been able to have children she'd have become softer and less domineering. So, what with one thing and another, we've stayed on here at Pendlehurst, where Pauline rules the roost. And I just don't count," he finished on a note of bitterness.

"I'm sure that's not true," Melissa protested quickly.

"No? I'll rephrase that. I count merely as one more person for Pauline to get organized. Sometimes everything builds up inside me, Melissa, and I feel like having a blazing row with her. But the impulse soon evaporates. I can't bear rows. Anything for a quiet life, that's me."

Melissa felt a great deal of sympathy for him, yet she couldn't resist saying, "That still doesn't excuse you from cheating on Pauline."

Edward gave her a twisted grin. "How prissy you sound! I'm not making excuses, Melissa, just trying to explain . . . as far as I can understand it myself. You probably think it's a matter of my wanting sex on the side, and it's hardly that at all, not really. But when I'm with another woman . . . well, for a brief moment I shine in someone's eyes. I actually matter to someone, instead of playing a bit part on Pauline's crowded stage. Does that make any kind of sense to you?"

"You ought to assert yourself more," Melissa said. "Why don't you tell Pauline how you feel?"

"That's easier said than done. She's not a woman who listens to other people's opinions, is she?" He smiled in a self-deprecating way. "I know darned well that I ought to assert myself more, but I'm *me*. And Edward Drake is not a very assertive character. Never was and never will be."

On impulse Melissa reached out and touched his hand sympathetically. "I'm sorry, Edward; I didn't mean to sound critical. I saw the danger of living at Pendlehurst when I married Toby. That's why I fought so hard against it. But then . . . Toby's accident made it seem the only solution."

"You and me both, Melissa; we've neither of us had it easy, have we?"

She flicked back a straying lock of hair. "Oh, I don't know. Compared with some people—"

"That's a no-go philosophy for me," Edward interrupted with a spurt of mild anger. "The fact that there are people much worse off than you doesn't make your own problems any easier to bear. To an outside observer, I've got it made. A satisfying profession, a fulfilling hobby. A wife who's universally admired and respected, and a home that's not far from being in the luxury class. But it isn't enough for me; it isn't what I dream about."

"Which is?"

"To be alone with Pauline. To be the one person who counts for her. But it doesn't look as if my dream will ever come true. Any more than yours will."

"You don't know what my dream is," Melissa said.

"Maybe I can hazard a guess." Edward gave her a straight look. "What went wrong between you and Maxwell? Why did he return to Portugal so hastily?"

Melissa found that her voice was only a husky whisper as she said, "I told him that it was all over between us."

"I see! Well, it seems to me that he gave you up very easily. I wouldn't have, in his shoes. You're something special, Melissa." Edward gave her another direct look. "Are you going to marry Selwyn?"

"Hey," she protested, "that's hitting below the belt."

"I thought tonight was cards-on-the-table time for us."

"Selwyn hasn't asked me to marry him," she pointed out.

"But we both know that he'll get around to it, don't we? So I repeat my question."

Melissa shrugged. "I can't give you an answer, Edward, because I don't *know* the answer."

"Pauline is dead set on the idea. Recently she's been urging Selwyn not to dillydally."

"I guessed that."

"There's plenty to be said in Selwyn's favor," Edward remarked musingly.

"That's what I keep telling myself. In fact, I can't think of any valid objection to marrying him."

"Except that you don't love him?"

"Does that have to be so very important?"

"Certainly." Edward's rather endearing, self-deprecating smile was back. "I suppose you're thinking that, with a record like mine, my opinion on the subject isn't worth a lot. All the same, I'm sticking by it. Two people loving each other is the only basis for marriage."

"You hit the bull's-eye, Edward. It has to be *mutual.*"

He gave her a surprised glance. "So which way round is it?"

"Which way round?"

"Oh, come on!" Edward shook his head impatiently. "We're talking about Maxwell now. The guy came rushing here from Lisbon, so the signs are that he's fallen for you in a big way. Right?"

"Wrong. Phil doesn't love me, not really."

"Give the man a chance. You've hardly known each other five minutes."

Melissa felt oddly short of breath. Wasn't she being foolish, talking so freely with her sister-in-law's husband? Yet somehow it helped to spill out her misery, and Edward was there and ready to listen.

"Phil asked me to marry him," she said quietly.

"Did he now? And you obviously turned him down flat."

"Naturally I did."

"Why naturally?"

"I already told you. Phil doesn't love me."

"But you love him. That's beginning to come over loud and clear."

"Yes," she admitted tonelessly. "I love him."

Edward rubbed his chin reflectively with his thumb and forefinger. "So you've turned down the man you love in favor of the man you don't. Takes some explaining, that."

"I *had* to turn Phil down," she insisted. "He asked me for all the wrong reasons."

"What reasons?"

"Well . . . it was mainly to prevent me from marrying Selwyn."

Edward regarded her in skeptical silence for a moment. Then he said, "Now that, if you'll forgive my saying so, Melissa, is pure garbage. A man can have all sorts of reasons for asking a woman to marry him, but merely stopping her from marrying another man isn't one of them."

"He came up with his proposal in the heat of the moment," she explained unhappily. "I expect he's relieved now that I turned him down."

Edward ridged his forehead, looking thoughtful. "You must have made a very deep impression on Maxwell in the short time you were together."

"Well, if I did, it's completely over between us now. Which is the best thing all round," she added with a burst of vehemence. Edward seemed unconvinced, and she went on rather desperately, "What else could I have done but put an end to it? Phil and I . . . it was an impossible situation."

Edward picked up a small piece of cherrywood and studied it sideways as if that would somehow help him to understand her. Finally he said in a serious voice, "I'm very fond of you, Melissa. I hope you know that. I'd hate to see you make a bad mistake. I realize how much pressure is being put on you to marry Selwyn—pressure from your own mind as well as from Pauline and Selwyn himself. I know there would be practical advantages, especially where Jenny and Mark are concerned. Selwyn is a good chap . . . a fine chap in many ways, but . . ."

"But what?"

"Can it ever work for a woman to marry one man when she's in love with another?"

"Love let me down before," Melissa replied sadly. "It would be pointless for me to pretend to you, Edward, that my marriage to Toby was a good one . . . I'm talking about before his accident, of course.''

"You were younger then, and more easily taken in. You're older and wiser now, so you wouldn't have given your heart so impetuously this time.''

Melissa laughed drily. "There wasn't much cerebral activity involved with Phil, I can tell you. As soon as I arrived in Lisbon he . . . well, he swept me off my feet, as they say.''

"As you did him, no doubt.''

She made a face. "Hardly. He's been around too much for that.''

"And that worries you? If a bachelor of his age weren't pretty experienced there'd be something wrong with him. But I don't imagine that Maxwell goes around throwing out proposals of marriage.''

From the direction of the house came the sound of a car door slamming. Pauline's visitors were departing.

"I'd better be getting back," said Melissa.

Edward nodded. "Before you go, promise me one thing. Promise me that you'll give it a lot of thought before you accept Selwyn. Don't be rushed.''

"Rushed?" she echoed ironically. "Can you imagine Selwyn rushing into anything?''

He grinned. "No, I guess not.''

Melissa went to the door, then paused and glanced back. "Edward . . . it seems such a pity that you . . . I mean, when you still love Pauline . . .''

He looked up from putting his tools away and gave her a slow, sad smile. "I think you imagine that I'm some sort of Don Juan. It doesn't happen all that often.''

"Need it happen at all?" she burst out impulsively, then made an apologetic gesture with her hands. "I suppose you think I'm being prissy again?''

"Just a bit!" He heaved a rueful sigh. "I probably seem a feeble sort of guy to you, Melissa, but that one small spark of defiance means a lot to me. It helps to keep me sane. Of course, if Pauline were to wake up one morning and realize what a perfectly splendid husband I am, the need for it would vanish instantly. But, alas, there's no chance of that happening."

"She ought to realize it," Melissa told him warmly, "because it's true. Maybe she will one day."

"Pigs, as they say, might fly." Edward's gray eyes held a wistful, faraway look. "You may find it hard to believe this about an unemotional character like me, but I'd be devastated if my marriage were to break up. Meeting up with you at that restaurant in Tunbridge Wells that day gave me one hell of a fright."

"But not enough of one, it seems."

Edward lifted his shoulders expressively. "We can none of us escape from our stereotypes, I guess. I'm not proud of myself, but neither am I particularly ashamed. I am what I am, Melissa, and Pauline is what she is. Yet I love her very deeply." He looked faintly surprised by his own forcefulness. "Yes, I truly do! And I believe that, in her own way, Pauline loves me in return."

"I'm sure that's true," Melissa said, believing it. "Oh dear, Edward, why is everything so horribly complicated?"

He grimaced. "It all makes for life's rich tapestry, I suppose. The winners among us face up to the complications and overcome them. The feeble ones, like me, just accept defeat. Be a winner, Melissa."

"How about us lunching together today, Melissa?"

It wasn't the first time that Selwyn had made the suggestion during the past ten days, and she couldn't go on making excuses. Yet she dreaded getting into any even vaguely intimate situation with him.

She glanced up from her desk and made an effort to smile. "It'll have to be a fairly quick lunch, Selwyn. I have to finish the copy for our autumn mailing so that Linda can get it typed this afternoon."

He came round to stand behind Melissa's chair and glanced down at the papers spread on the desk. "Surely there's no great rush for that, as long as the printers get it by the end of next week? I was thinking, Melissa, we might do ourselves proud for once and go to the Ritz. In fact, I've already booked a table for us."

"Oh, great!" She had to put a good face on it now. "I'll feel very pampered being taken to the Ritz."

"Why shouldn't you feel pampered, my dear?" There was a note of tenderness in Selwyn's voice, and Melissa cursed herself for giving him an opening. She laughed, and said in a brisk, practical tone, "I'll have to keep a clear head for work this afternoon."

In the painted and gilded splendor of the Ritz Hotel it was difficult to keep the conversation on a prosaic level. She tried raising the subject of a bid that Colville's had made for the custom of a large supermarket chain, but Selwyn made a disapproving face. "There's a time and place for everything, Melissa, and this definitely isn't the moment to discuss our sales program."

In her search for a neutral topic she turned to the children. "Mark is doing well at school. I had a chat with his teacher on Monday. Jenny is, too."

"They're both bright kids," Selwyn said fondly. "We'll have no worries with them, Melissa."

We! She almost wondered whether to challenge him on that, but decided instead to pretend not to have noticed it. She switched away from the children, though, and asked Selwyn how the local golf club's tournament was coming along. Looking pleased at her apparent interest, he expounded at length, while Melissa gave him less than half her attention.

Thank heaven that Selwyn—and, it followed, Pauline—seemed unsuspecting about her true relationship with Phil. Edward had proved a trustworthy confidant. It helped a little to feel that she had an ally at Pendlehurst. An ally, she thought remorsefully, against two people for whom she felt nothing but gratitude and admiration, even if not, in Pauline's case, affection.

She studied Selwyn covertly as he talked; his squarish face was animated, his gray blue eyes warm. He was tailor-made for any woman who wanted a considerate husband, an intelligent and well-informed companion, and a caring second father for her children. Most people would think she needed her head examined not to be giving Selwyn the subtle little signs of encouragement that he was clearly angling for.

Was she a fit and proper mother, she asked herself, not to be seizing, for her children's sake, the chance of such a thoroughly good marriage? Was she sacrificing Jenny and Mark on the altar of her own selfishness? Yet how could she accept Selwyn as a husband when she knew that, for every minute of every day, she would be thinking of Phil and comparing Selwyn unfavorably with the man she loved?

"What, may I ask, is the matter with you this evening, Felipe?" demanded Senhora Inez de Ribeiro Costa, a frown of displeasure marring the ivory smoothness of her brow. "You seem very preoccupied."

Phil sighed inwardly as he met the reproachful glance of the beautiful, raven-haired woman who sat with him in an exclusive Lisbon restaurant. Inez deserved the full attention of any man she favored with her company, and she wasn't getting it from him that evening.

"*Desculpe, querida,*" he said with an apologetic gesture. "You must forgive me. I guess I have a lot on my mind just now."

"You have problems with your new *vinho espumante?*" she inquired. "Was that why you rushed off to London recently?"

"No, not real problems. Just a few minor difficulties that needed to be straightened out."

"Then what are these things that weigh so heavily on your mind when you are with me?" The challenge was thrown out with a glint of anger in her fine, wide-apart eyes.

"I've said I'm sorry." Phil treated her to one of his most

charming smiles. "You won't have reason to complain again, Inez."

"I should hope not!" She gave him a shrewd, assessing glance that made Phil feel uneasy. It had always seemed to him that Inez, as an artist, was more perceptive than most people, and he didn't care for the thought that she could see into his mind at this moment. Inez de Ribeiro Costa was far removed from the typical Portuguese woman; she was a true cosmopolitan, chic and sophisticated and independent. She had formerly been married to a wealthy Swiss banker, but she had divorced him long ago, obtaining a handsome settlement. She had then returned to her native Lisbon, and was now thriving in her own career as a top fashion artist and illustrator.

Phil had first encountered Inez two years earlier at a cocktail party held in the presidential palace at Belem. He had met her gaze across the width of the glittering salon, realizing in that same moment that she had been eyeing him for some time. It wasn't unusual for Phil to find himself the object of a woman's admiration, but something told him that this was due to more than just the fact that the woman fancied him. When, a few minutes later, he had contrived to be introduced to her, she'd astonished him by asking point-blank if he would model for a magazine short story illustration she'd been commissioned to do. Immensely tickled at the idea, Phil had agreed. They fixed that he should go to her studio in the Alfama district the following afternoon. He was to wear slacks and a sports jacket, she'd stipulated firmly, with a pale shirt and a blue or green tie.

For an hour and a half Inez had kept him in a fixed pose that made his muscles ache while she worked at her easel and chatted to him knowledgeably about Portuguese literature. Phil had been starting to wonder if he'd misjudged the situation when, abruptly, she'd tossed aside her charcoal and said in a brisk tone, "That's enough." She had then walked over and kissed him quite thoroughly, leaving him in no doubt about her intentions.

Their affair, after a fervent start, had settled down to being an easygoing relationship on a nonexclusive basis. From Phil's point of view the arrangement couldn't have been better. In addition to Inez's energetic and imaginative performance in bed, he'd valued her intelligent friendship. Which he still did. But he was forced to acknowledge that at this point neither Inez nor any other woman in Lisbon aroused the smallest spark of desire in him.

Until just a few short weeks ago, before he'd met Melissa, dining tête-à-tête with Inez like this would have been a pleasure to be keenly looked forward to; every minute of the evening would have been savored, his mind sparking against hers, his body responding to her sensuous beauty. Until a few short weeks ago dinner with her would have been the prelude to a very satisfying night of lovemaking. But now Melissa entirely filled his thoughts and his dreams, allowing no room for any other woman.

"Your mind is wandering again, Felipe," said Inez in sharp rebuke. She gave him another penetrating glance. "Since you insist that it is not business problems that concern you, I can only conclude that it is another woman."

"How could any man in his senses be thinking about another woman when he's with you, Inez?"

That had sounded, Phil realized to his shame, more like the guilty evasion it was than a genuine compliment. For heaven's sake, it ought to be easy to carry through what he'd planned for this evening. When he'd called Inez on a sudden impulse and found that she was free it had seemed a fantastic piece of luck; now he was throwing away his luck by annoying her. He made a big effort to pull himself together, to respond to Inez as she expected him to respond. But as they continued to talk, exchanging witty, flirtatious repartee, a bleak picture took possession of Phil's mind. She was as clever and beautiful as ever, but he just wasn't interested in any woman but Melissa.

What on earth had made him get into this impossible situation? Phil asked himself angrily. He knew with chilling certainty that, somehow or other, he had to extricate himself. But he would have to try to avoid letting Inez feel rejected.

As it turned out, though, Inez proved to be quite capable of turning the tables on him. When Phil stopped his car outside the door of her studio he remained motionless and silent, hoping for a last-minute miracle. Then he said apologetically, "Inez, *querida,* I'm not feeling my best this evening, so perhaps I won't come in."

He heard her breath hiss sharply. "You would do well, my friend," she said, "to await an invitation before you refuse it."

"I only meant—"

"I don't wish to hear what you meant. Thank you for the dinner, Felipe, and goodbye."

He put out a restraining hand. "But *querida* . . ."

"What is it?" Her long-nailed fingers beat an impatient tattoo on the dashboard.

"Shall I call you soon?"

"If you decide that you are able, for the space of a few short hours, to give me your undivided attention, then by all means call me. I will then consider whether I have any wish to see you again."

"Inez, the last thing I wanted to do was to upset you."

"So you have succeeded, Felipe. I am *not* upset. Good night."

This time he let her go, waiting until she'd opened her front door and disappeared inside. He'd been holding his breath, he realized with surprise, and released it now in an explosive burst. Slamming the car into gear, he accelerated so hard that the wheels spun on the wet cobbles. Damn Inez. And damn Melissa . . . because his lack of interest in any other woman was undoubtedly her fault. Yes, damn Melissa for having blighted his life.

Ten minutes later he stood at a long window in his apartment, gazing out at the twinkling lights of the city spread below him and the swaying lights of ships riding at anchor on the dark waters of the estuary. Inez was forgotten; images of Melissa hovered in his vision, tantalizing and tormenting him.

His sigh was so long and heavy that it seemed to shudder through his whole frame. He had planned to drive away Melissa's haunting ghost by involving himself in a hectic social life, by assuaging his desire in the arms of other women. But now he wondered anxiously if he would ever again even feel desire. Had his virility been drained from him for good?

Phil's body responded to his agonized question with a sudden uprush of passion that startled him and left him breathless. He was burning in a fierce blaze of the male need that he'd feared he had lost. How long would this unwanted longing for Melissa last, he thought in despair, before it finally abated to a level that would allow his brain and body to function normally and give him back his peace of mind?

The only solution he could think of lay in hard work. Tomorrow he would head for the Silva Cunha vineyards and become a fiend for perfection and detail, down to the last grape in the last bunch of the millions that were now beginning to form. He would exhaust himself in hard labor, and perhaps in that he would find salvation.

"Now that you plan to be here for a few days, Felipe, you can take Josepha on the promised tour of the vineyards and winery." Dona Carlota's voice was censorious as she went on. "You have treated the girl very badly, you know, and you can be thankful that she has been so patient with you."

"Grandmama," Phil said wearily, "I have no time for giving conducted tours of the vineyard to all and sundry."

The old lady looked affronted. "Josepha is not 'all and sundry,' as you so crudely put it. She is a charming, intelligent young woman and—"

"I think it's time I told you," Phil interrupted, "that I

have absolutely no intention of marrying Josepha Carreiro. None whatsoever. She is the last woman in the world I'd want to marry."

"How vehemently you express yourself. What fault do you find with Josepha that she deserves such strong language? She may not be an outstanding beauty, but her features are quite good. It would only need better-chosen clothes and a little more grooming for her to appear entirely presentable. You would do well to think again, Felipe."

On the verge of giving a sharp answer, Phil held his tongue and pondered. Why was he so positive that he could never consider marrying Josepha? Probably, he thought, because Josepha was someone whom Melissa had met. There was a link between the two women which would inevitably invite comparison—to Josepha's fatal disadvantage. Each and every time he looked upon Josepha she would be a fresh and painful reminder of Melissa.

On the other hand, it might be sensible for him to start listening to his grandmother's constant urging and select a wife, a woman from the right sort of family who would give him children. So long as it wasn't Josepha, did it really matter much whom he married? Yet the thought of finding himself a wife seemed tedious beyond bearing. Why not, he reasoned, allow his grandmother to do the preliminary sifting? The choice was of almost total indifference to him, assuming that he didn't feel a positive dislike for the chosen candidate.

"Not Josepha, Grandmama," he said in a mild tone. "She's out of the question."

Dona Carlota made no comment, but Phil saw from the look of satisfaction on her lined, aristocratic face that she had registered the implication of his remark. Doubtless his grandmother would now start making mental lists with fresh energy, awarding points to her nominees on such factors as quality of family, good health and the likelihood of bearing strong babies.

As Phil strode off briskly to his day's work in the vineyards he told himself that he was acting wisely. His impulse to ask Melissa to marry him had been totally out of character. Suppose she had accepted? He shuddered; it would have been disastrous.

No, his priorities had been wildly wrong when he'd made that impetuous proposal. What it boiled down to in bald terms was that he'd offered Melissa marriage in return for the lovemaking it had seemed impossible to get from her any other way. Sheer lunacy. Thank heaven she'd turned him down flat. He gave an inward smile that carried with it a tug of yearning. He might have guessed that Melissa would immediately perceive the insanity of his proposal. She was such a clearheaded, intelligent woman. She was also so maddeningly stubborn and irrational, so fascinatingly complex, so emotional and caring, so warm and passionate, so sweetly tender. Oh God, how he wanted her!

He halted abruptly and stamped his foot on the hard, dry soil. A worker hoeing among the vines looked round at him with bewildered apology.

"Am I doing something wrong, Senhor Dom Felipe?"

Phil pulled himself together. "No, Santoz, you're doing just fine. I was angry with *myself* about something, that's all."

Phil jerked awake, bathed in sweat—a common occurrence these days. He lay staring into the darkness, listening to the faint sounds of the night: a breeze rustling the trees in the *quinta*'s gardens; a bird grumbling sleepily in the eaves; the slow, measured ticking of the alabaster clock on his mantelpiece. His body ached as if he'd fallen from a horse, or been badly beaten in a fistfight; every last bone and muscle seemed to have its own private pain. He'd never known such a fever of wanting, of longing. Not just desiring, but that, too . . . oh yes, that, too. He rose from his bed and went to stand naked at the open window, allowing the night air to cool the furnace heat of his skin. But the insistent, passionate need remained, a throbbing torture to him because it could not be assuaged.

In these vigils of the night, when his brain felt drugged from lack of sleep, it seemed to him that, paradoxically, he saw things with greater clarity of vision. He had been castigating himself as a fool for proposing to Melissa, and he'd thanked his lucky stars that she'd turned him down. But now he saw his proposal to her as the most sensible suggestion he'd ever made to anybody in all his life, and he cursed the ill fortune that had made Melissa refuse him. What bliss it would be if she were with him now, he thought wildly, light-headedly. What heaven it would be to spend each night holding her cradled in his arms, with her lovely body curled intimately against his own, both of them satiated and deeply fulfilled after making love. And then to wake in the morning with her there beside him—forever. Phil groaned aloud and distractedly ran his fingers through his thick hair. The insanity had been to imagine that he could ever marry anyone else. After Melissa, he could never tolerate any other woman in his bed.

He would return to England the very next day. He would see Melissa again—at her office, at Pendlehurst, wherever she might be—and repeat his proposal. He would demand that she accept him, plead with her, beg her . . . anything, just so long as he could win her as his wife. That was the only future he could bear to think about.

But even as he formulated these plans in his head, he realized with a fearful certainty that he wouldn't be success-ful. Melissa had refused him once, emphatically, and she would do so again. For her, nothing would have changed. She was determined to sacrifice herself for the sake of her children. Damn it, though, apart from the blood relation-ship, he could offer those two children of hers all that Selwyn Colville could and more. She could stipulate any-thing she wanted for Jenny and Mark, and he'd willingly agree.

Yet still he knew that she'd refuse him. It was as if, he thought savagely, Melissa had some masochistic urge to hurt herself. She had freely admitted that their lovemaking had been as wonderful and as meaningful for her as it had been for him. She didn't regret their affair, she'd said, but she'd insisted that it had been no more than an episode—an incidental segment of their lives with a definite conclusion. For him, though, it wouldn't end. Not ever. He would remember Melissa with longing all his days.

He had to do something! But if not go to England in pursuit of her, what then? Suppose he could somehow persuade her to come to Portugal again? Surrounded on all sides by memories of the happiness they'd known together, might she not then succumb?

It was an impossible dream; Melissa would never agree to come.

Unless . . . could he make use of their business involvement? Colville's and Silva Cunha had signed a contract, which meant that he had the right to insist on their cooperation with any reasonable request. Suppose he invented a minor hitch that needed to be ironed out. Suppose he suggested to Selwyn that since Melissa had come to discuss things with him before, it would make sense for her to come again; she had a thorough understanding of his setup. Phil's heart began to pound with renewed hope. It might work . . . it had to work! Failure was unthinkable.

Dawn was breaking, showing as a pearly radiance in the eastern sky. A signal? An omen? Phil glanced at the luminous hands of his wristwatch. It would be several hours before he could catch Selwyn at his London office. Knowing that he wouldn't sleep again, he hurriedly dragged on jeans and a rollneck sweater, and quietly let himself out of the silent house. Without any sense of purpose he strode through the mist-shrouded vineyards toward the crest of a hill.

Chapter Thirteen

"I simply don't understand you, Melissa," said Selwyn, looking perplexed. "What do you have against going to Lisbon again? Was it that you didn't like the place I'd booked into? Go to a five-star hotel if you'd rather."

"No, the guesthouse was charming. I loved it."

"What, then? You got along okay with Senhor Maxwell. And even if you didn't . . . this is business, Melissa, where the client calls the tune. When Maxwell phoned to say there was a small hitch about delivery quotas and he'd like to have a personal chat to iron it out, I naturally agreed. When he went on to suggest that it might be best for you to be the one to go, as you already know exactly how his operation works, I agreed to that, too. So I'm afraid that you're committed."

Melissa rose from her desk and began to pace around her office in agitation. This was dreadful. She felt tempted to tell Selwyn that the whole thing was a frame-up on Phil's part, but she threw the thought out as soon as it entered her head. She could never tell her brother-in-law the truth about Phil and herself, not even part of it. He would never understand.

Grasping at a straw, she said, "I'm sorry, Selwyn, but after what happened before I just can't go away and leave the children. It wouldn't be right."

Selwyn frowned at her. "You're not still feeling guilty about Jenny's little tumble? It would have been just as likely to happen if you'd been on the spot. A spirited child is always going to find things to do that carry an element of risk."

"I know, I know. I realize that I'm being silly and overprotective, and that Jenny and Mark are every bit as safe with Pauline as they are with me. But . . . well, I can't help it, Selwyn. I couldn't go away and leave them again."

"So take them with you," he said.

"What?" Apprehension crawled up Melissa's spine when she saw from the look in Selwyn's eyes that he meant it. "I couldn't take the children on a . . . a business trip," she stammered.

"I don't see why not, in the circumstances. Senhor Maxwell would understand, and he's already met them. When you need to be free of them to talk business it wouldn't be any problem getting a babysitter. There are plenty of English-speaking women in Lisbon."

"But—"

Selwyn cut across her. "If you don't like the idea of leaving them with a stranger, then take along someone you know and trust. I bet young Lucy Hatchley, for instance, would jump at the chance of a free trip to Lisbon. She's on vacation from college, isn't she? I'm sure Joy could be persuaded to let her have a few days off from the stable."

"Listen," Melissa said desperately, "I can't turn up in Lisbon with a sort of entourage."

"You're just making difficulties," said Selwyn in dismissal. "I told Senhor Maxwell that you'd ring him back later today to finalize arrangements, so I'll leave it to you. Okay?" With that he walked out of her office.

Melissa thought rebelliously, I won't go and that's final. But logic was on Selwyn's side. If she wanted to keep her job at Colville's Wines, then she couldn't shirk what the job entailed. He'd thrown in the suggestion about taking the children along to appease her oversensitive maternal conscience, and he'd even come up with a practical suggestion of how it could be managed.

Feeling thoroughly boxed in, she called Joy Hatchley and sounded her out about the idea of Lucy going with them to Portugal. Joy had no objection, and at once put her daughter on the line. Lucy was thrilled to bits.

"Wow! Sure I'll come, Melissa. I bet Jenny and Mark are excited."

"Well, I haven't told them yet. I wanted to check with you first. Thanks a lot, Lucy."

"That's neat, you thanking me!"

Pauline wouldn't be any too pleased, Melissa mused as she hung up. She'd feel slighted, as if her competence were being called into question. But that hurdle could wait until evening. Meanwhile, Phil had to be informed. Nothing would induce her to talk to him on the phone. Instead she buzzed through to her secretary and said, "Linda, please call Senhor Maxwell's office and say that I'll be there on Wednesday. Okay?"

Melissa went home by train, as Selwyn had decided to stay the night in London following the monthly meeting of a vintners' trade association. It was also Edward's evening to work late, when he always ate out, so it would only be herself and Pauline at dinner. Melissa put the children to bed without mentioning Lisbon. She preferred to tell Pauline about her plans without having their excited chatter breaking up the conversation.

Pauline seemed a trifle on edge as she served the beef casserole she'd prepared for them. She hardly seemed to hear when Melissa dutifully commented on how delicious it looked; she just gave a vague nod.

"Pauline," Melissa began, helping herself to beans, "I

have to make another trip to Lisbon. Selwyn told me today. I'm leaving on Wednesday and—"

"When will you be back?"

"I don't quite know. Sometime during the weekend, I imagine."

"Oh dear," said Pauline with a frown, "I was planning to be away myself for a couple of days at the end of the week."

"That'll be nice. Where are you off to?"

"Well, I shan't be able to go now, shall I, if I'm going to be looking after Jenny and Mark for you?"

"But you won't need to, Pauline. I'm taking the children with me this time. I've asked Lucy Hatchley to help me with them, and she's over the moon about it."

Melissa had expected her sister-in-law to react with a certain amount of pique at this news, but instead Pauline showed only relief.

"That's good," she said. "It should all work out quite nicely. I was feeling a little concerned about leaving you to cope without me, although naturally I'd have cooked things and left them in the freezer for you, and I was going to give Freda a list of instructions."

Melissa felt a gush of irritation. "Really, Pauline, anyone would think I was totally helpless. It wouldn't be beyond my capabilities to organize a few meals, you know."

"Well no . . . of course not." But Pauline's skepticism was heavily apparent.

Melissa suddenly found herself spilling out a thought which she had been turning over in her mind for the past week or so. She couldn't go on drifting the way she'd been doing; sooner or later she had to arrange a settled life for herself and her children. "While we're on the subject, Pauline, I've decided to look around for a small house somewhere in the locality . . . a place just a nice size for the three of us."

"What *are* you talking about?"

"Well, I can't just go on living here forever," Melissa explained. "It was necessary up until Toby's death, and I know there are lots of advantages where the children are concerned, but—"

"This is Selwyn's home," said Pauline sharply.

"That's what I'm getting at—it's not *my* home."

"Of course it is. It's the *family* home, for all of us. I could never understand why you insisted on dragging Toby away from Pendlehurst when you married him. Still, I won't say any more about that. As things are now, though, it would be pointless for you to leave for such a short time. When you marry Selwyn . . ."

"No!" Melissa groaned inwardly. She hadn't bargained on having to cope with this issue right now, but she couldn't let it go unchallenged. "I am *not* going to marry Selwyn," she said with quiet emphasis.

"You're not going to . . ." Pauline looked bewildered. "But we've all seen it coming for ages." Her violet eyes narrowed suspiciously. "Have you and Selwyn had a quarrel?"

"No."

"Then I don't understand . . . have you told *him* that you're not going to marry him?"

"The question has never arisen," Melissa said in a cool voice.

"Well, if that's all that's bothering you, I'll soon—"

"No, Pauline, you won't do anything," Melissa retorted crisply. "I'll handle my own affairs, thank you very much. One of the reasons I feel that I must get away from Pendlehurst is to put an end to Selwyn's expectations about me."

"But why should you want to? Where on earth will you find yourself a more suitable husband than Selwyn? He's very fond of you, Melissa, and he loves the children almost as his own. He *is* their uncle, don't forget. It would be an ideal marriage."

"Ideal in what way, Pauline? In sensible, practical terms? I must remember that I'm a widow with two young children? Not the best possible catch for a man?"

"I didn't quite mean that, Melissa, but facts have to be faced. Anyway, what more do you expect from marriage?"

Melissa laid down her fork. "Listen carefully, Pauline, and I'll try to explain. I'm fond of Selwyn, truly I am. I think he's one of the kindest, most thoughtful and considerate men I've ever met. But that's not enough. I don't love him."

"Oh, love!" Pauline's fierce gesture expressed scorn, but a wistful quality in her voice suggested a contradictory emotion as she added, "Love, my dear Melissa, can be very fleeting."

"That sounds as if it comes straight from the heart," said Melissa, meeting her sister-in-law's glance in challenge.

"Did it?" Pauline shrugged. "I was merely generalizing. You'd hardly expect a woman of my age to have romantic dreams."

"Doesn't every woman, at every age?"

"Perhaps . . . in one's weaker moments."

"Pauline . . . is there something wrong between you and Edward?"

"Wrong?" She glanced down at her plate. "What on earth could be wrong?"

There was a short silence between them, then Melissa ventured, "Do you love him, Pauline?"

"What a thing to say," she returned, looking affronted. "Edward is my husband; naturally I love him."

"Yet a moment ago you were scorning love as the basis for marriage."

"I was scorning silly, romantic notions about love. For mature people it's a nonsensical concept." She closed her eyes momentarily, and Melissa had a strong feeling that Pauline was holding back tears. Was it possible that she had discovered something about Edward's transgressions?

"By the way, where is it you're off to?" Melissa asked. "You didn't say."

"Edinburgh. It's the annual dental symposium that Edward goes to. He was talking about it at dinner the other night, you remember."

"Oh, yes. And this year you've decided to go with him? That's a good idea, Pauline."

"Well, I thought . . . I mean, lots of wives do, and I don't want Edward to . . . to be at loose ends." She became brisk again. "Right, then. As you'll be in Portugal with the children, I think I'll suggest to Selwyn that he stay over in London, and I can give Freda and Tom a couple of extra days off. Selwyn will be only too delighted to stay in town and go to the theater or a concert. He'd never have kept Pendlehurst on, you know, if I hadn't insisted on it. And then where would we all have been?"

"Yes, that's quite interesting, Pauline, isn't it? How would we all have managed if you hadn't organized our lives for us?" At Pauline's startled glance, Melissa plunged on. "Hasn't it ever occurred to you that maybe you concern yourself about the family too much? We're each of us competent in our own way, even if not half as competent as you are." She smiled to take the sting from her criticism. "You're so talented in all sorts of directions, Pauline, so capable and efficient. I don't suppose it's ever struck you that to ordinary mortals you can be a little terrifying."

"Terrifying?" The word was echoed in outrage.

"You make everyone else feel inadequate."

"Really! Just because I dislike incompetence—"

"Must you always make your superiority so apparent?" Melissa interrupted. "Please believe me, Pauline, I'm not trying to be nasty. I admire you a lot—that's quite sincere— but I do find it irritating the way you imply that everything I can do you can do a whole lot better."

"That's absurd! For instance, I don't pretend to have the same grasp of business that you and Selwyn obviously possess."

Melissa paused a moment, and then said quietly, "And how about Edward?"

"Edward? I don't know what you're talking about."

"No?" Melissa changed tack. "I think it's a great idea for

you to go to Edinburgh with him. You should do that sort of thing more often."

Pauline nodded. "Men are such weak creatures, so easily led astray." She stood up quickly and reached for Melissa's empty plate. "I haven't made a dessert tonight; there's just fruit and cheese."

"That's fine."

So it looked as if she'd been right, Melissa thought, as she helped Pauline clear the table. Edward's infidelity had been discovered, or at least suspected. Perhaps, she mused, despite what he'd said about his anxiety that Pauline shouldn't find out, it was what Edward had actually wanted. Perhaps involving himself with other women had been his way of crying out for help.

"I suppose you realize, Pauline," she said on impulse as they sat down again, "that Edward utterly adores you. More than anything in this world, he longs for your approval."

"How do you know that?" It was rapped out sharply.

"It's obvious. Also, he told me so."

"Edward told you?"

"Yes, why not? What's wrong with a man telling someone how much he loves his wife?"

Pauline sniffed. "He has an odd way of showing his love for me."

"Maybe, Pauline," said Melissa, treading warily on very thin ice, "Edward could say the same about you. He happens to be an exceptionally good dentist with a reputation for being very gentle with his patients. He's also very clever with his hands when it comes to restoring antiques, a subject about which he's quite an expert. Besides that, he's very well read and has an excellent brain. . . . Shall I go on?"

"Everybody knows those things about him," said Pauline, seeming to be at a loss.

"So it might be asked how in the world such an accomplished man could feel so inadequate."

"Edward feels inadequate? What nonsense!" But there was a slight tremor in Pauline's normally confident voice.

Having come this far, Melissa decided to go out on a limb. After all, she reflected wryly, it was partly in her own interest. "If you want to know what I think, Pauline, it's this. You and Edward ought to quit living at Pendlehurst and find yourselves one of those beautiful Georgian houses in Tunbridge Wells, conveniently near his office. You've never had your own home, just the two of you, and I reckon it's time you did."

There was a long pause while Pauline pleated her napkin. Then she said, "Freda and Tom have been talking of retiring for some time, so I might consider something of the kind—if I could be happy knowing that you were going to marry Selwyn."

"You can put that right out of your mind," Melissa said tersely. "And if you like, you can tell Selwyn I said so. It just wouldn't work."

"Well, if you're determined to be difficult, Melissa, that settles the matter. I could never abandon Selwyn."

"Selwyn isn't a boy any longer," Melissa pointed out impatiently. "He's a grown man. You said yourself that he'd probably have sold Pendlehurst and gone to live in London if he'd had his way. Why not let him do that now?"

Pauline smoothed back a strand of her ash blond hair. "Selwyn is going to be shattered when he learns that you won't marry him."

"I doubt it. He's made of tougher material than you think. You don't see him at the office—he's a different person there. No, Pauline, it's your husband who needs you now, much more than your brother does. That's why I'm so glad that you're going to Edinburgh with Edward."

Pauline gave her a long, searching scrutiny. "I believe you mean well, Melissa," she said at length. "Otherwise I'd be deeply offended at your harsh criticisms. It's just possible, I grant you, that there might be a grain of truth in what you've said. But for the most part it was wild exaggeration. Now, about this trip to Lisbon . . .''

"I have everything under control, thank you," Melissa said serenely. It sounded so self-assured, she thought; how would Pauline know that she was trembling inside, feeling more and more apprehensive as each minute that passed brought her that much nearer to her confrontation with Phil?

Throughout the flight Melissa hoped and prayed that Phil wouldn't be there to meet them at the airport. Yet she knew, deep down, that if he wasn't she'd be bitterly disappointed.

He was standing at the barrier as they emerged from customs, and her heart soared at the sight of him; he looked so incredibly handsome. He was dressed casually in pale fawn slacks that hugged his hips, and an open-necked cream shirt. For an instant their eyes locked in a silent duel before Melissa glanced away. Phil smiled at them all and greeted the children as old friends. Lucy was obviously thrilled when he lifted her hand to his lips; then it was Melissa's turn. She steeled herself to remain calm and not let him feel her electric response to their physical contact, but she saw the flicker of satisfaction in his dark eyes. She knew forlornly that if she'd been alone Phil would have taken her in his arms and kissed her lips, and she wouldn't have had the strength to stop him.

Though he took the heaviest of their luggage under his arms, Phil still managed to keep his hands free, one for Jenny and one for Mark. They walked ahead, the children dancing along happily on either side of him.

"Isn't he just gorgeous?" Lucy whispered with an extravagant sigh. "I thought so that day you brought him to the stable. He's the sort of man who makes you go all quivery inside."

"He's twice your age!" said Melissa sharply.

"Huh! Who cares?" Lucy darted a saucy look at Melissa. "What you really mean is, hands off, he's mine."

"Don't be silly," Melissa protested, wishing the color weren't warming her cheeks.

They had reached Phil's car, and he loaded the luggage. To Melissa's surprise he ushered her and Lucy into the rear seats, reserving the front for the children. She tried to feel glad that he was being so discreet, but couldn't.

"I gather that you're booked in at the same place as before," Phil said as he drove off. "I checked this morning. They had allocated you two separate rooms with twin beds, but I changed that to a double suite with a sitting room between. I thought it would suit you better."

"You're very kind, Senhor Maxwell," said Melissa stiffly.

"Oh, please . . . call me Phil, all of you."

"Sure thing," Lucy said, grinning.

"What I've planned," Phil went on, "is to drop you off at the guesthouse and give you time to settle in. Then I'll collect you and we'll see the sights. After that I'm taking you all out to dinner."

Melissa tried to apply a damper to the exclamations of delight from the other three. "But the children's bedtime is—"

Phil cut across her, saying with a laugh, "When in Rome, you should do as the Romans do. In Portugal children aren't packed off to bed nearly so early as they are in England."

Jenny and Mark, grasping that Phil was proposing they should be allowed to stay up, chorused their approval, so Melissa weakly agreed.

The tour was a great success with them. Phil had chosen an itinerary with the children in mind, leaving out monuments and churches, which they'd have found boring. They finished up by having dinner at a large popular restaurant right on the waterfront, where they could watch the ships as the sun went down.

"I've arranged to put a car and driver at your disposal during your stay," he told Lucy. "Miguel speaks tolerable

English. Just tell him where you want to go. Or, if you ask him, he'll make suggestions." He glanced at Melissa. "He's very reliable; take my word. The children and Lucy will be in good hands while you and I talk business."

Phil returned them to the guesthouse at a reasonable hour and politely bid them good night. It would all seem so utterly aboveboard to Lucy, Melissa thought with a sigh. But what lay in store for her when she met Phil alone the next day?

By 10:00 A.M. she was close to finding out. Miguel had collected Lucy and the children and was driving them to one of the resorts along the coast. He was a quiet, courteous man in his late fifties . . . deliberately chosen, Melissa guessed, to calm her fears. She had elected to walk to Phil's office rather than take a taxi, feeling . . . she didn't quite know what she felt. Butterflies were fluttering in her stomach, and she could hardly breathe. Her legs seemed as heavy as lead, yet it felt almost as though she were floating as she made her way through the familiar streets.

The receptionist at the Silva Cunha offices greeted Melissa as an old friend. Phil appeared immediately and ushered her up to his private office.

"What's this all about, Phil?" she demanded the moment the door was closed.

"I had to see you, Melissa."

"So you invented a problem with the contract?"

He shook his head. "No, there genuinely is a small hitch."

"But one that could be dealt with on the phone, or by an exchange of letters."

"Perhaps. A face-to-face meeting is always best, though."

She sat down in the visitor's chair and looked up at Phil, who'd remained standing. But she wasn't quite looking at him; she didn't dare to meet his eyes. Instead she stared at his mouth, studying its chiseled shape and remembering how, when they'd been staying at the chalet and sunbathing on the beach, she'd spent long minutes letting her fingertips dance over his lips lovingly, teasingly. "I warn you, Phil," she said in a stiff, tense voice, "this isn't going to do you a bit of good. I'm only here because you made it impossible for me to refuse to come—as I wanted to do."

Those sensitive, chiseled lips parted in a warm smile that, against Melissa's will, melted some of her determined hostility. "For whatever reason, Melissa, I'm very glad that you're here. And I'm glad that you decided to bring the children along."

"Why should you be?" she asked suspiciously. "You have no interest in Jenny and Mark."

"On the contrary, I have a big interest in them. My aim is to become their stepfather."

Her heart quaked, but somehow she managed to remain cool. "I thought I'd made it clear to you, Phil, that there's no chance whatsoever of my marrying you."

"I handled the situation badly in England," he admitted gravely. "Looking back, I'm not surprised that you refused me."

"However you had handled it," she told him in a biting tone, "my answer would have been the same. No! And now let's get down to the business I'm supposed to be here for."

"There's no hurry about that."

"I think there is. The sooner we can wrap things up, the sooner I can get back to England."

"And deprive your children of a lovely vacation?"

"They've just had a vacation, if you remember," she said tersely. "In Hastings."

"But coming to a foreign country must be so much more exciting for them. They'll be terribly disappointed if you rush them back home before they've had a proper chance to enjoy themselves."

She gave him a bitter look. "I suppose you think this is all very clever, maneuvering me into a situation where you can use my own children as a weapon against me."

"I didn't ask you to bring them," he pointed out.

"But you did say you were glad that they'd come."

"I am."

"Why don't you admit the truth, Phil? Your plan was to get me out here again on my own, wasn't it?"

Phil didn't refute the charge but attacked in return. "You accused me just now of using your children against you. Fair enough. But *you* were using them against *me,* weren't you, in bringing them with you?"

Melissa wasn't about to admit that it had crossed her mind that the children's presence would be a useful buffer between herself and Phil. She said fiercely, "It was Selwyn's idea to bring them. He forced me to come because, as far as Colville's is concerned, you're calling the tune. But that doesn't mean you can call the tune for me personally."

"I hope to persuade you to change your mind, Melissa."

"Well, you won't! You won't succeed, Phil," she reiterated to convince herself as much as him, "because my mind is made up."

"To marry Selwyn?"

"Not to marry you . . . not under any circumstances to marry you. Or," she added forcefully, "to have any other relationship with you than just business."

"That's not possible, and you know it. When two people have shared what we did, nothing can ever blot out the memory. It was something very special. Unique." Phil's tone suddenly changed, becoming low and pleading. "Give me another chance, Melissa; that's all I ask of you. Open the door of your heart just a tiny bit to let me through. Don't keep me shut out like this."

For long, throbbing seconds she met his burning gaze, praying that he wouldn't make a move to touch her, to take her into his arms . . . her heart hoping with equal fervor that he would do just that. She found herself saying, in a far-off voice that hardly sounded like her own, "You keep asking me if I'm going to marry Selwyn. For what it's worth, I'll tell you now that I've definitely decided not to—I think I always knew in my heart that I never could. But that still doesn't mean that . . ." She trailed to a stop.

"It's a beginning, Melissa," he murmured, and a smile softened the tautness of his features.

Chapter Fourteen

At Melissa's insistence she and Phil spent the next few hours discussing the minor problem with the contract, which was the ostensible reason for her presence in Lisbon. She succeeded in remaining cool and efficient and, to her great relief, Phil made no further attempt to get personal. Even during a short break for lunch at a neighboring café they stuck to discussing the wine trade, yet not for a single instant was Melissa unaware of the heavy emotional charge that flowed between them.

By midafternoon there was nothing further to be sorted out, so Melissa stood up and announced that she'd be going. Phil didn't demur, but offered to drive her back to the guesthouse.

"Thanks, but no. I shall enjoy the walk," she said distantly.

"As you wish." He crossed to open the door for her, then paused. "About tomorrow. I thought you might all like to visit—"

"We shall be returning home tomorrow," Melissa interrupted.

"But you can't. I thought you'd agreed that it wouldn't be fair to Jenny and Mark—or Lucy. You must give them a short vacation now that they're here."

She knew he was right, of course. "Well, if we do stay," she said defiantly, "there's no need for *us* to meet again. We've said everything there is to say."

He shook his head reprovingly. "You really are being difficult, Melissa. We'll discuss the matter over dinner this evening."

"No, Phil. Anyway, the children will be tired after their day out, so we'll be eating at the guesthouse."

"Okay," he said, with a shrug of his broad shoulders, "if that's how you want it to be."

Melissa's heart was hammering. Was this really the end? She couldn't believe, after all that Phil had said, that he was giving up so easily. She should be feeling glad, she told herself, but instead she felt torn apart by her conflicting emotions.

"I'll say goodbye, then," she muttered in a husky voice.

"*Até* à *vista*, Melissa . . . that's the Portuguese way of saying 'Until we meet again.'" He escorted her down to the street door and raised her hand to his lips in the gesture that always made her insides turn to jelly. "I'll be in touch very soon."

As she walked away Melissa could feel his gaze on her back, and it was all she could do not to turn around and run to him . . . to throw herself into his arms. Instinct, rather than conscious thought, led her footsteps back to the guesthouse. Once there she flopped into an armchair and covered her face with her hands.

Lucy and the children returned a couple of hours later, chattering about the wonderful day they'd had.

"I'm glad you all had such a good time." Melissa glanced at Lucy. "I hope you don't feel worn out, having had these two on your hands all day?"

"Not a bit. Anyway, I didn't have much to do. Miguel saw to everything . . . and paid for everything, too. I gather that Phil had told him not to spare the *escudos.*"

"Oh dear!"

Lucy glanced at her oddly. "Why 'oh dear'? I think it's very decent of him. He really is a fantastic man, isn't he?"

Melissa sidestepped that, becoming brisk about getting the children showered and into clean clothes. As soon as they were all ready they went down to the dining room, where they were shown to a table laid out for five.

"One too many," Melissa told the waitress with a smile.

"No, *senhora,* it is correct. You will be joined by Senhor Maxwell. He is waiting in the bar across the courtyard until we inform him that you are here."

"Oh, but . . ."

"What a lovely surprise," said Lucy, her blue eyes sparkling.

A couple of minutes later Phil came into the dining room. He wore a dark suit and a crisp white shirt, and looked so handsome that Melissa felt all the breath struck from her throat.

"Hi, everyone!" he greeted them. "I thought it would be a good idea for me to join you for dinner so we could make plans for tomorrow." He stood between the children. "How did you two enjoy your day? Was it fun?"

"Ooh, yes!" they chorused, and Jenny went on, "It was lovely up in the mountains, and Senhor Miguel told us the names of the wild flowers."

"I played football with some big boys on the beach," said Mark proudly, "and I beated them."

"I can tell that you're going to make one of the big teams when you're older," Phil said with a smile as he sat down in the empty chair between Lucy and Melissa. "We're very keen on soccer here in Portugal, you know. Have you ordered wine yet, Melissa?"

"Well, no . . ."

"Then allow me." He signaled the waitress. "And I know a rather special soda that Jenny and Mark will enjoy."

He kept up a flow of easy conversation all through the first part of the meal, and it was obvious to Melissa that the other three were delighted to have his company. When the dessert had been served, Phil said in a briskly practical voice, "Now, about tomorrow . . ." He looked at Melissa and Lucy. "I thought that you two would welcome a chance to browse around the shops. There are some really excellent ones in Lisbon, especially for shoes. So while you're doing that, why don't I take Jenny and Mark sailing on my boat?"

Before Melissa could open her mouth in protest the children were exclaiming with glee.

"But you can't," Melissa stammered. "Just you and the two children in a boat . . . it wouldn't be fair."

"I take it you really mean," he said with a smile of gentle reproach, "that it wouldn't be safe. But you needn't worry, Melissa. Jenny and Mark will be wearing life jackets, naturally, and I shall take along a young man of the utmost reliability. He's a member of the yacht club I belong to, and we often crew for one another. I've already checked that he's free tomorrow morning, so it's settled. I hope you two are good sailors," he went on, turning to the children.

Melissa only half heard him telling them about his boat and answering Lucy's questions about the best shops. She felt furious that Phil was manipulating her like this, but she didn't see how she could stop him without seeming a spoilsport. She knew what his game was: to win the children round to his side and thus undermine her defenses against him.

Well, he was going to discover that she wasn't easy to defeat!

Jenny and Mark chattered endlessly about the boat trip as she put them to bed, until she wanted to shout at them to be quiet. Lucy had gone off to the lounge to watch a pop music show on TV. Melissa sat in the sitting room of their suite and tried to concentrate on a book. Occasionally a streetcar clanked by on the street below. She tried to focus her thoughts on the sort of future she wanted for herself and her children. First off, she'd have to find a house—not too large, not too small, with a nice yard, of course, for Jenny and Mark to play in. It had to be near their school, and not too far from Pauline. She wanted to avoid daily visits, yet she mustn't cut her children off from their aunt.

But these thoughts only floated at the edges of her mind. The core of her thinking was dominated by images of Phil . . . the strong, clean lines of his face; those dark, compelling eyes; his rich-toned, sensuous voice; and the musky masculine scent of him . . . his powerful, athletic physique and the fluid rhythm of his movements . . . the hard strength of his muscles, and yet the exquisite gentleness of his hands when he touched her, caressed her . . . Dear heaven, would she always be haunted by memories of the bliss they had shared? How could she bear to think of a future that excluded Phil?

But nothing had changed since she had come back to Portugal, she reminded herself sternly. All her arguments against marrying Phil were just as valid as when he'd first proposed to her in England, and she mustn't let herself be swayed by his persuasiveness. It just wouldn't work; there was no hope that marriage between them would work. Phil wasn't the sort of man to take his marriage vows as a solemn commitment, and if she were ever foolish enough to let him talk her into marrying him—which he only wanted because she wouldn't agree to continue their affair—she would be selfishly risking her children's happiness. It would be uprooting them from everything that was safe and secure for a new life that would almost certainly end in disaster for everyone concerned.

"Oh, just look at that gorgeous sweater!" Lucy exclaimed. "I wonder if they have my size."

"Let's go in and see," said Melissa. "If so, I'll buy it for you."

"No, you mustn't. I've got plenty of cash. Dad gave me an extra fifty pounds spending money, and so far I haven't touched it."

"Well, why should you? You're here for my benefit, remember."

Lucy giggled. "Don't you believe it. I'm having a super time."

They were in the Chiado, the most fashionable shopping street in Lisbon, and every window was a fatal lure. To Lucy, anyway. Melissa found it impossible to concentrate on clothes, and she'd given up the attempt. Lucy, though, was having a super time. Her mood had been even livelier than usual since Phil had arrived at the guesthouse to collect the children, his crew member in tow. Carlos was a darkly attractive young man in his mid-twenties, and rather appealingly shy. But not too shy, in those brief few minutes, to have eyed Lucy with obvious admiration. "We could go dancing this evening, if you are free," he'd suggested hopefully.

Lucy had glanced at Melissa, who in turn had glanced at Phil. His tiny nod had satisfied her that Carlos was a suitable escort for the girl.

"Go if you want to, Lucy," she'd said with a smile.

"You really wouldn't mind?"

"Not a bit."

How strange it was, Melissa reflected inside the shop as Lucy tried on the sweater, that she trusted Phil's judgment about another man, when she didn't trust Phil himself. Of course, she didn't distrust his ability to take care of the children's safety while they were in his charge—not their physical safety. But what would be happening to their minds and emotions? It was too darned easy, she thought with a spurt of resentment, to win the hearts of children when your responsibility only extended over a few short hours. It would be a different matter if he had them around all the time. Phil wouldn't share her pride in Jenny and Mark, nor help her shoulder the problems and anxieties that children inevitably brought their parents.

"Hey, wake up, Melissa. How do you like it?" Lucy had emerged from the dressing room and twirled before her for inspection.

"It's lovely. That shade really suits you, Lucy."

"Great! Then I'll buy it. I'm going to wear it this evening."

While the sweater was being packed and Melissa paid for it, a new train of thought brought her a little shiver of dismay. Had Phil organized Lucy's date with Carlos this evening? He'd know that, with Lucy out of the way, once the children were in bed their mother would be alone.

The tall mast dipped gracefully before the wind as Phil changed course. Should he grab the opportunity that Carlos had so unexpectedly provided? It hadn't occurred to him that the young man might take such a shine to Lucy. He could go round to the guesthouse to see Melissa after dinner this evening, Phil thought. Would it be a wise move, or not? If only he knew how long she could be persuaded to remain in Portugal, then he'd know how much time he had to see through his campaign. Melissa was in a strange mood, and he knew that he had to tread warily with her.

A car had been hired for their morning's shopping, again chauffeured by the attentive Miguel. When Lucy had purchased all she wanted, and Melissa herself had bought one or two small items for the sake of appearances—a silk scarf and a pair of sandals—she asked Miguel to drive along the waterfront to see if they could pick out Phil's boat. In only a few minutes they had reached the district known as Belem, where the ornately carved facade of the Jeronimos Church, almost five centuries old, gleamed a dazzling white in the bright June sunshine. Miguel swung the car in at the yacht club entrance and was able to gain them admittance to the clubhouse as guests of Senhor Maxwell. He brought their drinks to their seats at an upstairs window, and after scanning the expanse of glittering water he pointed to a yacht with blue and white sails.

"There, *senhoras*, that is the *Bela Dona*."

"Belladonna?" queried Lucy, with a puzzled frown. "That's an odd name to give a boat."

Miguel considered this gravely. "I think in English it means Fair Lady, or Beautiful Lady, *senhora*."

"Oh, I see. I thought it was deadly nightshade—a very poisonous plant."

Melissa smiled. "I seem to remember, Lucy, that the juice of the plant was once used as a cosmetic. Hence the name."

And just the sort of name Phil might be expected to give his boat, she thought critically. A beautiful possession, like a woman. She strained her eyes and picked out the occupants of the graceful yacht: two men and two children, all wearing orange life jackets. She waved at the children, but of course they were too far out to spot her at the window.

Phil tried to imagine what Melissa would be doing at that very moment. Was she in one of the smart dress shops? Or had she perhaps stopped shopping to have coffee or a glass of wine? He smiled to himself. Wherever she was, he wished he were with her. It was a wish that never seemed to leave him.

They were scudding shoreward before the wind, and Phil watched Carlos pointing out landmarks to Jenny and Mark. They were a charming pair of children; intelligent, too. He hoped they'd soon settle down in Portugal and make lots of friends. The language wouldn't prove much of a problem for them. He imagined that Melissa would prefer to live mainly in Lisbon rather than at the *quinta*. His apartment wouldn't be large enough for them all; they'd have to find a suitable house. Melissa would probably choose to have Jenny and Mark educated in England when they were older. These matters would all have to be worked out when she agreed to marry him. *When,* not *if.* He refused to allow doubt to enter his mind.

"Look!" cried Mark. "There's Mummy."

"Where?" both Jenny and Phil exclaimed together.

"There, at that window. She's wearing her green dress. See, she's waving at us." He waved back in great excitement, and had to be restrained by Carlos from jumping to his feet and risking a fall over the side.

What did Melissa's presence signify? Phil wondered with a blend of fear and hope. Was she there to keep an eye on her children because she didn't fully trust them in his care? Or could it be that she wanted to be near him, as he did her?

They'd been spotted, Melissa realized, and she stood up and waved vigorously. As the yacht gracefully sailed nearer she could pick out the four figures with increasing clarity. Phil's gaze seemed to be fixed on her intently; she could almost feel its impact.

"How wonderful it would be to live here," Lucy said with a heartfelt sigh. She too was watching a man in the boat with yearning eyes. She was half in love with Carlos already, Melissa thought, after just a few minutes' conversation with him that morning. Life was so simple at Lucy's age, she brooded. Lucy would bask in the golden aura of Carlos's admiration while she was there, and she'd probably feel that her heart was breaking when the time came for them to part. But back home in England she would soon find a new boyfriend and be equally starry-eyed about him.

Why can't I be like that? Melissa thought with a surge of regret. Instead, meeting Phil and falling in love with him had condemned her to a bleak future. Yet she still couldn't find it in her heart to wish that she had never met him. She was a more complete person for knowing him, loving him, than she would ever have been had fate not brought them together. He'd given a new meaning to her life, a new dimension.

"He really is rather dishy," said Lucy breathlessly. "Don't you think?"

"Yes, oh yes!"

A violent blush stained Melissa's face as she realized that Lucy had meant Carlos. But fortunately Lucy wasn't looking at her. The color had still not quite vanished when they went downstairs to greet the returning sailors.

She's so incredibly beautiful, Phil thought as he skillfully swung the tiller to bring the *Bela Dona* round to a gentle halt. Each time I look at her I'm surprised at her loveliness.

The instant the boat was tied up the children rushed ashore and dashed over to their mother, both talking at once, full of excitement. She put an arm around each of them, hugging them close. She looks even more beautiful now, Phil found himself thinking. He wished with a spurt of desperation that he could join the close-knit family group and embrace them all. He strolled over and stood watching them with a smile.

"You two seem to have enjoyed yourselves," Melissa was saying.

"Ooh yes, Mummy, it was lovely," said Jenny, and Mark piped up, "It was ever so exciting, with great big huge waves."

For an instant she met Phil's glance in shared amusement at the child's exaggeration, but she looked away at once.

"I'm going to have a big boat when I grow up," Mark went on. "And Phil has promised to teach me how to sail it."

Phil watched her smile vanish and her brow crease in a frown. She muttered to him in an angry undertone, "You shouldn't make promises you can't keep."

"I don't. I'll enjoy giving Mark sailing lessons when he's older. Jenny, too, if she's interested."

"Phil . . ."

"What is it?"

She gestured helplessly. How could she talk to him with

Jenny and Mark tugging at her for attention? But talk to Phil she must. He couldn't be allowed to continue this underhanded strategy of winning her children over to his side.

Somehow or other they ended up eating at the clubhouse. "Join us if you like, Miguel," said Phil. "Or would you prefer to slip home to your wife for lunch?"

"I would, Senhor Dom Felipe," he said gratefully, and departed.

They were served with a huge platter of crisply coated fish fillets and another of golden french fries. "The bestest I've ever had," Mark pronounced.

Jenny wriggled in her seat. "Phil says there's a pony trap at the *quinta* that we'll be able to ride in, Mummy."

"At the *quinta?*" she repeated dazedly.

"I suggest," said Phil, "that we make an early start so as to get a nice long weekend in." He fielded the anxious question in Lucy's eyes by adding slyly, "Carlos says that he'll be able to join us for tomorrow, at least."

"I think Sunday, too," Carlos put in, looking at Lucy.

"Now see here—," Melissa began.

But Phil spoke across her. "It's a pretty little trap, Jenny, that used to belong to my two sisters when they were small, and I'll be able to borrow a pony to pull it. There's just room for two children and the driver—that'll be me."

Melissa gasped furiously. "Really, Phil, this is ridiculous. This is the first I've heard about going to the Quinta das Andorinhas."

"But we thought it would be a nice surprise for you, didn't we?" he asked imperturbably, turning to the children. "Mark wants to see the Cabo da Roca. That's the westernmost point of the continent. It can be very wild and stormy there, even on a summer day."

"Great big waves," said Mark, windmilling his arms expressively. "Bish, bang, crash, wallop!"

Melissa gave up trying to object. For her to refuse to spend the weekend at the *quinta* would be too cruel to the children. And, she mused, seeing Lucy's enraptured face as she gazed at Carlos, to her, too.

"Oh, very well then," she agreed resentfully.

Phil gave an inward sigh of relief. He had feared that by trying to hustle Melissa into spending the weekend at the *quinta* he might end up making her dig in her heels more strongly. Luckily, though, his gamble had paid off. Melissa's concern for her children's happiness had outweighed her objection to the idea. It was a respite, a breathing space. She couldn't think now of catching a plane home until Monday. By then, somehow or other, he had to convince her that it was in the best interest of all three of them— herself, Jenny, and Mark—that she should agree to marry him.

"Thank you, Melissa," he murmured fervently.

She gazed at him coldly. "You left me no alternative, did you?"

Mark screwed up his face. "What's alt . . . alternative?"

"Never you mind," said Melissa, breaking her rule of always answering her children's questions. "Have some more chips."

Chapter Fifteen

Phil came for them at nine-thirty. It was a glorious morning, with a milky summer haze that slowly rose to reveal the soft blue hills of Sintra ahead of them, mysterious and beckoning.

"Do you make lots of wine at your vineyard, Phil?" asked Jenny, who was sitting in the front seat with Mark, while Melissa and Lucy sat behind.

"Lots and lots," Phil replied cheerfully. "I'll show you everything at the winery, like I did your mother when she came to stay before. She found it very interesting, didn't you, Melissa?"

"Yes," she agreed, and left it at that.

"I 'spect I'll make wine when I grow up," Mark announced. He spread his arms expansively, nearly poking Phil in the eye. "A hundred bottles."

"A hundred isn't many, stupid," said his sister.

"It is! A hundred is ever such a lot, isn't it, Phil?"

"That depends on what you're talking about," he said diplomatically. "For instance, if I told you that I was a hundred years old, that would be a lot, Mark."

"Are you a hundred years old?"

"Not quite," Phil said, laughing.

"How old are you, then?"

"Mark," protested Melissa, "you mustn't . . ."

But Phil waved her to silence. "I'm thirty-eight."

Mark's tone suggested that he didn't see much difference between thirty-eight and a hundred. "Mummy's thirty-two. That's quite old, isn't it?"

"Not to me," said Phil with feeling. He ruffled Mark's fair hair affectionately, and Melissa felt a fresh wave of dismay at her children's easy acceptance of him.

Their arrival at the Quinta das Andorinhas was not marked with anything in the way of a welcome. Instead there was a general bustle of servants arranging little gilt chairs in the salon.

"I'd forgotten, Grandmama, that this was the day for one of your musical soirées," said Phil, having introduced Lucy and the children.

"Typically inconsiderate," Dona Carlota remarked acidly, "to both me and to your guests."

"Oh, come!" Phil protested. "We won't be in the way."

"It is to be a recital for oboe and strings," the old lady retorted. "Two noisy young children would be completely out of place."

"I agree, Senhora Dona Carlota," said Melissa smoothly, controlling her fury. "I'll make sure that Jenny and Mark don't intrude on your soirée; please don't worry about that."

Mark had been staring openmouthed at Dona Carlota's lined features. "Is Phil's granny a hundred years old?" he asked in a hoarse, penetrating whisper.

Melissa hustled him and Jenny out of the way before either of them could make matters worse, and they all followed the young maid who was waiting to show them upstairs to their rooms.

Phil caught up with them at the head of the staircase and drew Melissa to one side. "I apologize for my grandmother's rudeness," he said.

Melissa shrugged. "Dona Carlota was merely speaking her mind. She has no cause to like me."

"Oh, but she has. And I shall tell her so."

"I'd rather you didn't intervene on my behalf, Phil. I'm perfectly capable of looking after myself."

His dark eyes looked intently into hers. "Sometimes," he said softly, "I almost wish you weren't quite so capable. But you wouldn't be you if you were any different."

Melissa didn't reply; she simply hurried on to rejoin Lucy and the children.

Later that morning Phil escorted them around the vineyards and wineries. Remembering the tour he'd given her before, Melissa realized how skillfully he was adapting his explanations to interest Jenny and Mark. He had a real talent for mimicry, and she found herself listening as fascinatedly as the children and Lucy while he related a story, supposedly true, about the pixies who lived under the ground and came out at night. Depending on their mood they would either help with the vineyard work, or, if anybody had done something to vex them, they would pick off bunches of unripe grapes and leave them in piles as a warning.

At one point they came across a bright-eyed old man who, Phil told them, could do a lot of clever tricks. He obligingly performed some on the spot, making a coin disappear and reappear in the most startling places, like behind Jenny's ear and in the pocket of Mark's jeans. He had both the children in fits. Then came a ride on a tractor, and a visit to the bottling plant, where Jenny and Mark were allowed to stick on some labels, by hand and rather crookedly. Clearly those bottles would have to be redone later. Melissa found herself torn between admiration at the way Phil was keeping Jenny and Mark entertained, and anger at the way he was manipulating her through them. And, of course, she was angry at herself for letting it happen.

*   *   *

As arranged, Carlos arrived in time for lunch. Melissa was glad of his presence. He really was a pleasant young man, and he chatted throughout the meal in a very lively manner, which helped make Dona Carlota's stiff, disapproving attitude less noticeable.

"Mrs. Colville," he said at one point, turning to her eagerly, "will you permit me to escort Lucy to Pena Palace this afternoon?"

"Of course, Carlos." She smiled at Lucy. "You'll enjoy Pena, Lucy; it's a marvelous place. And you needn't hurry back if you want to do something afterwards."

"You're sure you don't mind?"

"Quite sure."

"Well, then, how would it be if I were to take charge of Jenny and Mark tomorrow and leave you free? Carlos says we could all go to his parents' home at Cascais. He's got a younger brother and sister, and . . . and there's a swimming pool."

"I'm not sure about that," Melissa parried. "I'll have to think about it, Lucy."

"Oh please, Mummy, *please!*" the children chorused.

"Well, I suppose it would be all right."

"While you're gone," put in Phil, addressing Jenny and Mark, "shall I take your mother out somewhere?"

They clearly thought that this was a brilliant idea. "Mummy likes going for long walks," Mark confided. "More than we do," he added with feeling, perhaps remembering the few treks they'd made around Hastings.

"Thanks for the tip," said Phil, laughing.

Melissa shot him an angry glance. Phil thought he was so clever, maneuvering her into situations that she couldn't easily escape from. She wished that she had refused to let Lucy take the children to Carlos's home, but it was too late now.

* * *

"Grandmama, I have to talk to you," Phil said, entering her bedroom when she'd called in response to his knock. "There's something I need to make clear."

Dona Carlota had retired upstairs for a nap as soon as lunch was over. She was stretched out on a chaise longue, a gray silk shawl draped over her legs.

"What is it, Felipe?" Her black eyes were wary, hooded.

"Melissa Colville is the woman I intend to marry," Phil announced in a quiet, distinct voice. "I expect you to treat her with the respect befitting my future wife."

He watched his grandmother fight to control her fury. "Have you asked her to marry you?"

"I have. Several times, actually, but so far she's said no."

Dona Carlota's eyes flashed in astonishment. "But I don't understand. It is some stratagem, undoubtedly, to drive a hard bargain. On behalf of her children, perhaps?"

"It is no stratagem, Grandmama. Melissa believes that she doesn't want me—not as her husband."

Conflicting emotions fought a battle on the old lady's age-worn face. Clearly, Phil thought with sad amusement, the possibility that any woman would turn down the chance of marrying her grandson seemed in her eyes to be a gross insult to the family. And yet . . . she was immensely thankful, too. If Melissa Colville had refused him, there was still a chance for her cherished hopes of finding him a suitable Portuguese wife.

"I have been thinking, Felipe," she said carefully. "You may remember the Teixeiras of Coimbra. . . . You knew the elder son at school, I believe. Apparently the daughter has turned into a real beauty and—"

"No, Grandmama!"

"But—"

"I said no." Phil still spoke quietly, but injected a warning note into his voice—a trick he had learned from her. "I have already chosen my wife. I am going to marry Melissa Colville."

"But if she has refused you . . ."

"She will be persuaded to change her mind by persistence on my part. And I won't tolerate any attempt at subversion from you. Is that clearly understood?"

Dona Carlota regarded him with a pained expression. "All I want—all I have ever wanted—is your happiness, Felipe."

"Then if you truly mean that . . . if you rate my happiness above your exaggerated sense of family pride, you will make my task easier by welcoming Melissa and her children and making them feel at home here. Because, understand me, Grandmama, the Quinta das Andorinhas *will* become home to them. There's nothing you can do to prevent that. So don't even try."

Her old eyes flared again, but there was reluctant admiration in the look she gave him. "You are so like your father, Felipe. Edwin Maxwell was a strong, determined man who would brook no interference in his plans. I warned your mother that he was unsuitable—"

"Just because he was an American," Phil interrupted. "Or rather, because he was *not* Portuguese. But don't you see, Grandmama, such narrow ideas of nationality are dying in the modern world. We are all part of the human race. My father was a fine man who happened to be American; Melissa is a fine woman who happens to be English. She will bring, just as my father brought, new strength to the family."

Dona Carlota smiled sadly. "You must allow me to cling to my prejudices, Felipe."

"So long as you keep them to yourself." Then he smiled and kissed her withered cheek. "You and I will never seriously quarrel, Grandmama. We understand one another too well for that. We're two of a kind, aren't we?"

"Oh? In what way, might I inquire?"

Phil grinned. "We're both fighters. Right?"

The old lady's blue-veined hand came up to cover his

where it rested lightly on her shoulder. Phil felt the soft pressure of her fingers. His grandmother was growing frail, he thought, but she still remained strong in spirit. He loved her, and he wanted her strength on his side in his fight to win Melissa. He believed he had it now.

Jenny and Mark were running up and down a flight of stone steps at the end of the terrace while they waited for Phil, who had gone to fetch the pony and trap for the drive he'd promised them. Melissa, from where she was sitting on a carved stone seat, enjoying the feel of the hot sun on her face and bare arms, could hear them squabbling amiably as to which of them should sit next to him. It was lucky, she thought, that Dona Carlota's bedroom was on the far side of the house; otherwise she'd feel obliged to keep the children quiet. As it was, they weren't doing any harm, thank heaven.

Melissa smiled to herself. Despite everything, despite her lingering fury at having been manipulated by Phil, she couldn't pretend that she wasn't glad to be there. There was something about the place that seduced the senses. It was so incredibly beautiful. She felt an ache deep within her that almost made her want to cry. With every breath came the fragrance of lavender and golden broom and roses, and there were birds everywhere, filling the air with their song. Looking up, she could watch the flight of the swallows that had given the Quinta das Andorinhas its name, and through the trees she could see a flotilla of swans gliding serenely across the sun-kissed waters of the lake. The lake where she and Phil had . . .

No, she mustn't dwell on that. She must keep a padlock on her emotions for the remainder of this visit to Portugal. Once she was home in England she would have to pull herself together and start building a new life for herself . . . start making things happen the way *she* wanted them. Melissa sighed. The trouble was that she felt so hopelessly confused now that she no longer had the slightest idea what she did or didn't want. Phil dominated her thoughts to such a degree that nothing else seemed to have any reality. . . .

Through the open french doors of the salon behind her came the sound of a piano—just a single, pure note. And then a simple little melody that was very familiar: Beethoven's "Für Elise." Melissa listened a moment, absently, then gave a gasp of horror as she realized that it was Jenny playing one of her practice pieces. On that fabulous antique piano! She leapt to her feet and rushed indoors.

"Jenny, stop that at once! You mustn't—" Melissa broke off abruptly as she saw the diminutive figure of Phil's grandmother standing in the shadows by the double doors. "I'm so sorry, Senhora Dona Carlota."

At that moment Phil called cheerfully from the hall, "Right, all set. Come along, you two; your carriage awaits."

Jenny slid down from the piano stool, casting an apologetic look at her mother as she closed the hinged lid with exaggerated care. Then she fled with Mark, who'd been hovering at her elbow.

"I really am sorry about that, Senhora Dona Carlota," Melissa said again. "Jenny didn't realize, of course. She plays at home whenever she feels like it, you see, and seeing your piano, she—"

"The child has talent," the old lady interrupted in her rich, imperious voice. "Are you aware of that, Mrs. Colville?"

Astonished not to be getting the diatribe she'd expected about ill-bred children, Melissa said hesitantly, "Well, I know that she's making good progress for her age."

"She has a musical sensibility that goes beyond the general run. It is quite evident to me. Does she not have a teacher who has informed you of her talent?"

"Miss Carstairs is quite pleased with Jenny," Melissa told her.

"Who is this Miss Carstairs? What are her qualifications?"

"I don't know, precisely, but she teaches a number of children in the village."

"That is worthless. Your daughter needs proper professional guidance. Something will have to be done about it, without delay. Talent must be continually stretched to achieve its full potential."

"I'm sure you're right," Melissa said, clinging to her temper. "But so far Jenny has shown no more than a moderate liking for the piano. I have no intention of forcing her unless she does."

"A child will always take the easy path and avoid hard work unless pushed," the old lady persisted. "You are her mother; you have the authority."

"Exactly! I *am* Jenny's mother, so I think it's up to me to decide what's best for her."

Oddly, Dona Carlota didn't look wholly displeased at this set-down. "Hah! Another obstinate one. So be it. Well, you'll have plenty of problems to work out between the two of you."

"I'm sorry, I don't understand you." But she was talking to an empty doorway. Dona Carlota was gone.

Chapter Sixteen

Sitting in Phil's car as they headed for the coast, Melissa felt as if she were being swept along by a swift-flowing tide. In part of her mind she still felt angry with Phil, yet it was becoming increasingly difficult for her to sustain that anger. His dynamic charisma had seeped into every last cell of her being. Her love for him surged and pulsed through her veins with every beat of her heart. Weakly, against all her intentions, she had found herself agreeing to spend the day alone with Phil while Lucy and Carlos took charge of the children. They would drive somewhere pleasant, Phil had said, and then walk and have a picnic.

It had been bright and sunny when they had prepared to set out soon after breakfast. Melissa had dressed in tan slacks and a pale yellow short-sleeved cotton top. She had been astonished when Phil advised her to take along a sweater and a raincoat.

"A raincoat?" She'd glanced meaningfully at the serene blue sky. "Surely it's not going to rain today?"

"There's a storm blowing up out at sea," he explained.

"It might well reach land before long." He grinned. "No, I'm not a prophet, Melissa. I heard it on the radio."

Difficult as it had been for Melissa to believe in an imminent storm back at the Quinta das Andorinhas, when they reached the coast road the wind was blowing fiercely, bending the trees. She could see massive waves rolling in and smashing against the rocky cliffs in a wild fury, throwing up great white plumes of spray that sparkled in the sunshine. When Phil parked the car and they got out, they had to fight against the blast. Melissa was glad now to have the sweater.

"Is it too much for you?" he asked, shouting to make himself heard from the other side of the car.

"No, I think it's exhilarating."

"Good! We always seem to enjoy the same things." Phil reached into the car and pulled out a knapsack containing the food he'd had packed for their lunch. "All set for our walk?"

At first they followed a clifftop path, only attempting to exchange the odd word or two against the din of the wind and the crashing waves. After a few minutes, though, Phil took another path that crossed the road and headed inland down a slope of scrubby pine trees, golden gorse bushes and various exotic wild flowers that Melissa couldn't name.

As soon as they were in the lee of the high cliffs the force of the wind was lessened to little more than a gusty breeze. Melissa's cheeks were glowing from the exposure, but luckily she'd tied her hair back in a ponytail, and only a few stray tendrils had escaped to whip about her ears.

"You look even more beautiful like this," said Phil, catching her eye as they scrambled over a broken wall.

"I wish you wouldn't say such things."

He lifted an eyebrow. "Not say what's uppermost in my mind?"

"I'd rather you didn't," she told him in a stiff voice.

Phil considered her silently, then said, "Jenny and Mark are enjoying themselves, aren't they?"

"I guess so," Melissa agreed reluctantly. "But that still doesn't make it a good idea for us to have come here this weekend."

"Why not?"

Because I find it too disturbing to be near you! she thought. But she couldn't tell him that. Instead she said, "For one thing, your grandmother isn't any too pleased—which is understandable."

"She hasn't been rude to you again?" Phil asked, frowning.

"No, not really." Honesty made her add, "Dona Carlota has been quite tolerant, all things considered. When she had good reason to be annoyed, yesterday afternoon, she wasn't."

"Yesterday afternoon? What happened?"

"It was while you were fetching the pony trap. Jenny wandered in from the terrace and started tinkering with your grandmother's piano. Of course I stopped her at once, but Dona Carlota had heard."

"Why did you stop Jenny?"

"Why? That piano is a magnificent instrument, Phil. It must be worth thousands of pounds."

"I daresay it is. But what else is a piano for except playing on? What did my grandmother say, exactly?"

"She told me that Jenny has considerable musical talent, and that she ought to be receiving proper professional guidance."

Phil smiled, looking pleased. "So that explains why she changed her mind and had Jenny attend her soirée. When it comes to music, Melissa, my grandmother knows what she's talking about. She's been responsible for launching more than one young person on a musical career."

"I'm sure she meant well, Phil, only . . . well, I had to tell her that I'd never force Jenny into anything that she didn't really want for herself. Up until now Jenny has shown only a moderate interest in the piano, though I suppose she could have inherited some musical talent from my mother. It certainly skipped me."

Phil felt well satisfied. This was another sign—he'd seen several already—that his grandmother was coming round to accepting Melissa. A complete volte-face would be asking too much of her, but the fact that she wanted to interfere in Jenny's musical education indicated that she expected them to be around in future. He wasn't in the least concerned about his grandmother's attempt to play the autocrat; he could handle that. If, that was, Melissa needed any help from him. She'd already proven herself more than capable of dealing with her domineering sister-in-law back in England. Perhaps, he thought with an inner smile, the old lady was in for a pleasant surprise in Melissa. She respected strength and despised weakness.

But time was running out for him, he remembered with a flash of panic. He still hadn't found a way of breaking through the barrier Melissa had erected against him. Whenever they were together, even in the presence of other people, the emotional current between them flowed strongly. He knew that Melissa was just as aware of it as he was, yet she still obstinately refused to acknowledge that the two of them were meant for one another.

Phil had a wild urge to grab hold of Melissa, to pull her into his arms and kiss her until they were both breathless. But he was terribly afraid that any such move would be fatal.

They walked on for a couple of miles, together but very apart, making stilted conversation as they descended into a wooded glen. The sun still shone, but fitfully now, as dark clouds raced across the sky. They found a sheltered spot for their picnic where they could sit with their backs against an outcrop of mossy rock—though he noted that Melissa was careful to keep a space between them.

The family cook, a woman who'd been Phil's secret ally since his boyhood, had prepared a splendid lunch for them:

crusty bread with spicy chicken drumsticks, tiny sausages and sliced smoked ham, fresh curd cheese, sweet custard tarts and a bottle of rosé wine that was wrapped in a cloth to keep it cool. Yet Melissa ate with no more appetite than he did.

Afterward, with the picnic things still spread around them, Phil summoned up his courage and began, "Melissa, we've got to talk."

"We've talked enough, Phil. More than enough." There was no concession in her voice, and Phil's heart plummeted.

"Are you still determined to return home tomorrow?" he asked. "Won't you stay a bit longer? Please, Melissa."

"I should have left before the weekend," she said coldly. "I only stayed because you made it impossible for us to leave without the children and Lucy being very disappointed. But it hasn't got you anywhere, Phil. Nothing has changed . . . not really."

"For heaven's sake," he burst out, "it's madness for us to part like this. Surely you can see that? I'm asking you once again to marry me, Melissa. We—"

She stopped him with a swift, scathing glance. "That seems to get thrown in as your trump card whenever it looks as if there's no other way you can have me. What is it with you, Phil . . . can't you bear to be rejected by a woman?"

"I can't bear to be rejected by you," he said in a low voice.

Nervously, with trembling fingers, Melissa broke a crust into pieces and tossed it toward the hovering sparrows. "Back in England, when you first proposed to me, that was a sudden impulse, right? I bet the thought of marrying me hadn't so much as entered your head till then." Phil made no comment, and she pressed him. "I *am* right, aren't I? Why not be honest with me, Phil? I bet that in your heart of hearts you were glad that I turned you down. But then your pride started needling you again, so you used this ridiculous ploy to bring me to Portugal. But you're quite safe, Phil; I'm not going to accept you, however much you plead with me."

Phil was silent for a long moment while he pensively gathered a couple of small pebbles and tossed them in his hand.

"Okay, I *will* be honest with you, Melissa," he said at last. "It's true that I felt a sense of relief when you refused me in England. When I got home I even called myself all kinds of a fool for having proposed to you. I argued that what you and I have between us, wonderful though it is, wouldn't be enough for marriage."

"Which is precisely what I've said all along," she reminded him.

"No, listen to me," Phil insisted. "I'm telling you what I *did* think, when I first got home. You asked me to be honest with you, and that's what I'm doing. In those first few days after I got back I made a list of all the objections against marrying you to try to convince myself that it was for the best you'd turned me down. You weren't Portuguese, you had two children who would have to be transplanted here, and—"

"They're valid objections," she broke in, "and they still apply. We're just too different for it to work, Phil."

"I don't agree. I've thought about this over and over, and there's nothing impetuous about my asking you to marry me now. Our differences don't matter, darling, not compared to the fact that we want each other, need each other. My mother and father were from different countries, different cultures, and it worked for them. They were wonderfully happy, and we could be, too."

"It's not a question of nationality," she said in a sad voice. "Our ideas about marriage itself are totally opposed. You've given me a good idea of the kind of wife you want when you eventually do get married. I'm not that kind of woman, Phil; I'm nothing like her."

"Obviously we'd both have to make adjustments, darling. But what married couple doesn't?"

"Adjustments? The things I'm talking about are basics, Phil. Our whole philosophies of life are different."

"But I need you, Melissa," he said with an imploring look. "I just can't imagine life without you. I'm ready to change in all kinds of ways. I'd make you happy; I know I would."

Oh, yes, she agonized, Phil would make her deliriously happy for a time, but what then? Inevitably his passion would wane, and he would start to regret his impetuosity. He'd become increasingly irritated with the two young children for whom he'd so rashly accepted responsibility. And then the pain would start for her . . . the unbearable pain of loving a husband who no longer wanted her.

Unnoticed by them both, dark clouds had drawn across the sky. Suddenly it began to rain, large drops that stung Melissa's face.

"We'd better get moving," Phil said, scrambling to his feet and hastily gathering up the remains of the picnic. From the knapsack he pulled out their rolled-up raincoats. "We'd better put these on before we get soaked."

Fortunately, Melissa discovered, their walk had been on a curving route, and the car was scarcely a mile away. But as they came out of the sheltered glen onto the clifftop again the full force of the Atlantic gale struck them. Giant waves were breaking thunderously all along the rocky shore.

Before they reached the car Phil halted abruptly and stared down, obviously alerted by something.

"What is it?" Melissa shouted. Phil raised an arm and pointed. At first she could see nothing but the water foaming over a line of rocks that looped out to sea. Then she discerned a small fishing boat that was stranded there. Its tall mast had snapped and lay at a drunken angle, and its hull appeared to have been badly damaged. The only sign of life was a small head raised above the pointed prow. As they stood there an arm waved in a frantic plea for help.

"He's no more than a boy," Phil said. "There's no sign of the men who would have been aboard with him. He'll be scared out of his wits. I must go to him."

"Go to him? But how . . . ?"

Phil broke into a run, heading for the car, and Melissa jogged along beside him.

"Thank heaven I've got a rope in the trunk," he grunted. "I'll use it to get down the cliff. I hope to God it's long enough. You'll have to go and fetch help, Melissa. You'll be able to handle the Jaguar, won't you?"

"Yes, but . . ."

"Now listen carefully," Phil said as they reached the car and he hurriedly unlocked the trunk. "There's no time for me to go over it twice." He pointed. "Follow the road here for about a mile, then turn left at the crossroads. Left, Melissa. You go over a stone bridge and past some farm buildings. Ignore them. After a grove of eucalyptus trees you'll see a small stone house with pointed windows. The man who lives there—he's a retired professor of history— speaks good English, and he has a phone. Tell him what's happened, and ask him to contact the coastal rescue people. We're at Praia do Adanaia—here, I'll write that down." He found a scrap of paper in his pocket and scribbled the name. "Can you manage all that?" he asked as he hauled out a large coil of rope.

Melissa nodded. "Yes, I can manage. But what about you? Oh, Phil . . . it'll be so dangerous."

He stepped up to her and, drawing her hard against him with his free hand, kissed her roughly on the mouth. Then he let go, slammed the trunk and unlocked the driver's door. "Now, get going," he said, handing her the keys. "There's no time to waste."

In a daze Melissa scrambled behind the wheel and started the car. She glanced back and saw Phil silhouetted against the steel gray sky as he looped the rope around a rocky projection. Then he was suddenly gone. She had a wild impulse to stop the car and run back to him, to check that he was all right, but she steeled herself to keep going.

She followed her instructions like an automaton, her mind locked on Phil. Even if he got down the cliff safely, how could he survive the scramble across those jagged rocks, lashed by the raging sea? And if he reached the boat, how long could that battered shell hold together? She shuddered and felt sick. . . .

Here was the crossroads. Left? Right? Left, he'd said. Two minutes more and she crossed the stone bridge, then passed the farm, a huddle of buildings and not a sign of life. And yet it was a temptation to stop there and seek help. But Phil had said not to. Here at last was the grove of eucalyptus trees. Just beyond it, as he'd said, was the house. Melissa drove in between a pair of wooden gates, which stood open, and skidded to a halt outside the front door.

The wind was less fierce there, but the rain beat down more heavily. Melissa ran up the steps to a small porch. There was a bellpull, which made a loud jangling inside as she tugged it, and she underlined her urgency by hammering on the stout wooden panels with her fists. She heard a voice from inside; then after a few moments the door opened an inch or two and a frightened face peered out. It belonged to a woman in her forties, short and plump, wearing a pink nylon overall.

"There's a fishing boat smashed on the rocks," Melissa gasped out. "Please telephone for help to be sent at once." She fumbled in her pocket for the scrap of paper Phil had given her, and held it out. "Here, at this place. Please hurry."

The woman glanced at the name Phil had written down and mouthed it silently. Then she looked back at Melissa with blank, uncomprehending eyes. Dear God, Melissa thought in anguish, she doesn't understand English. "Where is the professor?" she demanded. "I must speak to him." Desperately trying to recall the odd phrases of Portuguese she'd picked up, she rushed on. *"Onde é o professor?"* After she'd repeated it twice the woman shook her head and said something incomprehensible, gesturing widely. Melissa gathered that the professor was out—which meant that somehow or other she had to handle the emergency herself.

"Telephone?" she said. *"Onde?"* She mimed the act of dialing, then speaking on the phone, trying all the while to convey the urgency of the situation. The woman nodded and beckoned her to follow. The phone was in the living room, on a windowsill, and Melissa ran to pick it up—then she paused in dismay.

"English," she said, pointing to her mouth. *"Inglês.* Someone who speaks *Inglês.*" Oh heavens, how could she explain? She tried again. *"Policia conversa Inglês."*

The woman still looked blank; then suddenly she understood. She took the phone and dialed a number, then spoke in rapid Portuguese. There was a wait; then she spoke again. Nodding triumphantly to Melissa, she handed over the phone.

Her heart in her mouth, Melissa asked, "Do you speak English?"

"Sim, a little. What is your wish, *senhora?"*

"It's very urgent," Melissa said. "An emergency. There is a boat, a fishing boat, stranded on the rocks. Do you understand?"

"What is this stranded?"

"Shipwreck. Smashed on the rocks. Disaster!"

"Ah, *desastre! Onde* . . . where is this boat?"

She read out the name Phil had written down, but it seemed to mean nothing to him. She tried again, stressing a different syllable, but it was useless. Frantically, Melissa turned to the woman, conveying by gestures that she wanted her to tell the man the name of the place. Luckily the woman caught on at once this time and did so.

"Do you understand now?" Melissa asked the police officer when the phone had been handed back to her. "Will you contact the coastal rescue service?"

"Yes, yes, I understand. Help will come *pronto, pronto."*

"You're quite sure you understand how urgent it is?" she said agitatedly. "My friend and I just saw one person on board, and he looked like a young boy. There must be others—probably injured. My friend is trying to climb down the cliffs to them, but it's very difficult and dangerous. The sea is very rough." Suddenly inspired, she added, "My friend is Senhor Felipe Maxwell of the Quinta das Andorinhas. Maybe you know him?"

"Ah, yes indeed, *senhora*. Please do not worry. Help will come with all speed."

Melissa didn't linger at the house. With a gabble of thanks to the woman she ran out to the car and headed straight back to the coast. Up on the clifftop the gale seemed to have intensified, and when she climbed out of the car she was almost blown over. She fought her way to the edge of the cliff, feeling sick with apprehension. She felt an enormous flood of relief when she saw that Phil had safely reached the wreck. Through the spray that foamed over the boat it was difficult to see what was happening, but it looked as if Phil was attending to someone who lay concealed by the bulwark. At that moment Phil glanced up and caught sight of her. He waved his arm. Melissa shouted that help was on the way, but her voice was torn from her by the wind and whisked away. She gave a thumbs-up gesture, and Phil acknowledged in the same way. The boy, who didn't look to be more than twelve years old, was clinging tightly to Phil's shoulder in a state of desperate fear. And no wonder! The boat was being pounded by the brutal waves and looked as if it might break up at any moment.

Melissa hoped to heaven that help would come soon. But how would it come? Would even a lifeboat venture close enough to those fearsome-looking rocks in this rough sea? But within a few minutes the sound of a helicopter was borne on the wind to her; then she picked out its shape flying in low over the water. Melissa watched as the machine banked steeply, then seemed to hang directly above the wrecked boat. A door slid back, and a figure in a bulky life jacket stood briefly in the opening before descending on the end of a cable.

The rescue was by no means easy. It must have taken all the pilot's skill to keep the helicopter steady as it was buffeted by the gale. Once the man on the cable hit the water as the copter suddenly dropped several feet; then he was clear again. Swinging above his target, he dropped something to Phil on a length of rope—a cradle of some sort. Melissa watched, agonized, as waves broke continually over the stricken vessel, each one threatening to smash it to pieces on the rocks. Then at a signal from Phil the injured man was winched upward toward the helicopter. As soon as the lift was safely completed the whole operation was repeated for a second injured man. Finally Phil and the boy were taken off together, the boy seeming so numb with fright that Phil had to hold him in his arms. Melissa watched as they were lifted clear of the boat and carried upward, watched as helping hands dragged them into the cabin of the helicopter. At once the machine rose and headed away.

Phil was safe—that was the one thought that sang in Melissa's mind. Then she realized that the helicopter was circling, coming back to where she stood on the clifftop. Phil appeared at the cabin's door. He waved to her, then came dropping down on the cable. He landed close beside her, released himself from the harness and let it go, giving a wave of thanks. The next moment she and Phil were in each other's arms, and Melissa wasn't even aware of the helicopter's departure. Phil was wet through, his clothes beneath the waterproof jacket a sodden mess, but she clung to him joyfully.

"Oh, Phil," she sobbed. "I was so afraid for you. Were those men badly hurt?"

"They'll be okay. One had a broken leg, which I managed to splint. The other man had put his shoulder out and had a bad cut on his forehead; he seemed a bit concussed. Still, I think it was the boy I felt sorriest for. The poor kid was terrified. Thank heaven we came along and saw them when we did. That boat wouldn't have lasted much longer."

Melissa had been remembering what Phil had told her when she had first been in Portugal about the dangerous lives of the fishermen along the wild Atlantic coast. She was thankful that this was one time when tragedy had been averted.

"You've got to get out of these wet clothes, Phil," she said with anxious concern. "I think we could go to the professor's house, couldn't we? He wasn't at home, but—"

"Not home? That's very unusual. How did you manage, Melissa?"

"There was a woman—his housekeeper, I should think, not his wife—and I was able to make her understand enough to phone the police. Between us we told them to send help." She giggled, feeling light-headed from relief. "I thought that dropping your name might add a bit of weight, Phil, and it looks as if it did. That helicopter turned up mighty quickly, didn't it?"

"Quickly? I guess so, even if it didn't seem like that to me." He kissed her. "You did marvelously, darling. Look, the best thing is for us to go to the chalet. It's only about six miles along the coast."

"Oh, good!" She glanced at him anxiously. "Are you sure you're okay, Phil?"

"I'm fine." The look he gave her was charged with tenderness. "You were really worried about me, weren't you?"

"I was worried sick. I was terrified that you'd be . . ." She couldn't finish; she couldn't put her horror into words.

The drive took only a few minutes. Once they were inside the chalet Phil headed straight for the stairs. "I'll find something to change into," he said. "I won't be long. You know where the drinks are kept."

Melissa slipped off her raincoat and shook out her wet hair; then she went to pour drinks—a largish brandy for Phil and a smaller one for herself. She sipped it, trying to calm the trembling of her limbs. Now that the danger was finally over, reaction had set in. There was a large basket of logs by the old stone fireplace, and she noticed some kindling, too. A fire would be a good idea. Within a minute or so flames were curling and crackling around the dry wood.

"That looks great!" Phil had returned. He wore creased blue jeans and a navy sweatshirt, and he was rubbing his wet hair with a towel. He tossed this aside and came to her, taking the glass she handed him and downing the brandy in a single gulp. "That's better."

For a few moments they looked at one another, smiling tentatively. Then suddenly they came together in a joyful embrace, their mouths meeting in a deep, consuming kiss that made Melissa feel faint from the wild rush of emotion that surged through her. She could feel Phil trembling as much as she was. When at last their clinging lips broke apart, Phil buried his face in the rain-damp softness of her hair.

"Melissa . . . darling Melissa. For God's sake don't walk out on me now. If you were so afraid for me this afternoon, it means that you must care."

Melissa couldn't hold back her tears. "Oh, Phil . . . don't you understand? If it were only myself involved, I'd take the chance of marrying you . . . I'd be willing to risk it all ending in misery."

"Misery? What are you talking about?" His hands on her shoulders, Phil pushed her back to look searchingly into her eyes. "You and I would be happy for always, darling . . . always and forever. I love you so much."

Melissa's heartbeat faltered, and she felt as if everything were spinning around her. All she wanted was to sink back into Phil's arms and press herself against his warm flesh, to let him make love to her once again and to escape from reality in their mutual passion. But somehow she found the strength to hold fast to her determination.

"You don't love me, Phil," she said sadly.

"I do," he insisted, and his fingers dug into her flesh almost painfully. "I do love you, Melissa."

"Then the word means something quite different to us. I won't risk my children's future. That's what marrying you would mean."

"But I want Jenny and Mark, too. I really do."

"Just as a means of getting me." She heaved a sigh. "For heaven's sake, Phil, you can't play fast and loose with people's lives just to get your own way. Especially children's lives."

Phil started to protest once more, then broke off. When he began to speak again it was with quiet firmness. "Earlier on, before the rain started, I was trying to be honest with you, and I'll try again now. I admit that when I first asked you to marry me that day in England, I saw Jenny and Mark as a necessary encumbrance. If I wanted you, I had to take them, too. But it's not that way now. I've liked your children from the start, Melissa, but it wasn't until you brought them here and I got to know them better that I saw them in a totally different light."

"How do you mean?"

"I can tell you the exact moment the change happened. Remember on Friday after I'd taken them sailing? You were waiting on the quayside, and they ran to you, and you hugged them. I felt . . . it's difficult to describe what I felt. Sort of shut out. I had a longing to be accepted as one of you, the four of us as close as the three of you already were. I saw then what I'd never seen clearly before: that Jenny and Mark wouldn't just be an obligation that came along with you. They're an essential part of you. The you I want, the you I fell in love with, is the devoted mother of those two children. I want you all, *querida;* I want to make all three of you happy. I'll work hard to make Jenny and Mark love me. And you, too. Your love, Melissa, would be the most wonderful gift I could ever receive."

She made a small, inarticulate sound, then somehow found her voice. "You already have my love, Phil. I've loved you since . . . oh, how can I be sure when? The first day we met, I think. Certainly the next day. It was all I could do not to tell you how I felt."

"Why didn't you?" he asked with a tender smile. "If you *knew?*"

"Because I couldn't believe that you loved me. Not in the way that I interpret love."

"I think I loved you all along. But I didn't realize it myself. It seems unbelievable now that at first I actually imagined that I'd be able to get you out of my system." He gave a hollow laugh. "When I think how I . . ."

"Go on, Phil," she prompted him.

His dark eyes were clear and candid. "As I said, I tried to kid myself that I was actually glad you'd turned me down. I tried to convince myself that I didn't need you by dating other women. But it was a hopeless failure. . . . Thoughts of you completely filled my mind. It had to be you, you, you."

"That sounds like an obsession, Phil," she murmured.

"No," he answered soberly. "It's love. I didn't recognize it because I've never been in love before." He drew her closer. "I love you, *querida*, and I want to marry you. Having you and yours with me, to love and cherish, is the only future I can bear to contemplate. Say yes . . . if you have any compassion in your heart."

Melissa hesitated, scared by the very strength of her need for him. When her whole being, body and soul, yearned for him with this kind of wild desperation, dared she take such an irrevocable decision?

Phil must have read her mind. He said urgently, "The most important thing in the world to you is your children's happiness; you've made that clear to me. But think, darling, could Jenny and Mark ever be truly happy if you weren't happy too? If you were *miserable,* as you certainly would be, because you had thrown away your chance of happiness? I know that you're concerned about their future, and rightly so, but I promise you—I swear to you—that as their stepfather I'll devote myself to their well-being. I've had lots of time to think about this, and I know it can work. We can give them whatever they need here in Portugal. There are English-speaking schools here, and they'll soon pick up the language and make friends. And we can have Jenny's pony shipped over here. Oh, darling . . . you must say yes. I'm not trying to pretend that there won't be problems, complications, but we'll overcome them."

Melissa suddenly recalled Edward's words. "Be a winner," he'd urged her. The winners, he'd said, were the ones who faced up to life's complications and overcame them. But it wasn't the memory of Edward's advice that convinced her. She knew now that she could no longer hold out against the overwhelming strength of her love for Phil—and the knowledge that he loved her in return.

Tears welled up again as she nodded silently.

"So you will marry me?" There was still a hint of anxiety in his voice.

Melissa's throat was so tight that the words wouldn't come. At last she murmured huskily, "Yes, Phil, I'll marry you."

"Oh, darling. My wonderful, beautiful darling." He gave a little laugh of triumph, of relief. "You just can't know what terror I've lived through these past few days, afraid that I wouldn't be able to convince you, that you'd escape me again. But I would never have given up, *querida*. *Never!*"

Neither of them could quite believe in the happiness they had suddenly found as they clung together, not kissing, just holding each other. It was a moment to be savored slowly, the dawning of the realization that they had the rest of their lives together.

Phil's hand came up to caress her cheek. "Soon . . . it must be very soon, *querida*."

"Yes, soon."

Later, as they sat together on the sofa, arms entwined, with the fire blazing before them, Phil asked, "Will you want our wedding to be in England, darling?"

She smiled. "I think so. The only thing is, Phil, what about your grandmother? Will Dona Carlota be able to travel so far?"

"Try and stop her! She may be an old lady, but she has a strong spirit."

"And how about your sisters? I'm looking forward to meeting them, and their families."

Phil laughed. "They've been telling me for years that I should get married. They'll want to be on the spot to see the knot tied."

Melissa was content. "That's all I care about—your family and mine. Because, Phil, the Colvilles are the only family I have . . . the only family the children have."

"How will they take the news?" Phil queried. "Selwyn, especially?"

"I daresay that Pauline has already told him that I'm never going to marry him. I suggested that she do so to put an end to the idea once and for all. You know, Phil, I honestly believe that it will be the best thing all round for me and the children to leave Pendlehurst."

"The best thing? I don't get it. Losing you will be to lose so much. I must admit that I feel just a twinge of guilt about stealing you away."

"You're really doing them a favor. It's time they gave up that big house. Pendlehurst hasn't got a long family history like the Quinta das Andorinhas, and it isn't part of an estate, either. It was bought by Selwyn's and Pauline's grandfather, and it's outlived its usefulness. It's a liability now." She told Phil of her recent conversation with Pauline, and her suggestion that she and Edward would be happier living in Tunbridge Wells near his dental office. "As for Selwyn," she went on, "he could find an apartment in town, which would be much more his style. And if he wants to get married, I don't doubt that he'll soon find a wife, too. He has a lot to offer a woman, Phil."

"But not enough for you?"

"How could he have, compared with you?" she said with a grin.

They kissed again, lingeringly. "Do we tell Jenny and Mark straight away?" Phil asked.

"Of course. They'll jump for joy. They think you're the greatest."

"So they should! I worked hard to persuade them."

Melissa laughed. "And I made you work hard to persuade me, too. I must have been crazy."

He shook his head sternly. "I won't let you say a word against the woman I love. She's perfect in every detail." His voice had grown husky, and she felt his body quicken with longing. "I want to make love to you, *querida*. Are you going to make me wait?"

"Wait?" Melissa laughed incredulously. "Now you're the one who's crazy. I wish we had a few days to spend here, like we did before. But as it is . . . oh, Phil, how long have we got before we need to start back?"

"Long enough," he assured her as he pressed her gently back against the sofa cushions and stretched himself beside her, "to show you how much I love you, want you and need you."

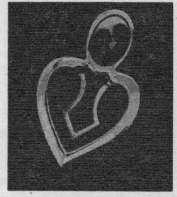

Silhouette Special Edition

MORE ROMANCE FOR
A SPECIAL WAY TO RELAX
$1.95 each

2 ☐ Hastings	21 ☐ Hastings	41 ☐ Halston	60 ☐ Thorne
3 ☐ Dixon	22 ☐ Howard	42 ☐ Drummond	61 ☐ Beckman
4 ☐ Vitek	23 ☐ Charles	43 ☐ Shaw	62 ☐ Bright
5 ☐ Converse	24 ☐ Dixon	44 ☐ Eden	63 ☐ Wallace
6 ☐ Douglass	25 ☐ Hardy	45 ☐ Charles	64 ☐ Converse
7 ☐ Stanford	26 ☐ Scott	46 ☐ Howard	65 ☐ Cates
8 ☐ Halston	27 ☐ Wisdom	47 ☐ Stephens	66 ☐ Mikels
9 ☐ Baxter	28 ☐ Ripy	48 ☐ Ferrell	67 ☐ Shaw
10 ☐ Thiels	29 ☐ Bergen	49 ☐ Hastings	68 ☐ Sinclair
11 ☐ Thornton	30 ☐ Stephens	50 ☐ Browning	69 ☐ Dalton
12 ☐ Sinclair	31 ☐ Baxter	51 ☐ Trent	70 ☐ Clare
13 ☐ Beckman	32 ☐ Douglass	52 ☐ Sinclair	71 ☐ Skillern
14 ☐ Keene	33 ☐ Palmer	53 ☐ Thomas	72 ☐ Belmont
15 ☐ James	35 ☐ James	54 ☐ Hohl	73 ☐ Taylor
16 ☐ Carr	36 ☐ Dailey	55 ☐ Stanford	74 ☐ Wisdom
17 ☐ John	37 ☐ Stanford	56 ☐ Wallace	75 ☐ John
18 ☐ Hamilton	38 ☐ John	57 ☐ Thornton	76 ☐ Ripy
19 ☐ Shaw	39 ☐ Milan	58 ☐ Douglass	77 ☐ Bergen
20 ☐ Musgrave	40 ☐ Converse	59 ☐ Roberts	78 ☐ Gladstone

$2.25 each

79 ☐ Hastings	87 ☐ Dixon	95 ☐ Doyle	103 ☐ Taylor
80 ☐ Douglass	88 ☐ Saxon	96 ☐ Baxter	104 ☐ Wallace
81 ☐ Thornton	89 ☐ Meriwether	97 ☐ Shaw	105 ☐ Sinclair
82 ☐ McKenna	90 ☐ Justin	98 ☐ Hurley	106 ☐ John
83 ☐ Major	91 ☐ Stanford	99 ☐ Dixon	107 ☐ Ross
84 ☐ Stephens	92 ☐ Hamilton	100 ☐ Roberts	108 ☐ Stephens
85 ☐ Beckman	93 ☐ Lacey	101 ☐ Bergen	109 ☐ Beckman
86 ☐ Halston	94 ☐ Barrie	102 ☐ Wallace	110 ☐ Browning

Silhouette Special Edition

$2.25 each

111 ☐ Thorne	133 ☐ Douglass	155 ☐ Lacey	177 ☐ Howard
112 ☐ Belmont	134 ☐ Ripy	156 ☐ Hastings	178 ☐ Bishop
113 ☐ Camp	135 ☐ Seger	157 ☐ Taylor	179 ☐ Meriwether
114 ☐ Ripy	136 ☐ Scott	158 ☐ Charles	180 ☐ Jackson
115 ☐ Halston	137 ☐ Parker	159 ☐ Camp	181 ☐ Browning
116 ☐ Roberts	138 ☐ Thornton	160 ☐ Wisdom	182 ☐ Thornton
117 ☐ Converse	139 ☐ Halston	161 ☐ Stanford	183 ☐ Sinclair
118 ☐ Jackson	140 ☐ Sinclair	162 ☐ Roberts	184 ☐ Daniels
119 ☐ Langan	141 ☐ Saxon	163 ☐ Halston	185 ☐ Gordon
120 ☐ Dixon	142 ☐ Bergen	164 ☐ Ripy	186 ☐ Scott
121 ☐ Shaw	143 ☐ Bright	165 ☐ Lee	187 ☐ Stanford
122 ☐ Walker	144 ☐ Meriwether	166 ☐ John	188 ☐ Lacey
123 ☐ Douglass	145 ☐ Wallace	167 ☐ Hurley	189 ☐ Ripy
124 ☐ Mikels	146 ☐ Thornton	168 ☐ Thornton	190 ☐ Wisdom
125 ☐ Cates	147 ☐ Dalton	169 ☐ Beckman	191 ☐ Hardy
126 ☐ Wildman	148 ☐ Gordon	170 ☐ Paige	192 ☐ Taylor
127 ☐ Taylor	149 ☐ Claire	171 ☐ Gray	193 ☐ John
128 ☐ Macomber	150 ☐ Dailey	172 ☐ Hamilton	194 ☐ Jackson
129 ☐ Rowe	151 ☐ Shaw	173 ☐ Belmont	195 ☐ Griffin
130 ☐ Carr	152 ☐ Adams	174 ☐ Dixon	196 ☐ Cates
131 ☐ Lee	153 ☐ Sinclair	175 ☐ Roberts	197 ☐ Lind
132 ☐ Dailey	154 ☐ Malek	176 ☐ Walker	198 ☐ Bishop

SILHOUETTE SPECIAL EDITION, Department SE/2
1230 Avenue of the Americas
New York, NY 10020

Please send me the books I have checked above. I am enclosing $_____
(please add 75¢ to cover postage and handling. NYS and NYC residents please
add appropriate sales tax). Send check or money order—no cash or C.O.D.'s
please. Allow six weeks for delivery.

NAME _____

ADDRESS _____

CITY _____ STATE/ZIP _____

Silhouette Special Edition

Coming Next Month

OPPOSITES ATTRACT
by Nora Roberts

•

SEA OF DREAMS
by Angel Milan

•

WILD PASSIONS
by Gena Dalton

•

PROMISES TO KEEP
by Carolyn Thorton

•

DANGEROUS COMPANY
by Laura Parker

•

SOMEDAY SOON
by Kathleen Eagle